MY ONLY FRIEND, THE END

1

ON THE LAST DAY, I went for a skydive. I'd been jumping for almost a year and was in love with the sport for all the reasons you might expect. There was the rush of adrenaline and the camaraderie with like-minded thrill-seekers—but most of all there was an escape from routine and some new self-awareness. I was somewhat surprised to realize that up to that point in my life I hadn't been at all adventurous. My idea of high times had been to ask for layered butter on my popcorn at the movies.

On this particular day I was an A license going on B license—still somewhat green. The group that I would jump with was new to me, eight urban cowboys up from Denver for a wedding. I tagged along, a solitary local who had finagled a spot among them because all the other times that week were booked.

Our jump master, Amelia, was guiding this group for the first time, so she was deliberate with her safety instructions before herding us onto the plane. Once we were all seated along the fuselage walls I was the closest person to the open door, the first jumper. This was good. There was something special about the sky when there was no one between me and the ground.

On the bench across from me sat a burly, moonfaced man who twice earlier had interrupted Amelia's safety lecture with off-color quips about the intelligence of the people up here in Montana. On the ground, this man had paid no attention to me. Up in the air, he held onto the safety rope with one hand and screamed at me over the whine of the Cessna's engine.

"Amelia says you're a writer!"

"That's right!" I shouted back.

"You get rich off of that?" he asked.

I laughed and shook my head. "I have a patron." He scrunched his nose, needed an explanation, so I said, "My wife. Patron and muse."

His questioning eyes told me he still didn't get it.

"I'm the opposite of rich," I said. "In fact, when I started writing, I didn't sell anything or make any money for more than two years."

He looked past me out the open door, seemed to be roughly gauging our altitude.

"Two years of nothing?"

"That's right," I told him.

"But you're making up for that now, right? I mean, you're still doing it."

"My wife out-earns me three to one," I told him.

He laughed and slapped his knee. "No kidding?"

"No kidding."

I noticed his chest strap was loose. If he jumped with it like that, when the canopy deployed his sternum would end up in his throat.

"You have kids?" he pressed on.

A voice from somewhere down the line hollered, "Leave him alone, Buck."

"I'm not hurting anyone," Buck said. Then he asked me, "Am I hurting you, guy?"

"We're good," I said.

"See, he's good. Everyone's good." He smiled at me. "So do you?"

"Have kids? I have a four-year-old son."

"So while Wifey's out bringing home the bacon, you're picking up Junior at preschool?"

"It's one of the best parts of my day," I told him.

He squinted as if maybe I was needling him. I wasn't. The preschool pickups were organized chaos and unvarnished joy. I knew that in my golden years I would look back on them with fondness.

Buck undid his seatbelt and leaned forward. He motioned for me to do the same so we could share a word in confidence—just him and me.

I leaned in. Our helmets almost touched.

Buck shouted so everyone could hear, "You sound like a Democrat! I thought everyone in this state was Republican!"

The woman to his right hollered to me, "If you ignore him, sooner or later he'll tire himself out!"

I reached out and snugged up Buck's too-loose chest strap. He took this as an invasion of his personal space and slapped my hands away.

"Don't you ever touch me, okay?"

Our pilot, Danny, hit a button on the dash and said something into his mic. He was linked to Amelia's headset. Amelia now shouted to all the divers, "We're nearing the drop zone, people!"

Buck forgot about me and I forgot about Buck. We undid our seat belts, rolled our necks, went through pre-jump checks. A few of the Denver jumpers exchanged high fives. When I looked back at Buck, I detected sourness in his hard-set features, so I initiated a high five and after a moment of doubt he slapped my hand and everything was cool. Then we all fell silent, all watched the red lights lining the fuselage ceiling. Before every jump, this was a moment heavy with expectation, with a stillness despite the shaking of the plane and the groan of the wind. Time stretched out.

The line of red lights blinked off and the green lights flashed on.

I pulled my goggles down over my eyes, edged off the bench, and spilled out into the open sky.

• • •

When you're knifing through the air at 115 miles per hour you don't have to work hard to find excitement. Despite this, I always put just a little too much effort into my dives. I was determined to achieve rapture, the glorious wind on my face, the freedom of my soul, that kind of stuff. On this dive there was even a notion to turn my controlled freefall into a trippy nosedive—maybe squeeze just one more ounce of juice from the drop.

But while I strained toward euphoria the jump plane dove in front of me not far in the distance. It was pointed straight at the ground as if

My Only Friend, the End

pilot Danny wanted to crash in the most geometrically efficient way possible. This did not make sense, not as an occurring event. It had to be a glitch of the mind, an adrenaline-fueled flash of recall from some novel I'd read or a movie I'd seen (dives did sometimes trigger crazy thoughts). Calmer heads would prevail and the ugly vision would blip away.

But it persisted. The Cessna screamed toward the ground. It took me a long while to sculpt a coherent thought:

Where are the Denver jumpers?

They were all still inside the plane.

I panicked, slapped at my pack, couldn't find the hackey to deploy the canopy. I pawed at my chest, gripped the main-canopy cutaway, came close to pulling it, but managed enough presence of mind not to. After more clutching and grasping, my hands found the right ball and I braced for the tear and felt the grab.

The average jump took four minutes once the tent was out. I told myself to swoop, to get to the ground as fast as possible, but the body wouldn't do what the mind commanded; a period of stunned suspension ensued, with me drifting, peering down at a ribbon of prairie highway where two cars crashed head-on into each other and other cars slowed and veered into the ditches as if a universal power switch had been flicked off. A half mile south of the road, a gas plant erupted in flames.

A short time after these things, the sewage plant on the edge of town leaked smoke and my jump plane disappeared into an earthy-black plume of Montana soil. There was no explosion from the impact, no flames. The plane simply crumpled in on itself as if Danny wanted to leave scant evidence it had ever existed.

All this destruction was accompanied by the peaceful acoustics of my billowing canopy, a rhythmic popping and slapping that had once signified control over deadly forces. Until this moment, it had been one of my favorite sounds.

• • •

I landed hard in a wheat field. If a knee was wrenched or an ankle twisted, the adrenaline overrode it. I clambered out of the harness, tore off my helmet and dug my cellphone out of my jumpsuit pocket. Calling 911 produced a busy signal, so I tried Ronnie, my wife, but the call wouldn't go through. Same with calls to her office's land line and to the dive office at the Great Falls airport. The phone screen showed one Verizon network bar—and then it showed none at all.

I stuffed the phone back into my pocket and thought about Buck and Amelia while I sprinted through the young wheat toward the parked cars in the drop zone. I had planned to ride back to the airport with Amelia, so I had no keys for any of the vehicles. This fact did not arrive immediately (no clear thoughts did), but when I grasped that I was stranded out here, I altered my course and ran toward the nearest farmhouse, which was far away through the field, a good half mile off.

Soon my lungs burned and my legs ached, but the pain was peripheral, cloaked by other, more significant things. A single thought played on a loop in my mind as I bounded through the knee-high crop: *This isn't what it looks like. It can't be happening.*

For a moment, from the vantage point of the farmhouse's front lawn, maybe I was right, because the scene looked normal: a sturdy clapboard house, a hammock strung between two poplars, a tricycle straddling porch steps. But as I climbed those steps, I saw a woman on her back close to the porch swing. She was maybe thirty years old, dressed in faded yard-work denim. She stared up at me with wide, unblinking eyes. A part of me sensed she could see me. There was an urge to look away from her, to distance myself—but a stronger need to stare more closely, as if something in those eyes might explain what was happening. I stood there gawking for what might have been minutes, until the sound of an approaching vehicle wrestled my attention away.

A solitary truck crawled toward me through the wheat. I crossed to the end of the porch to get a better angle on it. Through the windshield, the driver sat slumped over the steering wheel, his ball cap slightly askew and his face buried in the crook of his flannel-clad arm. His truck described a slow, steady arc through the crop as if it had its own will independent of human guidance. Unless something disturbed it, it would repeat its circular course until it ran out of gas.

I tore open the farmhouse's screen door and shouted something panicked and jumbled. This was met with silence, which in turn was broken seconds later by the distant rumble of a faraway explosion. The home phone, a terrestrial line, sat on a counter in the kitchen, but when I dialed 911 the result was a busy signal—and on my second try there was no signal at all, only a dial tone that soon gave way to a depthless, echoing silence that produced in me a sense of falling through space. This was too much to process. I stood there staring at the phone, couldn't choose a course of action. At some point, I dropped the phone on the counter and lurched around the house looking for still-alive occupants.

In the master bedroom, a woman lay on her stomach on the carpet, hands at her sides. She hadn't tried to break her fall and she wore the same expression as the woman on the porch, as if she had not been particularly bothered by her own death.

In the basement, a spindly teen in a gaming chair sat draped over his computer keyboard. I looked at his face only briefly, and he came across as incongruently bored. On the computer screen: a military shoot-em-up game with the rudderless POV soldier bumping repeatedly against a bullet-pocked Middle Eastern wall. Like the circling truck outside, the bumping would continue for as long as the power source did.

Which was for roughly four more seconds. With a silent blip, the screen died and the light in the room died with it. The windows were yellow slivers behind black-out drapes, so I felt my way along the wall to the stairs, then climbed up to daylight, to the kitchen, where I tried another light switch, then opened the fridge and saw no light on inside and heard no compressor hum. There was a cell phone on the dining room table. Maybe it was on a still-functioning network. But when I checked the screen, it showed no bars. I checked my own phone again—same thing. I put the phone back in my pocket and stood there a long, muddled time, again unable to move or do anything. In retrospect, there was something very obvious to do: find a vehicle, speed into town, check on my wife, Ronnie, at her office, and on our little boy, Evan, who was in preschool. But logic was gone; everything spun.

An explosion ended the confusion. The blast took a small chunk out of the day—maybe a minute, maybe more. When conscious thought returned, I was on the dining-room floor with a burning face and ringing ears. Shattered window glass lay sprinkled all around me.

I pulled myself to my feet and staggered through the kitchen and out to the yard. The barn was ablaze. Just outside it, what once had been a fuel tank was now a jagged metal art installation. And more explosions sounded on the horizon, distant popcorn pops that arrived with a diffuse faintness that produced no smoke high enough for me to see. I looked all around the prairie, saw no other houses. The wheat waved gently in the breeze. The woman on the porch still looked okay with the fact she was dead.

Something trickled down my neck. I felt around my face and pulled a shard of window glass out of my left cheek. This made the blood come faster. I pressed at the wound with my fingers, but the stream kept coming, so I lurched back into the house, to the bathroom. In the medicine cabinet, I found a medical kit with iodine and butterfly bandages. Despite my shaking hands, I squeezed the edges of the gash together, pressed on two faux stitches, and spent a moment staring at myself in the mirror. The tears looked foreign. They weren't me—or were distant elements of me, of little consequence. Tears were supposed to mean sorrow, but sorrow was absent, chased by shock, or by shock's antonym, a type of understanding that was degrees worse.

As I stood there, my mind flashed on a waking nightmare, a kind of fraught vision that superseded even the terror of the present: I saw my wife Ronnie and my son Evan leaning out of a twentieth-floor window of a skyscraper that climbed all the way to the clouds. They were trapped by a fire a few floors below, couldn't take the stairs. They cried out for me to save them…

I dashed outside. The farmer's truck was no longer describing a circle in the wheat. It nudged up against a rut in the soil, a gentle, repetitive attempt at locomotion. I opened the door, reached around the dead farmer and put the vehicle in park. Then I pulled the farmer back in his seat and looked at his face: open, peaceful eyes, gray hair, sun-browned wrinkles. No twisted facial expression, no cadaver paleness or evident trauma. If there was a good way to die, this was it. I pulled him out of the truck and left him face up in his wheat—then put his vehicle in gear and drove toward my wife and son in Great Falls.

2

THE MONTANA PRAIRIE is vast and empty. The people there liked it that way, but I always wished the views were more substantial. This was because I was a snob. I thought unbroken wheat-field vistas were impressive only if you didn't care what lay beyond them. Even worse, about the time of my freshman year at college I decided the admirers of those views, most of my fellow grasslanders in northern Montana, suffered from small-town small-mindedness, and it was my job in life, as a writer-to-be, to understand this fact and to be a kind of silent conscientious objector among them, a stealthy chronicler of their flaws and weaknesses.

The plan was to use my superior understanding of my peeps for my own literary benefit, but I wouldn't educate or edify my subjects because I knew how the math of the situation worked. They had tradition and numbers on their side. They had enviable energy and were doers, tilling the land, drinking whiskey and playing video slot machines in bars after football games. They worshipped the flag, distrusted big-city outsiders and proudly sent their sons and daughters off to fight in foreign wars. Their most striking quality was their unquestioned faith in themselves, which they wore with burnished pride, even if some of their sons and daughters didn't return from those wars.

"They" was a very big word for me—very convenient. The fact that I never challenged my fellow Montanans on their perceived faults—that I never provided an alternative that might lift them out of their sweeping heartland ignorance did not cost me any sleep. Activism had always struck me as a thing for other places, for east-coast Occupiers and rabid social justice warriors. This was the prairie, after all, land of ingrained stoicism. I was hardwired to bite my tongue and take a discreet approach.

Still, by the time I finished college I honed a safe yet insidious method of registering protest: I tried to infect my fellow Montanans with a virus of moral integrity, a quietly insistent drip-drip of small, progressive deeds in a sea of parochialism. I proposed gay-themed plays to the local community theater group, gave to Amnesty International, bravely admitted in steak houses and farmers' fields that I opposed increased funding for the military—and then went home and informed Ronnie (with a careful hint of humility) that I had made progress in my secret quest to win over a few—just a few—hardened hearts and minds. It never occurred to me that maybe my fellow Montanans were flawed not because they loved football and played video slot machines, but because I, writer and passer of judgment, needed them that way. Every hero needs someone or something to triumph over.

So now, as I drove the dead farmer's truck north toward Great Falls, the prairie was vast and unbroken, but for the first time ever that panoramic vista felt like a good thing, because all of its constituent elements appeared normal: the ochre wheat fields, the leaning pasture fences, the grain elevators. Even the clouds in the sky looked normal, bulky rolls of blacking mist that might or might not bloom into evening showers.

That meant maybe Ronnie and Evan were okay. It had to mean that.

I sped up a little and turned on the radio for reports from town. A deejay waxed poetic about Bruce Springsteen and the E Street Band, and that made no sense. While falling from the plane, I had seen the sewage plant start to burn. From the farmer's porch, I'd heard explosions off toward town. The music program should have been preempted by an emergency broadcast message or by a grave-sounding newscaster describing tragic developments. The programming had to be canned.

I switched to NPR, which I knew was broadcast live. Dead air sounded. The local sports station, same thing. I checked my phone yet again, and again there was no signal. A farm was up ahead on the right.

As I approached it nothing seemed amiss, so I leaned on the horn and prayed for a reaction while I told myself, *I'm alive, so others are alive. Ronnie and Evan are waiting for me.*

But as I honked the horn and neared the farmhouse the front door didn't open. No one inside pulled back a curtain or opened blinds to see who was making that racket out on the road. I stopped honking only when I saw the body in the yard, a man on his back still clutching a shovel. There was something languid about his supine posture, a kind of loose-jointedness that suggested he might yawn, stretch, climb to his feet, and dust himself off.

But I knew he wouldn't.

They're all gone.

Then:

No. Not everyone.

If you're here, others are here.

There were no cats or dogs at the farm, not a single chicken. The nearby fields were all wheat crops, no pasture, so no livestock was in view. The smoke now climbing up on the horizon said Great Falls was about four miles away, but it felt more like four hundred miles. I sped up to eighty and told myself to stay calm, to get to Ronnie and Evan, don't stop for anything on the way.

Focus. Keep it together.

Evan, my boy. He was four, but he told everyone he was five—the eagerness of childhood, the optimism of innocence.

He'll make it to five. He's alive. Just get to him.

But the people at the farmhouse. The Denver divers. Why hadn't Buck leapt out of the plane right after me? Amelia had instructed us to keep small gaps.

Try the phone again.

No signal.

Try Ronnie's number anyway.

Nothing.

See if anyone's alive in the cars in the ditch up ahead.

All this was happening too fast. Maybe I was home asleep. This nightmare was a product of the subconscious. Too many Steven King novels.

The truck clock said 12:46. I seemed to be getting no closer to town. I began hyperventilating, growing dizzy. Ronnie and Evan needed me, but here I was, literally about to knock myself out.

Stop it. Calm down.

Ty to think normal thoughts.

On a normal day at this time, what would Ronnie be doing? Lunch would be over and she would be back at her desk putting together a balance sheet or a profit-and-loss statement. Evan would be tearing around his preschool, wreaking havoc before the kids were rounded up for their afternoon nap. He would be…

This wasn't working. Cars should have been fleeing the fires in town. This road, this secondary highway, was empty.

I approached a car parked in a ditch. Something in the vehicle fluttered, a sign of life, a hand maybe, waving for help.

The driver was alive.

I sped past the car feeling a surge of hope for Ronnie and Evan.

But what if the person or people in the car were in trouble? What if they needed help?

I drove a few more seconds before hitting the brakes and turning the truck around. A half minute later, I stumbled through the ditch over knobby mounds of prairie grass to the driver-side doors.

Up close, I saw a woman lying sideways in the driver-side seat, saw the crown of her head, chestnut hair streaked with gray. Her door refused to budge, so I ran around to the other side and tore open the passenger door.

The woman stared at me straight on from this angle. There was no emotion in her features, not even a moment-of-death look of "Something wrong is happening." I hoped for a second her lips would curl into a mischievous smile that said all this was some impossibly elaborate prank.

You're wasting time here.

But I couldn't tear myself away from her. I felt her forehead, found it cool to the touch. She must have died when the others died. I poked my head over the headrest. Nothing there, clean back seat. I pulled out of the car and began running back up the ditch. I slipped on some gravel and found myself vaulting backwards through space. The sensation was detached from the terrors of the moment, more dreamlike than real, a snatch of context-free time with a faint but somehow familiar sense of something terrible about to strike.

Then there was nothing at all, an absence of the bombardment of the last eighty or ninety minutes.

There was a complete and perfect void.

3

I HAD ALWAYS BEEN a vivid dreamer, had always had a strong faculty for remembering my dreams. I chalked this up to a robust imagination, which was something I relied on and felt proud of, because the imagination was the tool I used for making my living. Up until that last jump from the plane, I wrote a series of private-eye mystery novels. Like I'd told Buck, most of the books were far from bestsellers, but they did pay some bills and did allow me to evade the travails of the real-world workforce, with the low wages and limited options that tended to befall people like me who had no marketable skills.

But right now the ability to dream wasn't a blessing. It contained a chilling element of astral projection. I found myself floating above my own unconscious body, looking down on the out-cold me with an airy feeling of detachment. The me on the ground was blissfully at ease. Blood seeped from a spot over my left ear. A football-sized stone lay inches from my head, apparently the thing that had knocked me out.

Odd how I could feel so calm while seeing myself like this. I might as well have been lazing in a deck chair or absently channel-surfing after a long day's work.

Wake up! You have to get to Ronnie and Evan!

My Only Friend, the End

The unconscious me didn't hear this.

Stop wasting time!

But screaming didn't help. The absurdity of Dreamworld deepened. A team of riderless horses galloped across the prairie—or, rather, above it, their hooves not quite touching the grass. They looked majestic under the setting sun, all sinew and grace, like freedom itself—until I looked behind them and saw why they were running: they were escaping a rolling billow of fire tumbling out of the southern end of Great Falls.

I panicked and started running after the horses, then stopped and looked back at my unconscious self in the grass.

But the me in the grass was no longer there.

Instead I saw Ronnie and Evan, flat on their backs just like I'd been, both losing blood from wounds over their left ears. But they weren't unconscious, weren't asleep or passed out. Ronnie and Evan were stock-still and ashen, very clearly dead.

A cry gathered somewhere deep inside me and exploded with a force that blotted out the fires, the galloping horses and everything else.

I have no way of knowing how long that cry went on.

• • •

Eventually there was a dream-free period before my mind inched back toward the waking world. This slow drift bled into an almost-lucid knowledge that I was leaving unconsciousness and should probably open my eyes. After that: a flighty lapse where I saw Ronnie stepping out of the shower, glistening and happy, and Evan tugging at my pant leg, asking to play *Operation*, and then I found myself blinking up at prairie darkness. The night looked serene, a blanket of distant suns, the brightness of constellations.

And meteors—shooting stars—a Jackson Pollock array of them. I breathed easily, glad to be out of Dreamworld but not yet fully awake or reconnected to the facts of the present. I watched the meteors come three at a time, then four at a time, from all directions, a celestial symphony of random beauty to ease me back into life.

But as my mind awakened, it became likely the sky lights weren't meteors; they were satellites burning up in the atmosphere.

I lifted my head and saw an orange glow along the horizon toward Great Falls.

An attempt to sit up sent a knife blade through my head and put me down on my back again. Past clumps of grass I spotted the dim outline of the rock that I'd hit my head on. It was wasteful, concussing myself when I needed to get to my family. It was extravagant—pointless. Somehow it was selfish.

I looked at the sky again and thought, "Maybe aliens did this." On the second attempt to stand I fought through the pain, stumbled to the truck and drove toward town. Whatever had looked alive in the dead woman's car no longer mattered. Maybe it had been a mirage, because as far as I could see there weren't even any birds in the air or bugs hitting the windshield. Everything was dead.

Only that pulsing orange sky was alive.

• • •

The secondary road joined the I-15 just outside of town. The ditches on the Interstate were lined with crashed cars, many of them with engines still running. The airport, ahead on the left, was dark save for a fire where a taxiing plane had hit a hangar wall and exploded. It was the same airport where I'd boarded my jump plane twelve hours ago; now, in the fire-lit gloom, it looked like something from a war movie. People outside the terminal lay dead. People in the parking lot lay dead.

Farther along, on the fringe of town, people lay outside the Old Navy and the Michael's like a grisly game of connect the dots. Even the golfers at the Meadowlark Country Club were dead on the fairways. I couldn't see them in the darkness, but they were certainly there, being feasted on by mosquitoes, unless those were dead too. At least the Missouri River, which bisected Great Falls on its way eastward—at least the river looked alive, because it moved. If anything, it looked a little high. If its fish were dead, if everything was dead, then—

Stop that. Just get to them.

I turned off the highway at Second Street, passed a fire at a gas station, and made my way downtown. The solar lights were on, spotlighting ways in which people's worlds had ended. An elderly man had been mangled by a riding mower, which now sat against a tree trunk slick with blood. A woman carrying groceries had fallen in a crosswalk; her head was encircled by a halo-like puddle of spilled milk. I tried to look away from such horrors, but there was always another solar light or another fire and a new need to stare. The scenes drove home the vein-freezing certainty that very soon I would find my wife and son in the same state as everyone else.

On Second Avenue, I navigated crashed and stalled vehicles. A backup light had come on inside the Walgreens. The light gave me a clear view of the high pharmacy counter. For a moment, my mind registered the fact that all sorts of very heavy drugs were there. The concept tried to linger a while, but I pushed it away, swallowed hard, and drove a winding path of fresh death to Central Avenue, where I parked next to a still-running cargo van outside Ronnie's office. Somewhere during this journey, the sense of horror mutated into a kind of leaden numbness that let only a few poignant facts through:

They will be dead when you see them.

That is when everything will really be gone.

I don't recall walking into the building. There must have been bodies in the lobby, and in the adjoining offices. There must have been ghastly versions of Wayne, her boss, or Pearl or Anand or the others. I don't remember seeing them. I do recall watching the fringed beam of my iPhone flashlight crawl the walls, highlight a printer, a cubicle, a water cooler—and then land on a woman who was maybe Ronnie, head on the keyboard, body limp.

I couldn't see her face from this angle. A fan of raven-black hair spread out over her cheek. I closed my eyes against this sight and gulped in a huge amount of stale, uncirculated air, and when the eyes opened again I had to look away. There was a stapler lying on its side at the edge of her desk. For some reason I had to put that stapler upright in what might have been its usual spot. After that, my legs gave out; I found myself slumping to the floor.

It was cool down there, dark now that my phone's flashlight was face-down on the engineered hardwood. I looked up at the dim outline of my wife's body and said her name out loud. The word felt weak. Foreign.

"Ronnie," I said again, louder, and she didn't answer because maybe this wasn't her. I picked up my phone and was careful not to shine it on her. I waited a long moment before reaching out to brush the hair from her face, but before contact was made I snapped my hand back.

It didn't have to be her.

Not her hair. Not her blouse.

I stepped back and away from her.

This was a coworker who looked like her.

An IT worker who'd been checking the printer cable.

This was the wrong desk. In the gloom of the unlit office I had ended up at someone else's workspace.

Stop that. What are you doing?

But clarity couldn't be risked. I found myself bolting from the office, bumping into walls and desks, bouncing off a cubicle and down the stairs, then installing myself back in the truck and screwing my eyes shut, afraid of opening them to see the corpse in the driver seat of the still-running cargo van beside me.

After a minute or two of this, an emptiness came over me, as if I'd taken a slow-working drug. I felt like a distant version of myself in a distant version of the world—none of this really real. How could it be?

I told myself to get it together, go back up, go be with her, but the command was weak—blotted out by the need to shut things down.

Now there was no plan to make and no goal to chase. Evan tried to enter my mind but was summarily evicted—too dangerous. Same thing with a new mental image of Ronnie at her desk. The one thing I did allow myself to ponder was Walgreens—those drugs behind that high counter. They were reasonable options, the only things that really made sense.

I started the truck and began driving, but I didn't go to Walgreens and I didn't do the right thing and go to Evan's preschool. I just drove, and yet again I replayed the image of Ronnie at her computer, only I visualized someone else—a woman with broader shoulders and darker skin. Twice the woman tried to turn into Ronnie, but both times I stopped the transformation in progress.

I wound up at the convenience store two blocks from my house. Inside the store, I saw a woman on the floor next to a dented box of wine. Marty, the store owner, was dead behind the counter, gangly legs sticking out into the aisle. I stepped over those legs, grabbed the first bottle of vodka I saw, and took three big, burning slugs—roughly a third of the bottle—before being slammed with vertigo, falling to the floor, then hauling myself back out to the truck.

Driving home, I saw a woman lying on the sidewalk behind a baby stroller. It was Ronnie's friend Rachel. I didn't slow down or peer inside the stroller (the baby's name was Ariel). I focused on the heat of the vodka, told myself Ronnie was at home waiting for me. I peered down at the road, away from other victims, no looking through living-room windows and seeing

Myrtle Jensen, who would have been squinting through thick glasses, knitting a sweater when the end came, or Tim Harald, who, like me, worked out of a home office and took long walks around the neighborhood to ward off the muscle stiffness produced by sedentary labors.

When I got home, I moved about quietly. If Ronnie couldn't hear me, she couldn't respond to my presence. If she didn't respond to my presence, maybe she was alive in one of the bedrooms or downstairs. I grabbed my old a.m. shower radio from the upstairs bathroom, then walked softly to the living room, sagged down into the sofa, and guzzled Smirnoff in the dark while weeping silently. I thumbed the radio's tune dial. The static up and down the range of frequencies sounded like an accusation.

Evan at his daycare.

Rachel and her stroller.

My mom in Scottsdale.

My brother and sister in Europe.

Go to Evan; he's alone.

But moving would have invited horror. The silence around me was a cocoon. "Ronnie?" I asked out loud, but there was a timid quality to the word.

Go get Evan, already.

For the first time I didn't chase the thought away. I ordered myself to stop feeling sorry for myself—go find him—but wanting to rise from the sofa and actually doing so were two different things. I sat there stuck, stars burning above me, the sun pulling farther away from the Earth, solar lights losing power and blinking off halfway through the night, leaving everything everywhere dark. I lingered over a million endings to things, until my mind landed on my first-ever encounter with death— my first real understanding of the concept.

That first death had occurred back in high school courtesy of Sean Vilmack, a boy who, halfway through lunch on a September day, jumped off the roof of the school gymnasium. Sean had been a friend and had worked hard to be good to me. I'd spent two summers just hanging with him, playing catch, fishing with him and his dad, going to movies, promising each other we would one day escape Great Falls and go live in a city where things actually happened.

I wasn't there to see his suicide, and I didn't see his broken body afterwards, but I did arrive at school in time to witness the residual blood and brain matter on the outdoor basketball court close to the hoop, as if

Sean had tried to make a gruesome three-pointer of himself. I watched while the cleaners power-washed away the last traces of him. Later there would be guilt, I would blame myself for his death and I would carry that blame for years, but for the moment there was something more visceral.

This was what was meant by death: not merely an end to life, not a cessation of being. Death was absolute in an unjust way, a full stop halfway through an unfinished sentence. There would be no revisions or additions, no mark provided for the work done so far.

Not for Sean and not for the multitudes who'd died today. As my thumb worked the radio's tune dial, I wondered whether the Sean of the afterlife had had a good view of today's events—then I told myself the thing that mattered most.

You just left her there.
You didn't have the guts to go to your own son.
So you have to do that now.

But I chose to wilt instead. I navel-gazed. Good people were gone, and I had been gifted an exemption. Listening to dead air on a shower radio wouldn't change anything, but getting active, seeking out a greater depth of horror, wouldn't help either. Only vodka would help.

The need to rise from the sofa softened into the fulfilment of a growing buzz. Things slowed down, dissolving in the murk of the unlit living room. Ronnie and Evan were still out there, but vodka built a wall in front of them.

Scaling that wall would have taken a thing called bravery, but I was beyond such considerations. Bravery—and everything else—would have to wait. Right now only one type of work got done.

• • •

When I woke again, it was still dark, maybe three in the morning. A nail twisted in my forehead. Smoke from distant fires suffused everything. I was still alive, still there, and that was not necessarily a good thing. I sought out last night's vodka and found the bottle on the floor, cruelly empty. Out in the kitchen, in the fridge, behind the pickles and mayonnaise, was a barely chilled beer. I opened it and started guzzling.

It was beautiful—a promise of a new curtain about to fall. While I caught my breath after gulping half the bottle, a snatch of my childhood bubbled up:

Apocalypse? I don't know what that means.
Who cares? It's not the end of the world!

I was eleven the first and last time I told that joke—a lifetime ago, during a brief flirtation with stand-up comedy.

At the end of the world, there'll still be one company selling books.
Amazombie!

Now a laugh that was more of a cry—then another rapacious guzzle, and the beer backing up on me, burning my sinuses. There were a million more one-liners, most of them groaners, most of them lifted from real comedians.

My parrot died yesterday.
It was a real weight off my shoulder!

A blast of nausea put an end to this. I leaned forward and vomited, spent a good long time fighting to steady myself, trying my best not to think. Recovery came in the form of another swallow of beer, then another full bottle, followed by a stagger to the bedroom and a crawl back into bed, where I pulled the covers up over my head. The throbbing in my temples was welcome. Maybe it was serious. With luck, it would end me. As I slipped back into unconsciousness for the third time in less than twenty hours, Ronnie and Evan remained safely ensconced on the other side of the wall. The smell of smoke carried a tinge of sweetness. I was still wearing my ridiculous skydiving jumpsuit.

• • •

This time when I woke up, the light of morning had arrived. I had wet the bed and was now shivering through an ice-cold fever. Despite the dampness and the nauseating odor, I couldn't move, couldn't even pull the blanket off. Too much reality awaited. My mind pinged from Ronnie to Buck and Amelia and then to the old man who'd been mangled by his riding mower. It bounced from Walgreens to the sight of my dive plane crashing and back to Ronnie again, this time Ronnie from yesterday morning, smiling and closing the front door behind her as she left for work—the last time I saw her alive.

In among this mental traffic was a memory of my first day of elementary school way back when, of my teacher consoling a girl who was crying because her mom had left her in a strange new place, and my mind flashed on a baseball coach when I was seven. Coach Lawson was African-American, the first one I'd ever seen in the flesh. When I stared at him he gave me a wink and said, "We aren't all rappers, you know." The memory was eons away from the present, random and unhelpful.

"Get up," I said out loud, but then retreated into another thought ping: an English professor back in university telling me J.D. Salinger had harbored a disturbing fascination with little girls.

Jesus, what was wrong with me? Where was my focus?

The thing to get me moving after these distractions was nausea. Dry heaves racked my body. I spilled out of bed and onto all fours on the carpet. The smoke was even thicker now, producing within me a tubercular wheeze. The air tasted industrial, like burning paint and upholstery. Through it, my eyes fastened on details: the Atwood novel that Ronnie had been reading, there on her nightstand. A hair brush. A box of tissues. A hair pin. On the dresser, a blouse she'd neglected to put in the hamper. It occurred to me that if I pressed the blouse to my nose it would replace the odor of smoke with the scent of Ronnie, so I did that, and her scent was there.

I imagined her speaking to me:

"Go to Evan."

"I know," I said.

"It doesn't matter that you can't bear to see him. You have to do it."

"I left you in your office," I said. "What kind of man does that?"

"You were in shock. You can't change that, but you can choose what happens now."

At long last I pulled my jumpsuit off and slogged my way to the bathroom. There I found the aspirin bottle in the medicine cabinet. I took two tablets, then two more, then guzzled water and put on Ronnie's bathrobe, which was on a hook on the bathroom door and which also retained her scent.

I sat on the tiles and hugged myself, fighting chills and fever and the fact that the new day was sure to be as hard as the old one; yesterday would not fade or melt away; it would be a part of all days to come.

There was a temporal cut-out here, a few minutes of lost time. There must have been some cleaning of my person and some pulling on of clothes, because I rejoined the narrative when I was driving my ageing Dodge Caravan to Evan's preschool. The Caravan's front end gave a light clunk when I turned right; it had long needed a new tie rod end and sway bar link. As I knocked my way from street to street, neglect in the matter of vehicle repairs somehow seemed to matter.

I found Evan lying on the floor of his daycare with his right arm around another boy, like they'd decided to fall together. I broke down and cried over him, but a small part of me was relieved he looked as tranquil as the other victims. When I felt I was able, I hefted him into my arms, cradled his head against my shoulder, and carried him out to the van. Along the way, I recited *Goodnight Moon*, word for syrupy word, even though he had outgrown it. The recitation was calculated—something to focus on and ward off knee-buckling emotions—but the further I got into the story, and the farther I walked with Evan's body, the more I felt like a part of him might hear me, might understand I was trying to connect to him. Hope is a strange thing that has unpredictable rhythms.

With Evan in the van, I drove back downtown to Ronnie's office, where finally I did look her in the eyes. The angle of the morning sunlight through the blinds left shaded hollows around those eyes, kept me from seeing any depth, and there were no longer any thought lines between the brows, no tension around the mouth. All strain had been removed, as if death had done at least that much for her.

"I'm sorry," I told her, and I closed those unseeing eyes and lifted her over my shoulder, then managed with great difficulty to carry her cumbersome dead weight out of the office and place her in the back of the van beside Evan. She cooperated throughout this process, knew I was moving her, because she refused to slip from my grasp and didn't shift or strike grisly poses while I took my careful, trembling steps. She knew I recoiled at the feel of the softness of her midsection on my shoulder, the rigor mortis already present in her arms and legs, the ease with which she would slide away if I didn't walk with a deep dip of my free shoulder toward the ground. It was hard to keep my balance on the stairs.

The drive to the cemetery was cautious; it demanded deft navigation of crashed vehicles and bumps in the road. The logic of the moment told me Ronnie and Evan could not be allowed to be further harmed.

There was an open grave near the middle of the graveyard, someone else's intended resting place. There were no dead mourners around, just a neat pile of earth and a Bobcat, with a lonely shovel beside the hole. For a long while I stood at the edge of the grave, Ronnie and Evan lying beside me facing the sky. I stared down into the hole, visualized insects feasting on them once I put them down there—which led to another freeze, another inability to move forward.

I stared into space, then recalled meals together, the three of us in the dining room talking about family things, about swimming at the Great Falls Wave Pool, with promises to Evan he could go on the big slide in just a year or two, when he was a little bigger. I recalled a time when Ronnie and I had been walking Evan—Evan still a baby in his stroller—and Ronnie had been clipped by an extended side mirror of a passing city roadworks truck. The driver had stopped and apologized profusely, had begged us to let him take Ronnie to the hospital. He was so guilt-ridden over the minor incident that in the end we worried about how he might pull through.

"Stop stalling," I heard Ronnie say. "There's no way to make this any less awful."

I buried them side-by-side in the hole, was gentle, made sure they were touching, would always be touching. For the longest while I offered no words and no attempt at ceremony. I couldn't look at the headstone, couldn't allow myself to see some other person's name over Ronnie's and Evan's final resting place. I stood over the mound for at most a minute, tried once to speak, but, still, words wouldn't come, so I walked back to the van thinking, *She's right. There's no good way to do this.*

I started the van but didn't put it in gear. The fuel gauge nudged the "empty" line. The radio, when I tried it, offered nothing, not even the distant a.m. stations from as far north as Calgary and as far south as Nevada.

A bee buzzed in through the passenger-side window. It landed on my lap, crawled around a little, then lit again. A Swainson's hawk circled overhead. I followed the ease of its path, the confidence of its bearing. The hawk didn't care what was happening down here. It cared only there were no predators and food was available.

The bigger point was slow to reach me:

The hawk was alive.

The bee was alive.

Only people were dead.

This sparked some relief, a ray of positivity, which in turn made me think of Ronnie and Evan lying in some other person's grave. A pang of survivor's guilt followed, then a new chain of dry heaves, right there in the van. The bout left me woozy and dry-mouthed. I spent a good ten minutes draped over the steering wheel fighting nausea, worrying about my wheezing, and ordering myself to put the vehicle in drive and leave Ronnie and Evan. But there was no strength for that. In the end, I climbed out of the van and grabbed a screwdriver from the toolbox in the back and a plank of wood from a nearby bench. I scratched their names into the wood, jammed it into the top of the mound of dirt at the grave, and told Ronnie and Evan how sorry I was while I walked without feeling my legs back to my worn-out tie rod end and sway bar link.

• • •

I drove through the smoke to the Albertsons across from the cemetery. There, I gulped bottled water and forced down the first food I saw: a banana from a stand inside the door and part of a day-old French loaf, dry. While I chewed and swallowed the tasteless sustenance, I grabbed a cart and navigated the bodies littering the aisles. This became easier once I reached Aisle 3 and found the flashlights and batteries, which were an upgrade from my iPhone.

I wasn't selective about the food I put in the cart—basically operated on autopilot. I did notice the junk-food aisle had more bodies than the other aisles. The health-food section had one lonely-looking woman in it. She wore a UPS uniform and held van keys in her outstretched left hand. Her hair had been dyed pink and she easily weighed two-hundred pounds, but as I looked at her I saw Ronnie in her place, Ronnie right in front of me in clear focus.

Outside the store, water from the Missouri River breached the riverbank and trickled onto the road. There were ten dams along the Missouri in the state of Montana. Maybe some of them were malfunctioning. Maybe the now-dead dam workers were supposed to close floodgates upriver, or open them downriver, or both. I drove the Caravan out of the parking lot and found a Conoco station on higher ground where there were no fires. But the gas pumps there wouldn't work. I checked the Caravan's gas gauge again. It told me I had thirty-two miles left, so I decided to fill up later. Right now I needed to get out of Great Falls before I gave in to temptation, drove back to the cemetery, and balled up in a fetal position beside that mound of dirt that I had shoveled down onto my wife and son.

But I didn't turn back and I did make one more stop before leaving town. The Walmart was across the river in Black Eagle. I hadn't shopped there in over a decade—my own mini-protest over its assault on Main Street. Now I moved around its aisles like an unthinking zombie and a still-functioning part of me took advantage of the Walton family's gift to retail commerce.

The pharmacy had painkillers, amoxicillin, dressing for my cheek.

Sporting goods had tents, sleeping bags, other camping gear.

The electronics department had a few shortwave and ham radios. I chose the biggest of each, located batteries, and stopped right there in the store to seek signs of life on the airwaves. The shortwave beeped and gave off static but raised no signals. Maybe I was operating it wrong or signals were blocked by the stanchions and metal roofing of the big-box store. Someone out there had to be sending a message. For a brief moment, I found myself listening for the sound of Ronnie's and Evan's voices.

I upgraded my Albertson's flashlight to a waterproof LED lamp with a compass and eventually I left both Walmart and Black Eagle without giving up and driving back to the cemetery. Heading north toward the prairie, I realized one good thing had happened: I had stopped lingering over the sight of dead bodies. Apart from the UPS driver in the health-food aisle, I couldn't recall a single face from the many corpses at both Albertson's and Walmart.

This felt like progress—a sign that maybe I was pulling myself together, moving forward.

More likely, every detail from every dead face had been etched on my brain but repression, that human tool of self-preservation, was telling me otherwise.

Whatever the case, I drove, and I didn't take any peeks in the rearview mirror. I did my best to look straight ahead.

4

AFTER A FEW MINUTES of driving, I had to slow the van and stop, had to rest. Otherwise, what was left of my heart would have blipped out between my ribs and sat smoldering on my lap like a dwindling briquette.

I sat there very still, parked on the shoulder, and tried to breathe deeply and just be still.

What do you call a meditating wolf?

Aware wolf!

"Wow," I said out loud, and resumed driving. Then I found myself saying, "You didn't do this. It's not your fault."

It was something Ronnie would have said.

"You have to take care of yourself."

Sounded reasonable, but Ronnie and Evan were still freshly interred, and my thoughts were a Rorschach blot of rain on their grave, coyotes clawing at loose soil, Evan rustling down in the dark mud because I'd buried him alive, and my bandaged cheek throbbed, my whole body still ached, and my wheezing made it hard to get air when I breathed. On top of this, post-concussion pain was a knife blade piercing my cranium just north of my eyebrows.

Oddly, though, despite the smorgasbord of woe, when I resumed driving there was a glimmer (just a glimmer) of something not entirely dreadful. There was the fact I *was* moving forward, I hadn't given in. The progress couldn't be denied. I was still around.

I could have gone to any number of farmhouses and thrown myself onto a soft bed, but then no, when it came down to it I couldn't. It felt unfair to the people there, and it would have called for the moving of dead bodies out of the living space. That type of task would have ended me, so instead I pitched my Walmart tent on the open prairie north of town, under a canopy of mature poplars on the edge of a wheat field. This gave me a panoramic view of Watson Coulee and the industrial west edge of Great Falls. Between eating canned food, checking the shortwave radio and (mainly) sleeping, I spent the next two days nursing a chill fever and watching the fires engulf pockets of the city slowly, more slowly than you might expect, with prodigious walls of steam wherever fire met the Missouri floodwaters. Despite the vivid show, there was something anticlimactic about the way the town died so gradually after everyone in it had died so fast.

The amoxicillin and painkillers aided the convalescence, but they did nothing for my mental health. Whether awake or asleep, I obsessed over Ronnie and Evan. I also immersed myself in a sea of questions that had no answers, questions that begat other questions, born of illness of the body and mind. Some of the more obvious ones:

What to do now? Go find survivors? Stay here and make sure I'm visible when the National Guard comes?

Some were darker: Did Ronnie and Evan suffer, or did everyone everywhere really drop dead at the same time?

The biggest question of all, which I asked myself every few minutes: *What the hell happened?*

And that question's obvious cousin: *Why didn't it happen to me?*

A fact that ruled out positive answers: No rescuers had come to the aid of the 60,000 souls of Great Falls, Montana. This, combined with the death of all radio signals from near and far, told me this plague or, I don't know, supercharged virus or whatever had a potentially planet-wide scope. But since I was alive, other people were alive too, right? At the very least another skydiver. A deep-sea diver. Someone who was immune to this ... to this what? *Was* it a virus? Bioterrorism? How could it kill the people on the ground and the people in my plane but spare me? Did my high-speed fall—115 miles per hour—was that what saved me? My unique movement within a certain pocket of air pressure shielded me from a blast from an otherwise apocalyptic pathogen or radiation pulse or microwave beam? If so, were other jumpers still breathing? Or climbers up on Everest? How about miners and spelunkers and sailors in submarines? I couldn't be the only one left.

Two days of such thoughts. Two days of sorrow and unrest, with an always-returning thirst for more time with Ronnie and Evan. On the third day, the fever persisted, but I could lie there no longer. I drove down the hill to a Ford dealership in Black Eagle and swapped my van for a Ford F-150 truck with a full tank of gas. Off toward the heart of Great Falls, I saw wisps of steam and smoke from now-dwindling fires.

Mosquitoes had been harassing me at the campsite. Hawks and crows had been circling overhead, keeping tabs on the sluggish late-spring gophers. Did their presence mean all animals were alive? Maybe some non-human creatures had died along with homo sapiens? The ones with almost-human biologies?

I drove to Pet Paradise on 10th Ave. to do a survey, and was surprised to see the building still standing. The Pizza Hut next door smoldered. The Exxon station across the street looked like Ray Bradbury's firemen had been at it. I remembered buying gas for my first car at that station, back when it was a Shell station and I was seventeen years old. I paid with $3.16 in change, mainly dimes and nickels, and the gas jockey, a burly old man with a "Moose" nametag stitched to his overalls, took forever to count the money and gave me a smile that said, *Ah, to be young again.*

Inside the pet shop, there was only one human corpse (an explosively pungent body that I did my best to avoid). The animals sounded alive—at least the birds and the barking puppies did. I left the front door ajar and walked down the aisles opening cages. The kittens were the first to be freed. They welcomed this, springing from their enclosures without showing much interest in me. The puppies, two Jack Russells, yipped and whined. They nipped at my fingers while I opened their cage.

They were impossibly cute, which terrified me. I lowered them to the floor, watched them jump at my legs, and soon felt melted by their need. I opened a bag of Purina, dumped it on the floor and used a dog-food bowl to scoop water out of a fish tank so the puppies and kittens could drink.

While the animals gorged themselves, I walked the aisles and liberated rabbits, guinea pigs, ferrets—even a gopher, of all things

($39.95, when the gophers just outside the door had been free and easy to snare for prairie boys who felt the need). Almost all of these creatures had survived, and they leapt at the chance to leave the shop.

About half the birds left, too, but the other half just peered at their open cage doors with bemused looks, like they didn't understand the concept of freedom.

The store's lone primate, a pig-tailed macaque from Thailand, was dead. What did big-city zoos look like? Dead orangutans? Dead lemurs and gibbons? What other animals were genetically close to humans? Or maybe immune to whatever had killed all the people?

By the time I reached the reptiles, the two Jack Russells were at my heels again, demanding attention. I tried to ignore them because their need was dangerous; it could trigger weakness.

"You're not coming with me," I said, though I knew the opposite was true, and I walked the rest of the aisles with both of them biting at my shoes and pant legs.

(The kittens, meanwhile, must have sensed my instability; they were gone.)

The reptiles were dead, including the snakes, and about half the fish. Four days without food, without heat lamps or oxygen pumps. Urban-fire smoke in the air. Many things could have killed them. The hamsters and hedge hogs were still alive, as was one of the two gerbils. Was opening their cages providing them with anything more than a brief reprieve? I went back to the truck, my two new charges close behind me.

I had to pick them up to put them in the cab. This I did without really looking at them. Still, tears welled up. I was their friend and master; they would shower me with affection no matter what.

As I drove away from Pet Paradise, the two Jacks stopped capering just long enough for me to feel them staring at me. I kept my eyes on the road, tried to ignore them, but they kept staring; I saw judgment in their focus.

"I can't do it," I told them. "I let them out of their cages. What more do you want?"

The smaller Jack yipped.

"I'm not even sure I can save myself," I said, "and you want me to go back and feed rabbits and guinea pigs?"

It wasn't until I was almost out of town, popping Advil while driving past a motorcyclist in shredded leather, that the two Jacks' guilt trip worked. I drove back to Pet Paradise and liberated cat food from the shelves and veggies and pellets from a back room where two aproned employees lay with greenish faces and flies starting to gather. I hefted all the animal sustenance outside the front doors, slashed the bags with a utility knife, poured everything onto the street. One of the two kittens was there. She dove right in. There was no sign of the rabbits or gerbils or ferrets. Some of them would show up sooner or later. The ones that didn't—and even the ones that did, now that I thought of it—would soon become prey for the local coyote population.

By pouring this food onto the street, I had laid out a big buffet for the predators of the animals I was trying to save.

I tried to pick up the kitten, but she jumped away—and jumped every time I tried to close the distance on her.

I told her, "You know what'll happen if you stay?" and tried some *here kitchy-kitchy* talk, then half-lunged to pick her up—but she leapt out of reach and bounded down the sidewalk and around the corner of the building.

I walked back to the truck convinced I had saved her only in order to kill her.

5

AFTER LEAVING PET PARADISE the second time, I moved the two Jacks to the passenger seat and kept my eyes on the road. My thoughts flashed again on that high counter at Walgreens, but I deleted the image before it could take root. I spent two more days recuperating at the camp. For much of that time, I kept the dogs zipped inside the tent with ample food and water while I stayed outside and tried to give my body the rest it needed. My cheek deflated to its normal shape, but the feeling of being alone cut to the bone. The presence of the two Jacks didn't help—and if it did, at times when I forced myself to be with them, the yearning for Ronnie and Evan stamped out any creeping amelioration. These cold emotional winds brought with them the obvious, crippling dread that this was it, this was all the human company I would ever have: me, myself and I.

If that turned out to be true? What then? On a practical level, food and shelter would be abundant. I could learn to survive winters, to treat illness, maybe even to set a broken bone, if it came to that, but solitude would be a challenge. Man was not meant to live alone. So I retreated to a refuge of manufactured hope, telling myself it was only a matter of time until others came on the scene. I found myself scanning the prairie for signs of life. I longed for high-school girlfriends and distant relatives and a boy who'd beaten me up after a Little League game (Lukas Jaworski; I had called him a dweeb after he dropped a routine infield fly). I started hearing noises in the night. Twice I scrambled over sleeping puppies and bolted out of the tent believing I'd heard a vehicle.

When the solitude got closest to overtaking me, I talked to Evan but he refused to respond, so I invited Ronnie in and she showed up and gave me some tough love.

"Stop feeling sorry for yourself."

"I'm here with you as long as you need me, but please stop whining."

"Get yourself together. Go find other survivors."

On the morning of the fifth day at my camp—now six days after the world ended without me—I bundled up the two Jacks and drove back to the roadside car where I thought I'd seen a sign of life. This time I stepped very carefully around the big rock that had tripped me up. Even before I reached the car, the smell of death announced itself. The woman inside was bloated and ashen, with her shirt pulled taught across her back. Bloody foam leaked out of her nose and now-gaping mouth. I held my breath and checked the back seat again.

Empty—like it had been cleaned shortly before the end. What was it I'd seen here? A fluttering of sorts. A hand waving. An arm giving a last, truncated flail. That's what I remembered; I hadn't dreamed it up. My eyesight was good (I'd never needed glasses). This woman had to have been alive for a while after the others died, at least long enough to signal me when she heard the sound of my approaching truck. Maybe the killing agent hadn't affected everyone at the same time or in the same way. Maybe, again, it hadn't affected some people at all. Since it hadn't killed me, that was more than a theory; it was obviously true.

And how about this: maybe there was something in this local environment—something here in Great Falls, Montana, the air or the water or the angle of the planet on that particular day of the year—something that had delayed this woman's death for a few hours and that had saved my life altogether.

I sought rational answers while driving back to the campsite, and on the outskirts of town I came across the Episcopal Church of Salvation—Ronnie's church. It looked proud of itself, with its pious steeple and its stained-glass Jesus giving all the corpses out front a look that said, *Sucks for you, but we all knew this day would come.*

I parked and stared at Jesus a long time.

"A lot of good you did."

The smaller of the two Jacks, Little Jack, yipped in agreement.

When I first met Ronnie, back in college, she was a regular parishioner at an Episcopal church in Bozeman. In recent years, she'd attended the church here in Great Falls only sporadically, usually on religious holidays, until tragedy entered out lives and she leaned on her faith, plunking herself down in a pew every morning of every day of the week in order to address the pain.

I never accompanied her. I was a life-long agnostic who'd never truly understood what it meant to have faith. I climbed out of the truck and found myself regressing to childish behavior: I gathered three big rocks from the alley around back and started throwing them at Stained Glass Jesus. Once his head was punched out of the glass, I muttered "That oughta do it," then told myself to get a grip, don't fall apart so easily.

I drove to the Walgreens and left the two Jacks in the truck while holding my breath and seeking out Vicks VapoRub and surgical masks.

After dabbing the Vicks under my nostrils and donning a mask, I tiptoed through the bloating corpses and reupped on food, water and other essentials: Bic lighters, batteries of various sizes, sunscreen, insect repellent. The combination of the Vicks and the mask soon began to burn my sinuses. I pulled off the mask, stepped over a distended teenager in a gangsta cap, and asked myself what provisions I was forgetting.

Then I heard a groan, a low hiss of someone too injured to move, too weak to speak. It came from the next aisle, and it reminded me of my friend Jason's father, who'd died of a rare brain disease the summer before I left for college in Bozeman. I had watched Jason feed the withered man homemade soup shortly before the end, and the sound of the tortured slurping and labored throat clearings and the pungent tang in the room told me this not-yet-elderly husband and father would soon be joining Sean Vilmack in the great beyond. But this—this moaning sound here today—was not the sound of death; it was a miraculous indicator of life. I dashed to the end of the aisle and called out as I went, "Who's there!"

Another hiss. Another breathless moan.

When I reached the next aisle, I saw a dead woman lying face-up on the floor. She hissed and groaned again, an open-mouthed, post-mortem retch as gas escaped. I gagged and stumbled out of the store without any of the supplies I'd gathered.

As I recovered in the parking lot, I said to Ronnie, "I need a plan."

She replied, "You need to go find survivors."

"Maybe I can find them here."

"That'd be a neat trick. There's no one left."

"No, there's me left. Something killed everyone, but something also kept me alive. It had to have kept others alive, too."

"But you're the only one here," Ronnie said.

"But how do we know that? How do we know people aren't waiting for help not far away?"

"The devastation is pretty thorough."

To which I replied, "I can't be alone. I won't accept it." While walking to the truck, I added, "And I can't leave town because that would mean leaving you and Evan."

She laughed at that. "Then take us with you, dummy. Family life, at this point in the game, is clearly a state of mind."

She always had a way of cutting to the core of the matter, but she was also wrong. Someone else on these prairies was alive. Someone was holed up in their house, in shock, crippled by fear, praying for help.

And I had an idea of how to reach them.

6

BACK IN THE TRUCK, of course the two Jacks wanted to play. For the first time, I let my defenses down, roughhoused them a little, let them crawl up on me and nip at my nose.

"You're right," I told them. "Let's end the funeral." I paused to clear my throat, then summoned my eleven-year-old self, the wannabe Steven Wright:

I was walking my dogs when a guy stopped me and said, "Beautiful dogs. Are those Jack Russells?"

I told him, "No, they're all mine!"

I remembered telling this one at my sister Joanie's birthday party. The audience was a dozen or so nine-year-olds, and the joke flew over their heads—but it slayed the two Jacks now. They play-growled and bit at my pants, the smaller one, Little Jack, falling off the seat and onto the floor mat.

"You like that, huh? Then how about:

What did the Dalmatian say after he finished eating?

That hit the spot!"

They applauded in their puppy-dog way. I mined my memory for more eye-rollers as I drove back to the camp. When the joke telling started to feel forced, I took a different tack toward positivity, telling them they would have loved Ronnie. "She was your type of woman. She would have showered you with affection."

I told them how she approached everyone she met with kindness and a belief that we were all fundamentally good; to her mind, the bad people in the world were not born evil; they were damaged by misfortune or mistreatment. She never succumbed to cynicism or petty grievances and was always willing to put her money where her mouth was. Case in point: the fact that she supported me while I wrote my first novel—was happy to do so, even eager for her new husband to give up his fairly steady drywalling job while he chased his dream—and she knew I didn't want kids but she also knew that if she could cajole me into having one anyway I would go gaga over him or her almost to the point of turning the stomachs of everyone who saw me transform into a saccharine SuperDad. Her faith in people was a logic that was both naïve and prescient. To her mind, having a child would be a profound and life-changing thing for me because there was no other logical option—and it played out just the way she knew it would.

When we reached the camp, I tired the dogs out with a half hour of wrestling and rolling in the grass—and a few more very bad jokes that now sounded like a desperate man talking—and then zipped them in the tent while I set about preparing to find survivors.

First item on my to-do list: move all of my things into the farmhouse across the field from the tent. This was preceded by the necessary relocation of three corpses from various points in the house. In dragging out one of the bodies, I slipped while straining to pull her down the stairs: I fell and she landed on top of me and black liquid oozed out of her mouth and stuck like gummy charcoal to my neck.

This sent me back to the tent for the afternoon, where I ignored the two Jacks, zipped myself inside my sleeping bag, and screwed my eyes shut in order to sleep the new world away. After the horror ebbed, I forced myself to keep doing what had to be done. I opened windows and bleached the house, then spliced/soldered a gas generator into the power line. There were no sparks or explosions when I turned the lights on, but since I was no electrician and a kaboom was not entirely unlikely, I kept the generator a good thirty yards from the house, just in case.

Then I started visiting radio-station transmitters out on the prairie. The biggest one, WLVY, "Montana's Best Talk," had back-up broadcast panels through which I planned to send a voice message far and wide. All I had to do was learn how to power up the transmitter and record and send a message.

"All I had to do." I thought I had good tech skills, but getting a radio station running was no easy task. There was more to the job than haphazardly splicing in a generator and hitting "broadcast" on a control panel. There were things like "kilohertz frequencies," "megawatt power storage," "demodulation" and "remodulation." So I got busy researching. I scrounged tech documents from the WLVY station downtown, and when the language got too technical, I found explanations in books at the Great Falls Public Library (it buoyed my spirits to see that that particular building had escaped the floods and fires).

It took me four days to solve the power issue (I learned to charge not the transmitter itself, but its back-up battery, which called for yet another dicey-seeming cable splice). The lights came on, the panels buzzed, but whatever had been playing one week ago did not resume playing now.

But fine, I could record a message and play it on a loop—if only I could find a panel with a "record" option. The hardware looked spaceship technical and the words and numbers on the machines might as well have been in Klingon. Back to the books I went.

Meanwhile, in the evenings, the lack of human company gave rise to painful yearning. I spent those hours trying my best not to wallow in the past or in all that had been lost. I played with the two Jacks and taught myself how to juggle (a strangely effective strategy for escaping my own mind) and read other books from the library, books that might give me plausible theories on what had killed everyone.

I spent the first two nights with volumes on pandemics, environmental catastrophes and astronomical cataclysms. There were some lethal, indiscriminate killers in the world and out in space, but nothing like what had happened after I jumped out of the plane. Also, it stood to reason that if some flash annihilation had happened at some time in Earth's past, I would have read about it or heard about it by now. Hollywood would have made a movie about it starring a hot young actor from some superhero franchise.

While reading these books, I sensed I should have been researching something else, but that "something else" was not readily available to me—hadn't been for years; I'd tamped it down, filed it away at the back of my mind in order to ward off pain, even if it had bubbled up from time to time (after reading a particular book or hearing someone's offhand, triggering comment or encountering two impossibly cute Jack Russells in a pet shop after the apocalypse). Now my defenses were down and the thing actually rose close to the surface for a split second before I managed to evict it.

The thing was this: Ronnie and I had had a child four years before Evan was born. His name was Oliver (the same baby whose birth had turned me into a fawning SuperDad). When he was fourteen months old, Oliver died, just like that. I was fixing the handle on the child gate at the top of the stairs when I heard him fall. The autopsy finding was no finding at all. Oliver had died of a thing called SUDC—Sudden Unexpected Death in Childhood.

Abrupt expiry from an undetermined cause.

After he died, Ronnie and I fell into a deep, dark hole that took two years to climb out of. We almost didn't make it (nearly killed each other instead), and now, today, the obvious potential connection between Sudden Unexpected Death in Childhood and Sudden Unexpected Death in Everyone tried to assert itself—and in fact should have been front of mind the first moment I gathered everyone was dead but, again, as soon as it arose, I stuffed it back down. Sometimes one part of your brain tells another part, *No, that's not a good place for us; we are not going to go there.*

I reimmersed myself in the books on various disasters and then turned to books on the effects of altitude on the body. I'd jumped out of the plane at 12,000 feet. That was considered "very high" by mountain climbers because at that altitude there was an instant decrease in hemoglobin. But I was only up there a few minutes, didn't need an oxygen mask. My body compensated for the lack of O_2. I would have had to climb to 26,000 feet ("the death zone") for the altitude to have had an irreversible effect on my body.

And anyway, if altitude had kept me alive, why hadn't it saved the other jumpers?

I put the altitude books aside and started consuming books that would help me keep my head screwed on straight despite the challenges posed by solitude:

How to Live with Yourself: Wisdom Through Meditation

Cruel and Unusual Punishment: The Case Against Solitary Confinement.

The most intriguing book was *Alone with My Thoughts*, about the Oregon Hermit, a computer-science student who, at the age of nineteen, decided that, all things being equal, he hated people. He dropped out of his own life and spent twenty-four years in a poison-ivy-protected camp in Oregon's Sun Pass State Forest. For food, he ate highway roadkill and committed petty burglary at summer cottages and campsites just outside the park. The gist of the book was that this man's solitude didn't mentally maim him; he actually sought it out, reveled in it. But why? How did he make the lack of human contact work? If I could answer that question, I could arm myself to survive in this grim new world until people heard my radio signal and we all got together and sang *Kumbaya*.

I would broadcast on AM, just a hair under 28 MHz. My library research told me signals at that frequency could bounce off the ground and the ionosphere for up to six hundred miles in all directions. That would take my message all the way north to Edmonton, Alberta, west and south to the Rockies and east to about the Minnesota border, maybe farther at nighttime. That translated into roughly ten million people (more, if the signal slipped through some mountain valleys). There had to be survivors within that radius. The alternative was too bleak to consider.

When I wasn't researching radio-station equipment, I maintained my pre-end-of-the-world exercise routine: a four-mile run in the mornings, but this time along the prairie blacktop, not at the corpse-littered track at Great Falls High School.

I also forced myself to play with the two Jacks every two hours and to watch at least one hour of TV per day. The farmhouse had an old DVD collection of *Wheel of Fortune* and *CSI: Miami*. I watched both shows not because I liked them, but in order to hear human voices. Solitude would not get the best of me.

But mainly I worked at the transmitter. After a week of studying and one day of trial and error, I learned how to record and send a message. I read into the microphone:

I'm a survivor in Great Falls, Montana. Or maybe I'm dead and I'm recording this in Hell.

I could change the wording later; the main thing was to get a message—any message—to play.

When I did hear my voice in the headphones, I felt like kissing the console. I dashed outside, turned on the radio in the truck and found the station.

—*I'm dead and I'm recording this in Hell.*

Genius! I deserved a Nobel Prize! Now all I had to do was record a useful communication and keep the generator full of gas and wait.

No. More than that. If anyone heard the message, they still had to know how to find me once they got to Great Falls.

I found paint in the barn, climbed up on the roof of the house, and slopped on a bright red SURVIVOR, then I went and painted the farmhouse's rural-route address on billboards on all big roads leading into town. Then I recorded a new message:

I'm a survivor in Great Falls, Montana. I'm unhurt but alone. If you can broadcast, do so at close to this frequency. If you can operate a ham radio, I'll check mine at nine a.m. Mountain Standard Time each day.

Also not the best message in the world, but I could hone it whenever I wanted to. Over the next two weeks, I did that almost every day, providing location details and tips on everything from how to do a poor man's cable splice to how to start a stubborn generator—but mainly to indulge in the redeeming hope that I was talking to someone.

I also followed a fairly stringent daily schedule: the morning run, play time with the puppies, then a transmitter check, books on solitude, more puppy play, and radio checks for signals from other survivors. After that, TV, puppies, and fine dining in the form of non-perishables from Walmart, followed by a nighttime transmitter check before climbing into bed with the two Jacks and reading myself to sleep.

I didn't summon Ronnie during this period and I didn't go home, didn't even drive past the house. Home was like a bare wire. If I touched it—zap, instant thoughts of the high counter in Walgreens. Only twice did I deviate from my daily tasks, and that was to go look at the car in the ditch just south of town, where I thought I'd seen a sign of life. I couldn't not go look at it, like a cryptographer puzzling over a cipher, but the corpse there served up only a stomach-churning odor and advancing stages of bloat and putrefaction.

On the Fourth of July, I drove to a gas station on the west edge of town and grabbed some Twinkies and cherry soda from the shop inside, then ran a line of gas from the curb to the tanks. Then I sat back in a lawn chair and ignited the liquid fuse and watched the station blow.

What do you call a duck that celebrates Independence Day?

A fire-quacker!

The pyrotechnics did nothing for me—didn't pick me up, didn't depress me (and the explosions traumatized the two Jacks). This was just another senseless episode in a senseless world, a manufactured waste of time, though time, under these conditions, wasn't exactly precious.

Fifteen days after I started sending my message, the signal disappeared from the home stereo. I went out to the truck and turned on the radio. It wasn't playing there, either.

It was also gone at the transmitter itself. Everything else worked. The power stayed on. The consoles and panels worked. I could erase and re-record my message. I just couldn't get it to broadcast.

So I hit the books again, but it felt different this time. The puppies were no longer a new thing, and I wasn't new to them (their need to play abated a little, which felt like a very cruel insult). And I'd run out of *CSI* episodes. And the farmhouse toilet was backing up (I'd been flushing manually with buckets of water). My earlier hopes of finding people were fading to a dull, slow-burn anxiety that I would never achieve anything this way. Maybe Ronnie had been right. Maybe survivors were *out there*, not here in Montana, and I should have been going to them, not doing poor man's cable splices and sitting in a library consuming knowledge of questionable utility. Maybe I was staying in Great Falls not in order to reach people through a radio signal, but because I was too scared to find out just how utterly dead the rest of the world was.

Maybe all of that, but it wouldn't make sense to leave now, not after all the work I'd done. Not until I at least got another message on the air.

So I stopped bogging down in what ifs and worked towards doing that.

• • •

A week after I lost the signal (and still couldn't get it back), I was downtown, walking from the library to the truck, when I saw that the two Jacks weren't right behind me. While in the library, I usually gave them some newspapers to chew on and to play-fight over. On the way out, they usually stuck close to me, but this time I was almost to the truck and they were still back at the library steps wrestling, having a ball not far from a moldering businessman with a still-wrapped Subway sandwich just beyond his outstretched fingers.

"Come on, guys!" I hollered. "You can play in the cab!"

Big Jack stopped wrestling and looked up at me.

"Atta boy! Let's go! Double-time!"

He started prancing, then stopped and tilted his head, confused.

"C'mon! Food in the truck! Milk Bones!"

Little Jack stayed on the stairs and licked himself, but Big Jack started toward me again in the cutest little puppy gallop imaginable.

But as fast as he'd started running, he stopped. He whined, lowered his head close to the ground.

I understood what was happening just before a coyote sprang out from behind a parked car, scooped Big Jack up into his mouth, and made off with him without breaking stride. Big Jack yipped as the coyote shook its head and loped somewhat casually down the middle of the street.

I dropped my books and launched myself toward Little Jack, who was still on the library steps, too scared to move. Two more coyotes darted out from behind vehicles and chased him halfway up the steps, then one of them deftly scooped him up by the neck like a mother dog carrying her pup and ran off toward its pack mate. Another coyote materialized half a block away and soon all four coyotes were trotting down the street toward the Dairy Queen.

I gave chase for two blocks before giving up and just standing there, stricken. I couldn't get any air, couldn't breathe. My chest felt constricted.

A little later, when I could breathe again, I burst into a wretched, sobbing kind of laughter. The thing that had happened slotted in perfectly with the days that had preceded it and all the days that seemed likely to follow. Death was the humor of the new times. Thick skin couldn't deflect it. Notions of safety and permanence were arbitrary.

My man-losing-his-mind laughter went on for a good long time before it lost its edge and turned into a saner brand of straightforward sorrow.

• • •

By that evening, I was blind drunk on Canadian Club whiskey and driving toward the transmitter with one eye closed (the only way to keep the road in focus) when I heard my gas generator explode.

So much for amateur cable splice jobs.

When I reached the transmitter, I saw the shack engulfed in flames, though the tower itself was untouched.

This time there would be no crying or emoting of any kind; there would be a detached, whiskey-aided taking of stock—an acknowledgement that things wouldn't work out the way I'd planned (in the days that followed D-Day, booze sometimes offered truths free of distracting counter-arguments).

My mind turned to Ronnie dead at her office. The image of her was clear as day; I discovered her all over again, her facing away from me, doing me that courtesy, me too afraid to approach her and really see her.

I also thought of my first son, Oliver, who arrived in my consciousness like a haunting intruder. This was the first time since Evan's birth four years earlier that I didn't try to think him away. I relived the feeling that had gone through me when I'd heard him fall down dead while I fixed the spring on that baby gate—and it was at this point that the booze ceased to help. Oliver was no longer something to be kept at arm's length. His capabilities expanded. He could overcome any strategy I employed against him.

So while I watched the transmitter shack burn, I let the overcoming occur: I sat in the truck and reeled. It was like dreaming while awake, the past mingling with the present, dead Oliver returning to life.

Even if it was only so he could die again.

7

FOR TWO YEARS after Oliver's death, I couldn't say his name out loud. For the first couple weeks, I couldn't say much of anything. I also had trouble looking Ronnie, my brave and loving wife, in the eyes, because his death was my fault, because I was there when he died. And because at times it was her fault, too, because despite her many virtues she was his mother and yet he was still dead. The solace that came our way, the wave of support from friends and family and acquaintances—it was a blur. Just as I recall only a few haunting details about finding Ronnie dead in her office, Oliver's funeral remains a hazy memory.

Ronnie coped with the death better than I did. She took strength from her church—early-morning visits to The House of the Stained Glass Jesus for thirteen days straight—and from her sister and her mother, who came up from Billings to stay with us for two weeks that to me felt like two years. Ronnie had long heart to hearts with them, in fact spent most of her time with them, while I spent my time pestering hospital staff for an autopsy report and accusing the doctors of not looking into the death certificate finding (which was that Oliver's cause of death "could not be determined"). While I sought a clear cause, I was coldly relieved that my brother and sister would not be visiting (they both lived in Europe and couldn't make the trip just yet) and that my mother, who'd retired to Scottsdale, came up to Great Falls for one day only, the day of the funeral. She headed back to Arizona the next afternoon not because she was cold, but because her son was reacting very poorly and clearly needed to be alone.

Meanwhile, Ronnie coped too well for my liking. She took care of the funeral, the notice in the paper, the phone calls and unannounced drop-ins. When I heard the home phone ring or saw someone approach the house with comfort food in hand, I retreated to my home office and let her deal with it. And she never judged me for that, never accused me of hiding or of not holding up my end of the bargain—which only made me resent her. Her grief was no less real than mine, but what right did she have to fight through it so valiantly? There was something devious about her strength. Her kindness, that wonderful, life-sustaining benevolence was no longer beautiful; it was a kind of character affliction that prevented her from seeing just how overwhelming this whole thing was.

But I dwelled more on other things. I needed that autopsy report. When I did get it, it gave me the worst possible conclusion. Sudden Unexpected Death in Childhood killed about four hundred children a year. It meant just what it sounded like. Even an autopsy and full investigation of both the death scene and Oliver's medical history (to say nothing of his potentially homicidal parents) gave the cops no clues as to the cause of death. All we knew was he was alive one moment and dead the next.

To make matters worse, everything I learned about SUDC suggested I would never find a cause. The closest potential cause—theoretically—was, as one doctor told me, "an undiagnosable neurological condition." The same doctor added, "I know it's hard to accept, but sometimes people die and we don't know why."

Or: sometimes all people die and we don't know why.

When I shared the SUDC diagnosis with Ronnie, she gave me some pointed silence.

"Well?" I said. "Are we going to just accept this?"

"What do you want to do, sue someone?"

"I don't know what I want. I just know I don't want *this*. What do *you* want?"

She nodded gravely at the question, gave it extended thought. "I think I'll send Mom and Lisa back to Billings. I need to go back to work."

Again, that ability to move forward—to at least try to transcend the tragedy—felt disrespectful. We had unfinished business here. Anger had to be served.

"And you should go back to your novel," she added. "I know it will feel wrong, and maybe you won't write anything good for a while, but we have to get back to life as soon as possible. Otherwise, we'll end up as junkies or something."

To which I replied, "It's too soon, I can't just turn it off."

"Doesn't matter what you can or can't do. It's what has to happen."

She sent her mom and sister back to Billings and returned to work two weeks to the day after Oliver died. I didn't try to stop her. Instead, I silently judged her, drank myself half-dead, then cobbled together enough sense of purpose to try it her way for a while. Better to force acceptance than to embalm myself with Bacardi. I stuffed the autopsy report in a drawer and threw myself into my new novel (the second in the series) with desperate gusto. It worked, too, kind of. I began to experience periods in each day in which I didn't think about Oliver. I was able to escape him—it—for fleeting moments. And common sense told me that with practice I would get better at this.

This was the start of a cool détente period between Ronnie and me, each of us concentrating on work and on the ability of time to blunt our pain. A part of me accused us of trying to kick sand over a raging inferno, but another part said there was bravery in fighting to move on, in focusing on the future. Only problem was, we didn't focus on each other. Contact between me and Ronnie had a faintly sour taste; we avoided it whenever possible, devolved into roommates. I had my office; she had the rest of the house. We ate all our meals together, but in near silence. Conversation was short, polite, practical. Leisure time became a chore that we were quick to fill with separate agendas. Sex became a memory. We both wanted so badly for the specter of Oliver to grow smaller that we would kill our relationship to do it.

In response to this method of coping, my dead son took a short break, then morphed into a presence more concentrated, more nuclear. He announced, many times and in many ways, that he wouldn't be beaten, we *were* kicking sand at a big fire, we were being foolish. So now, knowing this, were we still naïve enough to think we could erase our own memories?

I mentioned to Ronnie that this was how it was going for me—and I suspected it was going this way for her too—and she responded with, "Maybe. But we have to have faith."

"Please don't say that word to me."

"We have to stay the course," she said.

"I don't think I can."

"We have to give it time."

"That's what I've been doing," I said.

"Then give it more time. And if you can't do that, then…"

"Then what?" I asked.

"Then maybe it would be better for both of us if you moved out—at least until something starts to change."

The statement was a shock, but within the shock was a tinge of relief. To this day I don't know why it felt good to hear her say that to me.

8

AFTER WATCHING the transmitter shack burn, I opened another bottle and poured the alcohol into me while driving home to my little house on the tree-lined avenue in town. The neighborhood fires had stopped four doors down. They took out Ed Walden's house and garage but left his fancy RV unscathed in the driveway. In the living room, I paused over Ronnie's photo albums. I didn't open any. I chugged whiskey and staggered to the bedroom. Her hairbrush was still on the dresser. Her Atwood novel was still on the nightstand. There was no more scent of her in the bedsheets or in her clothes. My skydiving jumpsuit was still at the foot of the bed.

The next morning, I guzzled two warm beers for breakfast, stepped into my office, and a threw a nicely cathartic fit, bashing my computer monitor with the keyboard, ripping my books out of the bookcases, busting my ergonomic chair over the desk. While I did these things I bellowed:

So long, Microsoft!
Goodbye, Mr. Writer!
Useless! Can't use you!

The latter statement was directed at *The Complete Pelican Shakespeare*, which until then I had considered the best book in the history of the English language. When the spasm of pointless book beating played itself out, I picked up some vodka to go with the whiskey and quaffed both as if they were water while I drove around town. I looked with blurred, maudlin vision at the park where Evan used to play, then went out to the cemetery and blubbered over Oliver's grave, and then over Ronnie's and Evan's double grave, and when I was done, I drove to Malmstrom Air Force Base, on the eastern edge of town, and looked at how dead the fine members of the United States military were, with their uniformed bodies twisted in myriad ways.

All this woe-is-me wandering made me hungry, so I ate a bag of potato chips in the truck, vomited out the rolled-down window, and wiped the dregs of upchuck off the door with my shirtsleeve.

My mom used to tell me that barfing was hard.

But I got through it with flying colors!

The next two days were the same: junk food at mealtime, booze at all times, more reckless anger, no sustained thoughts. I didn't wash or shave, didn't change my clothes. Twice I returned to my home office and tore up more books because they were items of old meaning that had led me absolutely nowhere. While struggling to rip pages out of *Moby Dick*, I saw a coyote in the street out front.

"Murderer!"

I darted out the front door and threw a rock at it. I missed. The coyote didn't flinch, so I scrounged in the flowerbed for a bigger rock. By the time I found one, the coyote was gone and I was covered in dirt.

On the third day of this binge, I sat on Ronnie's chair in the bathroom and stared at myself in the mirror. Ronnie's face looked back at me. She was beautiful but pale, a corpse bride. I took a slug of booze, then found some blush and started patting it on her cheeks. She gave me a caustic look that could have flash-frozen a tidal wave.

"Stop it."

"That's what I'm doing," I said. "I am stopping it in spectacular fashion."

"Get yourself together," she said. "Go find people."

"I've never seen you this pale," I said, dabbing some blush on her chin.

"The closest big city," she said. "Calgary."

"If they were alive, they'd be broadcasting."

"Then Salt Lake."

"Too Mormon."

"Oh. So now you want to start hating, is that it?"

"I'd never make it to Salt Lake," I said. "The Interstate'll be packed."

"Then Seattle—and stay off the Interstate. You can make it if you plan right."

I gave her silence.

"You can drive it in two days. Four million people."

"Four million former people." I worked the blush around her eyes, careful with the brows.

"And Lewis-McChord," she said. "It's one of the biggest army bases in the country."

"Clearly you haven't seen Malmstrom. The military is no different from anyone else."

"But if you're so sure everyone everywhere is the same as here, then why hang around here waiting to be found?"

I grabbed the mascara from the counter. "Should we move on to mascara now?"

"I bet when it happened paratroopers were jumping out of planes."

"Maybe," I said, and took a hit of whiskey. "If they were, they're now pancakes." I started working mascara into her lashes. "I do think I have a flair for this."

She gave me a sad chuckle. "You think this is happening to you? Nothing is happening to you. You've been given a pass." She let me think about that, then added, "I'm not sure you're the man I married. Good fortune is wasted on you."

She disappeared, leaving me looking at myself in the mirror; with all the makeup, I was halfway to bride-of-Frankenstein status.

No, I wasn't the man she'd married. I wasn't the man of a month ago, or even three days ago, before the Jacks were taken.

There was still whiskey on my lap. I placed the bottle on the counter very gently, like it held highly corrosive acid.

Then I toweled some of the gunk off my face and went out to Ed Walden's RV to see if the shower's hot water heater worked.

• • •

The next day was spent finding a Humvee and trailer at Malmstrom and loading them with supplies. This included 12 gas canisters, dozens of MREs, water and supermarket food. I also gathered drugs: three different

My Only Friend, the End

antibiotics, two antivirals, Vicodin, Dilaudid, old packages of Percocet and a few other heavies that easily qualified as overkill. Plus more aspirin and ibuprofen. A broken arm without painkillers would not be pleasant, nor would a serious infection. There was a concern that things might get rough and I might go running straight for a cocktail of hard drugs, but I couldn't bring myself to hit the road without them. As a hedge against rash decisions, I also packed an unhealthy but nonlethal amount of rye whiskey and vodka, though the thought of more alcohol after the three-day bender was enough to bring back roiling nausea.

One last category of supplies for the journey: weapons. The world was now a wild place: coyotes, wolves, bears, snakes. A certain brand of survivor might also not be friendly. Therefore: knives for utility and protection, and two Rossi 352 handguns, both of them old-fashioned revolvers, because pistols tended to jam. And two SKS carbines, which would ward off animals and provide me with fresh meat if I decided I needed it. I didn't keep any of the weapons in the Humvee with me. They all travelled in the trailer. I needed them but didn't want them. They were as attractive to me as the alcohol.

On the way out of Great Falls, I stopped at one of my billboards and crossed out the farmhouse address with black spray paint. Underneath, I sprayed:

Survivor driving to Seattle
CB channel 9

The emergency contact channel. Calling the end of the world an "emergency" seemed not so much like an understatement as a weak attempt at humor. Still, I kept the Humvee's CB on while I drove and I listened hard, with a hope that at times almost made me feel okay.

I also kept VapoRub under my nostrils, because the open prairie smelled almost as bad as the city. There was dead and dying cattle, pig farms, chicken farms. These had a taste as well as a smell, so I sucked on citrus Vitamin C tablets and asked myself how long human decomposition took. How long before the bodies liquefied? Out on the roads and inside the baking vehicles, probably not long, maybe a matter of weeks. In the buildings in the cities, in dark basements, in places with dead air and little or no light— much longer. Seattle would smell a lot worse than Montana. Would it have a host of diseases to worry about? Was I driving toward a fatal, cadaver-borne illness? These things would have to be researched as I went.

I drove at low speeds, especially when approaching crashed cars and blind corners. After an hour on the road, I joined the Interstate at a rural junction called Ulm. To get there, I had to cross a bridge over the bursting Missouri River. In the middle of the bridge was a Greyhound bus lying on its side, with passengers splayed across the blacktop. The sight was grisly but instructional. One month after death, race was no longer a thing. Everyone had the same end-of-bloat color: greenish-red.

Though I drove slowly, my thoughts raced—mainly with Oliver at their core. SUDC. The doctor had suggested a neurological cause—and that felt plausible, maybe a neuro cause linked to an external condition. Maybe the human brain was hardwired to stop working once some tiny, planet-wide state of disorder arose: a gamma-ray burst, a solar flare, a ballooning supernova millions of light years away.

Or physics—not genetics or biology—maybe that was the culprit. Subatomic particles in one location could influence particles miles away in defiance of conventional laws of motion and force. What if everyone had died because of a fundamental law of nature that we humans simply didn't have the intelligence to comprehend?

What if God did this?

No. There was no God—at least not one that cared to make any sense.

But driving felt good. To drive was to approach life, to draw closer to the start of a new future. For the next three hours I followed the I-15 south along the Missouri. The prairie gave way to rocky foothills and then to full-blown forests—the kind of Montana that romantic people thought about when they thought about Montana. The road crisscrossed meandering mountain runoff that trickled through culverts and under small bridges. Most of the vehicles had been considerate enough to veer off the road before crashing. Even the smell of death eased off, absorbed in the needles of the roadside pines. I wiped the VapoRub from my face and sought life on the CB while I drove.

I reached Helena in mid-afternoon. What normally would have been a ninety-minute drive had taken five cautious hours on the obstacle-course highway. At this rate, reaching Seattle would take at least three more days.

Helena sat at the base of the Big Belt Mountains. It had been founded as a gold-rush town and had once been one of the richest cities in America. When things cooled down after the gold rush, the place settled into typical Montana obscurity, clean, comfortable, home to thirty thousand people—a nice town to raise a family.

Right now it didn't smell too good.

My Only Friend, the End

I slathered on more VapoRub and began driving cautiously into the death. I honked the horn every few seconds, scared two cats off the hood of a truck, kept my eyes open for signs of life among the burned gas stations and eerily dark storefronts.

The road obstacles were few. I passed an Episcopal Church that looked like Ronnie's church in Great Falls, only this stained-glass Jesus was holding a lamb rather than showing us his palms. I felt an urge to make a statement, something snarky about God really teaching man a lesson, but I nipped the anger in the bud, told myself instead this building was no different than any other man-made monument. It was a statue of Lenin in Siberia, or a marble arch in France, or the Sidney Opera House. The line of reasoning calmed me a little.

Minutes later I ended up downtown, drove past the capitol building, and pulled up in front of the Montana State Library. As I put the Humvee in park, the door to the library moved a little, closing slowly, probably just the wind. I watched it a moment, then turned off the engine and walked toward it.

Inside the library, there were only a few corpses and a dusky type of natural lighting that unnerved me. Behind rows of books, an echoing *click-clack-click* sounded, followed by silence.

A horse.

An animal got in here.

I inched toward the sound, and a male mule deer stepped out into the aisle. My presence spooked him. Trying to run, he slipped on the tiled floor and knocked books from a bookshelf. On his feet again, he loped past me and got a good run up before crashing through a glass wall and disappearing down the street.

I walked to the window and looked out. There was a blood trail. The deer would end up hunted by coyotes. Only coyotes seemed to be faring well in the new world.

I drifted around the library, checked what the people had been reading. Magazines, mainly, and a few newspapers. Only one of the dead patrons had been reading a book (one of the Harry Potters). At the far end of the library was a good newspaper morgue, as big as any I'd seen, with ample big-city dailies mixed in with locals such as *The Montana Standard* and *The Billings Gazette*. I picked out a *Helena Independent Record*, removed the sticks, started leafing through it.

On page 2 was a letter to the editor. Owen Marks, of the Marysville Militia, had mailed in a complaint—snail-mailed it because he eschewed the Internet, which according to him was an immoral disseminator of pornography and fake news. Marks railed about the greed of the IRS office in Missoula and promised not to pay back-taxes because he no longer recognized the United States government as legitimate.

A city councilor wrote a response in a column just below the letter: "Surely a man as principled as Mr. Marks should know better than to send letters via the U.S. Postal Service, which is a creature of that illegitimate government."

Marysville. Montana militias. Maybe some loner extremists had survived. The Unabomber had lived in a cabin just a few miles up the road (the kind of Montana that cynical people thought about when they thought about Montana). Maybe a man like him was hunkered down deep in a mountain nook and had somehow missed Armageddon. Maybe he didn't even know yet it had happened. The next time he forced himself to suffer the company of others (say, on a trip to town for supplies), he'd be in for a surprise.

This was entertaining, in way, reading about real-life outliers rather than the contrived antagonists of *CSI: Miami*; it felt like harmless respite from the soul-sapping dirge that accompanied most of my thoughts these days. Despite the smell of corpses, I gathered a stack of newspapers, took them to a table, and settled in to skim for more larger-than-life Helena-area characters.

They presented themselves soon enough. High up Old Baldy Mountain, just west of town, according to the *Independent Record*, was the "Fellowship of Agrarians of Montana." This was a community of vegan pacifists who grew their own food in mountain meadows, home-schooled their kids, and kept to themselves. They were in the paper because their vegetables won most of the prizes at a fair in Missoula.

The Agrarians impressed me; they had taken the brave decision to walk the walk in all of their daily actions. I doubted many of them were mired in petty complaints or futile regrets when the end came.

In a three-week-old issue of the *Independent Record* I found a third eye-catching sort, one Alvin Stinghold, a man who had spent a hundred thousand dollars building a Doomsday bunker in the back yard of his home outside Piltzville, just east of Missoula.

My Only Friend, the End

Stinghold was immensely proud of the place. He offered tours to all interested parties. Fox News had even sent a camera crew and had beamed the resulting footage nationwide.

I read more and learned that Stinghold was a semi-retired fifty-something electrician who admitted the end was probably *not* nigh, but he figured hedging his bets in that regard was a good way to engage in a challenging hobby. He built the entire bunker himself, with a little help from friends who referred to him as Noah.

"My buddies don't know much about the Bible," Stinghold told the paper. "Noah did no digging underground."

Twenty feet underground, to be precise. The place had everything, including a waterless incinerator toilet and a microwave oven. One feature in particular caught my eye, a ventilation system with nuclear-grade HEPA filtration. The place was completely self-contained. Alvin Stinghold told the newspaper he spent a lot of time there, lived in it as much as he lived in his house just a few yards away. At one point during the previous year's summer holidays, he had locked himself inside for two full weeks in order to test the systems and see how he would respond to solitude.

The reporter asked him how that went for him.

He replied, "The bunker and I both passed with flying colors, but my wife nearly killed me."

The end of the world had occurred at 11:30 a.m. on a Friday. Alvin Stinghold likely would have been at work at that time. But he was semi-retired. Maybe he had Fridays off. Maybe he was inside the bunker when the end came.

Ronnie would have shared my excitement over this. I asked out loud, "Are you thinking what I'm thinking?"

"I sure am," she said.

"If anyone's alive, he is."

"Then what are we waiting for?" Ronnie said. "Piltzville's on the way to Seattle. Let's make a pitstop."

I left the papers in a pile on the table and started navigating bodies on my way to the doors. A glossy magazine on a rack near the book check-out aisle caught my eye. The cover read, "Once the bees die, we die." Well, that was at least half-right.

I continued walking but then stopped, doubled back, grabbed the magazine. The story inside didn't solve the bee mystery, which meant, by extension, it shed no light on SUDE. It offered causal theories—pesticides, mites, immunodeficiency, unidentified pathogens—but no answers. The only thing certain: the bees were having a hard time, though not as hard as the humans.

A blackbird squawked outside an open window. The sound made me flinch. I looked down. My right foot was mere inches from a still-bloated library patron with a knapsack twisted around her chest. How had it happened this fast? How had I grown so casual with dead bodies?

I could hardly even smell this particular woman. I looked closely at what once had been a young and very alive face: rotting mouth pulled back around overly-bleached teeth—post-mortem blackface. A fly crawled out from between those teeth and all at once I could smell both this body and every body within a five-mile radius. The VapoRub under my nose might as well have been margarine.

I backed away from her and looked around at the others in the library.

So many of them. So many people, all of them gone, just like that. Strangers. Friends. Brothers, uncles and cousins. Instantly extinct.

That word gave me pause.

Extinction.

I checked the library map, then took the stairs to the second floor, to the earth sciences section. There, I picked out four books on the planet's major biological annihilations.

At a table near an open window (far from corpses), I dabbed on more VapoRub and started reading *The Earth's Five Great Extinctions*.

The most recent mass eradication was the Cretaceous-Tertiary Extinction, sixty-five million years ago. A comet or an asteroid pummeled the Earth, but that alone did not kill the dinosaurs. There were also massive volcanic eruptions, fast-changing sea levels and possibly other factors at play, and in the end, the extinctions were hit and miss, killing half of all species on the planet, but *not* including the dinosaurs, because some dinosaurs survived and evolved into birds.

Maybe I would evolve into a bird.

But there were still four other extinctions. I gathered the books under my arm and started toward the stairs.

Then something bubbled up from my subconscious and stopped me from leaving.

"What?" I sensed Ronnie asking.

I went back to the rows of books and started searching for the human-health section.

"You're not serious," Ronnie said.

After Oliver died, she had shot down all talk about SUDC, said investigating unsolvable medical mysteries would only prolong our misery. That sounded callous to me, so I gave her the silent treatment while I sought books on my son's killer.

"You're creating quite the library for yourself," Ronnie said, then added, "Do you realize how much time you spend sitting in one place? Just reading?"

I found a book titled *Case Studies in SUDC*. I blew the dust off, took it to a table far from the corpses, and sat down to open it.

"And when you're not reading, when you're actually doing stuff, you're doing it without well-thought-out purpose. You're moving not in order to find people, but to keep yourself from having to think—I mean, really think."

"And what is it I'm supposed to think about?" I asked.

"For starters, how about your family?"

"I'm reading this *because* I'm thinking of my family."

"Not this family, your first family: your mom and your brother and sister. You're acting as if they never existed."

She wasn't wrong. My family had of course entered my thoughts, but I didn't let them stay long. Like Oliver, they were potentially dangerous objects of emotion best kept at bay.

Still, Ronnie's tone felt wrong. She had morphed into someone else—someone colder than the real-life Ronnie. She had possibly troubling intentions.

I said, "Why are you being like this?"

"Why is anyone the way they are?"

"You don't really believe I was a bad son or a bad brother."

"It doesn't matter what I believe, it matters what you believe." The tone said she was enjoying this. She went on: "Why do you only hear me? Why don't you ever hear Evan or Oliver?"

I covered my ears with my hands, but her voice grew louder: "You've been hiding from reality ever since you found Oliver dead. Since before that. Since you helped kill Sean Vilmack."

I gaped at her. "I didn't help kill—"

"Then who did?"

"His father. Montana. And I'm not ignoring Oliver if I'm researching the cause of his death."

"All right," she said. "You've got it all straight in your mind."

"Thank you, I do."

"You have nothing to worry about."

"Yes. *Thank you.*"

"Why are we even talking about it?"

"Because you brought it up."

"But did I really?" she said. "Did I bring it up?"

Okay. This was the point she'd been leading up to: the cheese was slipping off my cracker.

I scooped the books off the table, dashed back outside, and got the Humvee going west toward the I-90.

While I drove, Ronnie stayed away, probably because I was slugging back whiskey yet again, Canadian Club, which gave me a beautiful throat burn and a palliative buzz.

This habit of getting sloshed while driving was far from wise, but crashing the Humvee into a pine tree wasn't the worst fate I could imagine. At that particular moment, it wasn't even in the top five.

9

MY FICTIONAL P.I. would have known how to handle the newer, colder version of Ronnie. His name was Mike Stone. No kidding: Michael Anthony Stone. I chose that handle in a perhaps too-transparent attempt to fit into the private-eye genre. Mike Stone was poised, brave, graceful under pressure—everything I wasn't. He had the fight skills of an MMA champion and the deductive shrewdness of Sherlock Holmes. Ronnie got a kick out of how I used him to make up for my own shortcomings. Every scrape I placed him in, he earned his way out of it. Every obstacle to goodness in his world, he vanquished it. Mike Stone was proof there could be order in the universe. He was dark, conflicted and cynical, but in the end, he set things right—or at least to a hardboiled version of right. That was what crime-fiction readers wanted and it was what most people everywhere wanted. I saw Mike Stone's travails as gritty fables on how to triumph over the destructive aspects of the human condition.

Living with this fictional character had been helpful to me on many levels. He was the antithesis of inaction. Without him, I would have lost the initiative against uncertainty. Without him, I would have been rudderless.

But now—while I swigged whiskey and bombed down the highway with the post-extinction Ronnie's accusations still blaring in my ears—I asked Mike Stone how he would respond to the things she'd said to me in the library.

He didn't answer, refused to put in an appearance.

Mike Stone was gone.

A month after everyone had keeled over, people were still dying on me.

• • •

It took five hours to drive to Alvin Stinghold's house. The Interstate between Garrison and Missoula had car-crash obstacles that forced me to take detours through the ditch. This I did with inebriated relish, pushing the Humvee's off-road capabilities, making the trailer bounce wildly behind me. I spilled whiskey in my lap and shouted exultantly at the cars, "You can't stop me!" By the time I reached Piltzville, dusk was falling, my clothes were soaked with rye, and I was illustriously blitzed.

Alvin Stinghold's house is gonna be hard to find.

But shucks, I know Armageddon closer to it!

The newspaper had stated he lived on a leafy cul-de-sac on Hellgate Street (a perfect name for both his hobby and the current circumstances). I drove to the end of the cul-de-sac, parked, and staggered from back yard to back yard. The bunker was easy to find. The solar panels in the yard gave it away. There were panels everywhere: on the fence, in the trees, atop a big shed. Their power lines led to a heavy steel plate near the trees. Just behind the plate: barrels of water, must have been 2,000 gallons, with plumbing lines leading down into the ground.

I stumbled to the plate, saw it was padlocked. I knocked on it and shouted, "Alvin, baby, how's the Apocalypse treatin' you!"

Of course he was dead; the bunker was locked from the outside. I decided to inspect the hobby-home anyway. One does not visit Disneyland without at least moseying over to Main Street.

I found a sledgehammer in the shed, broke the padlock, and pulled open the heavy steel door. Then I shouted down into the darkness, "He—ere's Johnny!" I laughed at my incomparably sharp wit and lost my balance, nearly falling into the hole.

Iron rungs led down to the bunker. When I got the merrymaking under control, I started down, had just enough light to see the bottom.

Once there, I pulled out my phone and tried its flashlight, but the battery was dead. But Alvin Stinghold had provided a light switch at the base of the ladder. I flicked it on and an LED bulb showed me I was standing on another steel plate, this one without a lock. I opened it and looked down into a dark hole. More ladder rungs. The air from the hole was musty. Stinghold hadn't been here for a while. I climbed down feeling like Indiana Jones investigating the catacombs.

A switch at the base of the ladder triggered a row of LED lights along the bunker's ceiling. I saw a plywood floor. The walls were lined with shelves stocked with canned and packaged food, blankets, every manner of post-apocalypse essential. The room ran to another door twenty feet away. On the wall, I saw a crank handle. I grabbed it and started cranking. A cool breeze hit the back of my neck. Above me, in the ceiling, was one of those HEPA-filtered vents. The hand crank had to be a back-up option to Alvin Stinghold's solar-powered system. I tottered down the length of the room to see what was behind door number two.

This one was a bedroom-slash-kitchen-slash-TV-room—but not just any TV room. The TV screen had to be sixty inches. It came with a Blu-ray player, a wall lined with movies and books and three theater chairs—actual theater seating with drink holders. Stinghold had been ready to ride out the apocalypse in style.

The kitchen had a microwave oven, a small electric stove and a dining-room table with two chairs. The bed was queen-size. The air in here was damp and stale.

The last room was the mechanical room, with a dozen lithium-ion batteries, power lines everywhere, esoteric panels and switches on the wall. I hiccupped and slapped at a few switches. Something rattled, a hum grew, and I felt a breeze from overhead. The incoming air felt Arctic fresh.

I laughed at this because laughing was easy, then I went back to the first room to see if there was any popcorn. It was movie-time. I couldn't settle in for a flick without popcorn.

And, of course, Stinghold had laid in a good store of Orville Redenbacher—a truly prepared prepper. While the kernels heated up in the microwave, I scoured the movie wall for something to watch. The movies were in alphabetical order, starting with *Ace Venture: Pet Detective* and ending with an obscure Ben Stiller effort called *Zero*

Effect. I would watch *Zero Effect* on Hellgate Street a month after the apocalypse. There was giddy, drunken meaning in this. I took a swig of booze, popped the disc into the Blu-ray player, and settled back in a theater chair to eat straight out of the still-hot microwave bag.

I wasn't five minutes into the flick before I passed out. The whiskey was still in my hand. The popcorn bag warmed my lap.

• • •

When I woke up, I was still drunk and my iPhone was still dead, so there was no way to tell what time it was.

The bunker washroom was in the utility room. I used the incinerator toilet, stumbled back out to the kitchen and gulped down a full bottle of water. Then I turned off the TV and Blu-ray player, put the popcorn in the garbage and doubled back into the utility room and turned off the air.

Climbing the ladder, I entered an unnerving darkness. The steel plate up at ground level was closed. Impossible. I hadn't closed it.

Had someone else?

Someone else?

I pushed on the plate but it wouldn't budge.

"Hello?"

There was no real hope someone would answer. But if there were survivors up there, why would they lock me in? And how would they do it? I had hammered away both the lock and the lock bracket. They would have had to close it gently, quietly, and then place something heavy on top of it. That made no sense.

Maybe someone feared that I carried the bug or disease that had killed everyone?

Maybe solitude had driven him or her loco?

Or maybe the plate was spring-loaded, like a fence gate; it had closed on its own while I checked out the bunker. Maybe things had shifted after it was closed; it got jammed, faulty construction.

Then there was the another possibility: while hopped-up on giggle juice, I had slammed it closed for God knew what reason and just couldn't remember it now.

I went back down, found a flashlight, and returned to the plate and pushed again, put my shoulder into it. The plate was jammed into the wall, stuck, as if someone had stomped on it from the top.

"Hello!"

No answer.

"Is anyone there!"

Of course there wasn't—so down I went again. I found a tire iron among the batteries and tools. I wedged it between the tunnel wall and the plate, tugged on it, but the plate held firm. I hammered on the tire iron, then pulled with all my might, at one point taking a foot off the rung to achieve more purchase. The plate stayed where it was.

I descended the ladder yet again. Stinghold had to have better tools, something to cut the corrugated steel near the plate, but there was no blow torch, no grinder, no power tools.

But he would have planned for something like this. He would have built an escape hatch—and I found one next to the bathroom in the utility room. It was another rubber-sealed door, this one with a Plexiglas window that showed me another set of rungs. I opened it and began climbing.

At the top, the steel-plate door was just like the one at the main entrance. It jangled loudly but wouldn't open—no doubt padlocked. Alvin Stinghold didn't want squatters in his theater seating.

I returned to the kitchen and guzzled more water. This didn't make sense. Someone had locked me in here but there was no one up there. And getting stuck here felt pointlessly redundant. I was already alone.

A third thorough search for tools produced one hammer, two sets of screwdrivers, two chisels, a mallet, nails, screws, nothing electric, nothing useful. What was Alvin Stinghold, Amish? I expected to hear a voice from the *Saw* movies: *You have one hour to escape or I will take away your oxygen...*

The next two hours were spent banging at the plate, prying at it, oiling it with a pastry brush from the kitchen.

No decent tools but the guy has a pastry brush?

I worked until my arms cramped. Only then did I retreat to the living room, huffing and puffing, the previous night's whiskey sweated out of me. I slumped down into the same theater seat as last night. In front of me, the blank TV screen, such a joy to find a few hours ago, was a cold and lonely companion. If only I could turn it off when it already was off.

I envisioned Ronnie sitting in the theater chair next to me.

"Potato potahto," she said.

"I don't know what you mean by that."

"I *mean* what's the difference? You're up there alone or you're down here alone—potato potahto."

"Why are you talking like this?"

"But I *suppose* the fact that you're now confined in a small space might make you a little crazier a little faster. Does that make sense to you?"

"You're never going to be like her again, are you?"

"Dunno," she said, "still thinking about it." She leaned closer to me, smiled mischievously. "But let's spend some time together, shall we? Let's talk."

10

WHEN RONNIE TOLD ME to either start getting over Oliver or move out of the house, I considered leaving and then said thanks but no thanks. I stayed right where I was because I think a part of me wanted to hurt her, to bring her down to my level, where flailing around in bitterness was the chief activity. I figured she owed me some passion. Her son was dead, for God's sake, and she was getting conveniently ascetic about her emotions? It gratified me that my inability to mourn gracefully was at least starting to pierce her armor, but I still had to punish those wildly unfair attempts to stay stoic. There was still work to do on her.

Things didn't go the way I wanted. She went all but mute, focused on her work, ignored my attempts to draw her out. Her resolve was actually quite impressive. Eventually I tired of trying to best her and went on a mission to get back at the world instead. I got into minor spats with deli clerks, with waiters, mailmen, always over nothing. But verbal conflict didn't quite scratch the right itch, so I went to bars alone and insulted big, angry men—and grew attracted to that whole package of pain and self-loathing that comes from getting punched out. I broke my nose twice, and both times Ronnie said not a word. She preferred to let her facial expressions do the talking.

My Only Friend, the End

There was the *you get dumber by the minute* look, and the *how does it feel now?* look and the *you are too pathetic for words* look. After a while, the looks weren't hard to ignore. I adopted her penchant for keeping it all inside (maybe she'd been right to tune out and turn off; things were simpler that way). In terms of dealing with grief, she went her way and I went mine, and for reasons that didn't get explored, it felt appropriate to remain physically together while this played out.

Meanwhile, Mike Stone, my fictional P.I., took a ridiculous detour. Book one in the series had been dark but conventional, but in book two Mike Stone turned into a major-league cynic. Yes, there was still a moral code, but he stopped believing the selfish, corrupt rulers of the world could be reformed or defeated by goodness. He became a self-pleasing vigilante, followed evil-doers down dark alleys, punished them. He offered a touch of kindness to no one—not to the cops, not to his informants on the street, not even to the brittle, bereaved woman who hired him to find her husband's killer. He cleaned up garbage and gave everyone the middle finger because he was pure while the world was corrupt.

When I sent the manuscript to my agent, she called me up and said, "Are you kidding? Do you *want* to lose this publisher?"

"Just send them the pages," I said.

"They won't publish it."

"They will. We have a contract."

"But the contract," she said, "is contingent upon you turning in good work."

"This is good work. It's real."

"So are those big, city-sized clumps of plastic bags in the ocean," she said, "but no one's going to write an ode to them."

I told her to just send it in, which she reluctantly did, and the publisher asked if I was off my rocker, but then published it near the bottom of their list after I threatened legal action.

Then the unthinkable happened. The critics loved the book, gushing over the ways in which it … I don't know, the ways in which it meant something. The first print run sold out in presales. One reviewer called it "a daring literary odyssey."

Literary. I didn't even really know what that meant.

It was only then that I realized I had wanted the book to fail. While writing it, I had assumed it would happen. People would hate the thing. They had to. If not, if Mike Stone's stomach-bile view of the world struck a chord, then my Post-Oliver worldview was correct: the world we lived in was horribly broken to the point of being unfixable.

Everything sucked, so why not suck right along with it?

The whole thing was confusing. I was writer who knew deep and meaningful things about life? Puh-lease. The critics, the publishing industry, this writer himself—we were all absolute phonies so immersed in our phoniness that we no longer knew where the real world ended and the world of self-indulgent emoting started.

And during all this, Ronnie and I were still living in a toxic emotional space—two full years after Oliver died. She cracked one day after I upbraided her for leaving the milk out of the fridge. She opined that we had to either get help, or help ourselves, or get divorced. And she said she had a plan.

"Let's hear it," I said. "Now the font of wisdom will speak to me of salvation." (Such boorishness never had the desired effect; Ronnie always refused to take the bait.)

"New York," she said.

"What about it?"

"A trip," she said, then, after a pause, "a holiday—together."

I responded with the obvious question: "Why?"

"Because we need to stop indulging in our pain."

"Is that what we've been doing?"

"Yes. And we need to see if there's any way at all we can still stand each other."

That latter point made sense, but: "If we can't?"

"I've been to a lawyer. I'll divorce you and we'll each get the help we need or we won't get the help we need or maybe something in-between will happen. But we'll stop slowly killing each other. One week together in New York or we're finished."

The ultimatum hit me in a place I hadn't felt before. I needed her to stay with me. Who else was going to listen while I railed against the world? I couldn't be alone; other people were essential to the process. So I decided to give the trip a try, to see if I could concoct a way of conning her into maintaining the status quo. I was smart, after all, the critics had said so. I had all sorts of *literary* weapons up my sleeve.

So the first thing we did when we got to New York, we went to a play—and not just any play, but a revival of a thing called *Rabbit Hole*, about a grieving couple struggling to come to terms with the death of their son. Ronnie chose it, thinking it was a comedy because the playwright had also written *Good People*, an uplifting, life-affirming play about class that we'd seen and loved in Great Falls. It was anything but.

Yet a funny thing happened. We sat through the whole play, and it was dark and hard-hitting, and we fumed from start to finish; then we went back to the hotel and laid into the writer, David Lindsay-Abaire, as if he was there with us. I launched the tag-team tirade with some know-all scorn:

"That twerp knows something about losing a kid? Well, maybe he does know something, but he doesn't know what it's like for *me* to lose a kid."

"For *us*," Ronnie corrected me.

"For us," I agreed, feeling a tinge of communion. "I mean, what was that ending about? The pain never goes away? Just gets smaller with time? What an awe-inspiring panacea for grief!"

Ronnie added, "I wonder if that jerk even knows anyone who lost a child. I really doubt he does."

"Did you see his bio on the Playbill?" I shouted. "Did you *see* the thing?" I ran to my blazer, grabbed the Playbill from the pocket, tossed it in her general direction. "You know what he did after he wrote this play? The joker turned around and wrote *Shrek*. *Shrek!* Might as well have sashayed over to the cemetery and danced on some graves!"

"You're choosing the next play," Ronnie said, and her delivery was so deadpan that after an odd, silent moment, we both laughed for the first time in two years.

Then we just stared at each other for a long, confusing while. Something was happening. I was embarrassed by my behavior and judging from the way Ronnie now looked down at the floor, she was embarrassed by hers, and the fact that we could be embarrassed together helped.

Without exchanging a word, we had a drink from the bar fridge, wary of where this might lead. And one drink did not turn into two; this thing was too important to be clouded by alcohol. Saying nothing, she reached out and caressed my face. I can still feel that hand, the warmth of it, the feeling behind it. We ended up making love with a new kind of awkwardness, a sense of discovery.

And after that things did become more manageable; the pain did grow a little smaller. We started talking again, not eloquent proclamations, but simple kindness, each of us starting again to care what the other felt. It was so much easier to drop our weapons and cease the offensive. The divorce talk ended. She suggested we attend a support group for parents. I agreed, and at group they gave us permission not to let the past poison the future. They allowed us to have raged against the world for as long as we had. It was natural; everyone operated based on their own internal clocks. Strong-willed people tended to have strong clocks—for us, two full years' worth. They told us some people took decades—and some never escaped bitterness at all. Two former group members had killed themselves.

So the sun could shine again so long as we committed to be honest and open irrespective of the related pain.

We had to decide to live with SUDC.

We couldn't have done it if Ronnie hadn't taken the initiative to save our marriage.

If only she would be like that now and help me to live with SUDE.

11

B UT OF COURSE, the new Ronnie didn't want to help. I sat in Alvin Stinghold's subterranean theater chair, drained from hammering at the bunker's steel-plate door, and she wanted to play mind games. This I deduced from the snarky tone in those two crisp words: "Let's talk."

"About what?" I asked her.

"About you, of course. You're starting to lose it."

"I'm losing my mind?"

"Afraid so. This talking-to-ghosts business isn't healthy."

"I'm choosing to talk to you," I said. "Who else do I have?"

"But you've made me a little toxic, haven't you? And you can't always shut me off. Is that what a normal, sane person does after a month of being alone?"

I had no answer to that, but since this wasn't really Ronnie, I didn't owe her one. I climbed out of the chair and slogged my way back up the ladder, where I hammered the stubborn steel plate some more. And Ronnie disappeared. For the next three days, I hammered and rested and tried to dream up other ways of escaping. After meal breaks, I oiled the plate. I heated it with a blow dryer (Alvin Stinghold, bless his heart, had no good tools yet he had a blow dryer). I tried various jimmying angles, but it wouldn't budge. I listened for lubricating rain, but there wasn't any. I hacked at the hinges with a hammer and chisel. I swore at the plate with a great many juvenile varieties of the f-word. Nothing worked.

In one of my resting moments, I scoured Alvin Stinghold's wall of movies again. Despite the *Ace Ventura* and the *Zero Effect*, most of the DVDs were for literate grown-ups, with complex themes and unapologetic amounts of dialogue. But I didn't watch any of them. The fact that I would have to watch movies alone made movie-watching seem pointless and depressing.

Instead, I checked out the nooks and crannies of the bunker. I learned how to tell day from night by peeking out at a sliver of light when I pushed up on the escape-hatch plate. One night when the last trace of evening twilight had faded to black, I set the clock on the microwave at 9:30 p.m., my best guess at the time. It worried me that I wasn't certain of the date—either July 24th or July 25th.

On the fourth day, I hit upon a new approach: hack my way out, punch slits in the corrugated steel tunnel wall just under the plate— manually cut a semi-circle in the wall, scoop out the dirt, then climb up onto terra firma and skip to my Lou my darling.

The only tools for the job were the hammer and a chisel (there were two chisels, one large and one small). If I could put a dozen punctures in the steel per day, I would be out in two days.

But hacking slits in the wall was back-breaking work. It took me most of the morning of the fourth day to punch two holes in the steel. At this rate, I would be stuck here for weeks, assuming the chisel held up, which it certainly wouldn't; it would soon dull or break, forcing me to use the smaller chisel, increasing the number of holes I would have to punch.

But I couldn't come up with a better plan, so I hammered with the rhythm of an old-time railroad worker, and my hands sprouted painful blisters, which I popped with a needle at the end of the day while sitting in front of the blank TV screen.

Ronnie left me alone. At first, I was relieved she was gone, then I found myself missing her, because I missed everyone. On the evening of the fifth day in the bunker, I broke down and drank the rest of the bottle of whiskey, and the booze sent me to a parallel universe. I tried to summon an array of ghosts.

"Marsha?" This was my agent, always good for a memorable quote. "Wanna gab?"

No answer. But agents were busy people, so her silence was forgivable.

"Mickey?" The guy who'd taught me how to skydive: spry and positive—totally undemanding.

But Mickey wasn't there.

"Where is everyone?" I asked the empty room. "What's a guy have to do to talk to someone?"

This bouncy mood was rewarded not with a friendly ghost, but with a surprising and unbidden memory: I was sixteen years old and at a summer-evening movie with Sean Vilmack, my friend who come September would jump off the roof of the school gymnasium. The movie was *Enter the Dragon*, a Bruce Lee classic at the Bijou, where they ran old movies on Monday nights until they tore the place down. We'd been to maybe a dozen flicks together (*The Exorcist* and *Apocalypse Now* were our favorites). Noteworthy about this particular movie was that shortly after Bruce kung-fu'ed some ill-humored bad guys into submission, Sean reached into my lap and took hold of my hand.

He did this naturally, his eyes glued to the screen, like it was something that happened all the time. I stared at his hand for a long while as anger and shame mixed into a noxious stew in my stomach, then I pulled his hand away and placed it back in his own lap. Still, he didn't move—just sat there staring at the screen as if nothing had happened.

I gaped at him, knew he could see me watching him, and maybe a minute later a single tear gathered at the corner of his eye. I couldn't stay there to watch that tear fall—just couldn't handle it, had no tools for the task. I climbed out of my seat and hurried out of the cinema without looking back.

I relived the day as if the hand-holding were happening anew, with all the old emotions, but there wasn't time to absorb it or analyze it because now Evan pranced into the room licking an unwieldy, triple-decker ice-cream cone. Evan in shorts, four years old, with a face pocked with rubber tire pellets he'd picked up from the new playground down the block. The sight of him sent shivers through me. He sat beside me and licked at the ice-cream melt running down the side of the cone.

Not him. Not my boy.

"How come you're not dead, Daddy?" His gaze remained fastened on the cone.

When I was able to answer, I said, "I don't know. I've been thinking maybe I am dead. If this is hell, then maybe not knowing it's hell is part of the punishment." This I said to the imagined ghost of a four-year-old boy.

My Only Friend, the End

Evan kept licking the cone.
"What flavors are those?"
"Did you do something, Daddy?"
"What do you mean?"
"Did you do something bad?"

The image of Sean tearing up in the cinema flashed in my mind. I said, "Who told you I did?"

Evan shrugged while lapping at the cone.

"Do *you* think I've done something bad?"

He didn't answer. He climbed to his feet and walked slowly out of the room, still ultra-careful with the ice-cream.

Lovely. Ronnie would have a field day with this one.

But after Evan left, Ronnie didn't pop by, and neither did anyone else. That was a mixed blessing. No ghosts meant no ghostly mind games, but it also meant I was alone, with the walls closing in.

I tried to strike Sean and Evan from my mind by being busy. My non-hammering moments had to be filled somehow. I rummaged through Alvin Stinghold's books, planned to loosen up my mind with a flashy, escapist novel with simple themes and larger-than-life characters. Problem was, Alvin's taste in fiction was dark and literary. The guy was a prepper and yet he kept a library of works by Faulkner, George Orwell, Tennessee Williams, Jack London and John Updike. Serious dead-white-male stuff. He had the complete works of Ernest Hemingway, which felt at least marginally more in line with prepper sensibilities, but right next to *Death in the Afternoon* was a copy of *Miracle of the Rose*, by Jean Genet.

Who *was* Alvin Stinghold, anyway? How did his mind have room for his contradictions? This was a prepper who told newspapers he didn't believe the end was coming. Who watched *Ace Ventura* but read Jean Genet. Where was the Tom Clancy or Elmore Leonard, maybe a little Ludlum—unchallenging page turners? Failing that, give me a stereotypical screed like *Mein Kampf* or *The Turner Diaries*, a gawd-awful tome of racism or half-baked conspiracy theories or thinly veiled class rage—something I could feel superior to. There wasn't even a Bible, which surely is featured on The Official Prepper Reading List for the Apocalypse.

And if not one work of fiction suited my desire for escape, the nonfiction books were worse: *The Rape of Nanking*, *Five Past Midnight in Bhopal*, *Shake Hands with the Devil*—books that could haunt you. *Stalin*, *Words to Outlive Us*, *The Ballad of Abu Ghraib*—books to commit suicide by. Where was the true crime and the Anne Coulter and the Tucker Carlson—or even the Bill Maher making fun of Tucker Carlson? And meanwhile, my books on SUDC and the world's five extinctions were all in the Humvee, might as well have been on Mars. I needed another way to escape the present.

As I stood there at the wall of books, the lights blipped off for half a second, then flickered back on. Then the soft whir of the bunker's ventilation sputtered and stopped. I looked up at the now-silent vent. The lights blipped off for good, blanketing me in a darkness deeper than any shade of night.

For a long while it was hard to process the new reality, hard, even, to breathe. The air felt physically heavy, like it could be cut and folded. My next movement, a tentative shuffle-step forward, was perilous, like dangers awaited: sharp objects, electrical wires, bear traps.

Where had I left the flashlight? At the ladder leading up to the steel plate. Two more shuffle-steps forward brought me to the bookshelf. From there it took me four full minutes to follow the wall to the doorway, and from there to the end of the bunker, where I found the flashlight.

When I turned it on, it cast a bright amber beam fringed by a dull gloom. The bunker looked like a night-time crime scene or a pacified war zone that soldiers had fled in a hurry. I crossed to the ventilation hand crank and gave it a few turns. The air that came down was rich and revivifying. If the power didn't return, this would be my only way of getting air.

In the utility room, everything was in order—no blown fuses or disconnected lines. I hit all the "off" buttons, reset the system, but flicking the switches on again had no effect. I followed power lines to their terminals at the oven and TV, at the vents, at the incinerator toilet. Everything looked operable. Maybe the problem was outside the bunker, but since the water was gravity fed and the only parts of the system outside the bunker were the lines to the solar panels, that seemed unlikely. Here inside the bunker, none of the power lines were buried behind the bunker's steel walls. Everything was visible and available, so where was the problem?

The only thing certain was creeping claustrophobia: the bunker's air grew harder to breathe. Common sense told me there would be good, breathable O_2 for at least a few days, but that didn't kill the urge to return to the hand-crank and work it until green grass and ferns sprouted up all around me.

I found back-up batteries for the flashlight, then perched the light against the base of the ladder, pointing up at the plate. I went back to

My Only Friend, the End

hacking the corrugated wall under the steel plate. On the ninth or tenth hammer strike, the chisel handle splintered and broke. After a few steadying breaths, I retrieved the smaller chisel and punched two small slits in the metal in less than ten minutes. The shorter blade was perfect. I didn't need power or fresh oxygen. If this kept up, I'd be out of here in less than a day.

So I worked at it, merrily punched holes, kept a close eye on the chisel handle, prayed it wouldn't break, because if it did, there were no more chisels; there were only screwdrivers.

A half hour later, my hammer-holding hand cramped up. I should have taken a break at this point, should have gone down and cranked some fresh air onto my sweat-soaked forehead. Instead, I kept working—and eventually misfired with the hammer, mashing my chisel-holding thumb with the precision of a medieval torturer.

The pain was other-worldly. Even worse, after the aching ebbed I couldn't move the thumb, couldn't reliably hold the chisel. But I tried anyway, cupped the chisel at the V between the thumb and the index finger. This seemed to work. Two test swings punched a new slit in the wall—victory!—but the third swing splintered the chisel's wooden handle in half and deflected squarely down onto the same throbbing thumb—exact same spot.

This was too much. I howled and flailed away at the wall like a toddler throwing a tantrum. The burst of anger felt good, so I rode the cathartic wave for a long, blue-languaged time. In doing so, I flattened some of my hard-won Morse-code chisel dashes, widened others. Who cared? The dig-myself-out plan had been dumb. I would die here in this bunker. Fools like me *deserved* to die, because only fools tried to hack through corrugated metal with a hammer and chisel. Only self-absorbed, ghost-seeing failures saw Elmore Leonard as a solution to their psychological prob—

Crick...

I stopped swinging the hammer, froze without looking up. After maybe ten seconds, I let go of the hammer and heard it clunk against the metal at the base of the ladder. Then—still not looking up—I raised my aching arms and pushed up on the steel plate. Metal scraped against metal as the plate moved—but stopped after a few inches. I pushed harder, and the plate sprang open, splashing me with beautifully frigid nighttime air.

The next instinct was fear. Someone had closed the plate. Someone was waiting not far away, maybe pointing a rifle. For a moment, I considered going back down to the bunker where things were at least established, without surprises.

But I climbed up into Alvin Stinghold's back yard, spent only a moment looking around for signs of life, then drank in the rich smell of pines in the summer night, the beauty of gently rocking tree branches, the outline of mountains crisp under a waxing moon.

An eaves trough on the garage had come undone. It dangled halfway between the roof and the patio. The lawn also looked overgrown and unruly. These minor developments dampened my joy. I'd missed much by being down below. With each new sunrise, lawns had grown wilder and things had crept closer to a state of everlasting disrepair. Each new day killed more of the world made by people.

The aching thumb snapped me out of these thoughts. I walked out of Alvin Stinghold's yard and followed the sidewalk to the Humvee, where I scooped one of the medical kits from the trailer. Opening the bag with my good hand, I paused a moment, my gaze lingering over the boxes of drugs now in view. The Dilaudid looked inviting, but I downed two low-dose codeine/caffeine pills instead, then leaned back against the truck and studied my thumb. If it didn't heal right, I would have to live with the left-hand digital functionality of a primate.

Don't worry about things you can't change. You're out of the hole. Go find people.

I stuffed the medical kit back into the Humvee and climbed into the driver seat. As I was about to close the door behind me, something made me pause, the kind of sound you hear without really hearing. I listened hard but it didn't repeat—there was only the soft breeze in the trees and the perfect scent of the pines. I closed the Humvee door and started the engine—then heard the sound again, clearly this time. It was the sound of a child crying.

I turned off the engine and peered down the street toward Alvin Stinghold's house. In the shadows, the figure of a child slowly took on definition. It was walking toward me.

Euphoric, I scrambled out of the truck and ran toward the boy.

"I see you! Stay where you are!"

But when I neared the child, I had to stop. The child was Evan. He sniffled, held his thumb in front of him, his left thumb—held it exactly as I had held my own left thumb just moments earlier.

"It hurts real bad," he said. "Make it stop."

The tears were real and the whimpering was real. The way he looked at me, confused about why I'd hurt his thumb, that was the realest part of all.

"Please, Daddy, don't hurt me anymore."

All I could say was, "Don't come any closer."

He shuffled toward me. "Make it stop, plee-ease."

My legs stopped working. He approached to within arm's reach and stared up at me with lost, little-boy eyes. He also smelled strongly of something that at that moment was every bit as bad as the smell of rotting corpses: my little boy's breath was pure Canadian Club rye whiskey.

I backed away from him slowly, then ran but tripped and fell, then scrambled to my feet and sprinted to the Humvee, which wouldn't respond to my turn of the key. Evan shuffled toward me, still crying, still begging for help.

"You're not him," I said. I started the truck, stomped on the gas, and left him there on the pavement.

Driving away, I watched him in the rearview mirror. He didn't mutate into a horror-movie monster, didn't disappear into a mist. He just stopped walking, stood there with the slumped posture of defeat. The last thing I saw before I turned off of Hellgate Street—Evan, my dead little boy, turned around and trundled miserably back toward Alvin Stinghold's house.

12

DRIVING, I TRIED to slow-breathe away the hammering in my chest. Ghosts. How could I know they were my mind's creations and yet see and feel them? Crazy people didn't know they were crazy, but sane people didn't smell whiskey on the breath of their dead children.

A mile from Hellgate Street, I brought the Humvee to a stop, pulled my stock of whiskey and vodka out of the trailer, and with my good hand tossed the bottles far into the trees. Driving again, I checked and re-checked the rearview mirror. If Evan could materialize, other ghosts could—and seemed likely to. Or maybe, like I'd said earlier to Evan, I *was* dead. Maybe *I* was the ghost here. My parachute hadn't opened during that jump. My body lay in the morgue in Great Falls and my post-life mind could not adapt to this new realm. Evan hadn't been in that street holding his thumb. Ronnie hadn't sidled up to me and said, "Let's talk." I'd created them. I was a master at imagining things, but in death my mechanism was misfiring, boomeranging my various life issues back onto me as random bits of skewed experience.

Or solitude was the culprit, not the booze I'd just tossed away. Solitude was robbing me of my usual pressure-release valves.

My Only Friend, the End

It calmed me to roll through answers and reasons. The enemy was cunning and devious, but so was I. As a writer, I had spent an entire life not letting people see the real me, and with a writer's discipline I could fight back, research my way out of this thing, arm myself with books on how to combat isolation—better books than the ones I'd read in Great Falls. I could build a strategy for outwitting my own mind. I would just have to be determined and reasonable—refuse to accept crazy for an answer.

Insanity is when you're cheating at solitaire and a fight breaks out!

My heartbeat eventually slowed to normal. I stopped checking the rearview mirror. I even felt sorry I'd ditched the whiskey. The codeine pills had yet to kick in, and the craving for a drink right now was strong enough to suggest that my fondness for binge-boozing was starting to become an issue.

The clock on the Humvee said it was 10:16 p.m. It was good to know the time. At a gas station outside Missoula, I grabbed two watches from the rack by the door. Both of them said the time was 10:48 p.m. and the date was July 27th.

So the world had ended forty-two days and eleven hours ago. Spring had turned to summer. I would never lose track of time again. I would find wind-up watches at a jewelry store and I would always keep them wound. I would always know where I was and when I was there—a small weapon in the battle to outwit solitude.

I drove on a highway that hugged the northern edge of Missoula. It was easier than usual to ignore the death outside the vehicle. Mercifully, most of the visuals were obscured by vegetation and the highway's distance from the town proper. Warehouses on the outskirts gave way to gas stations and generic bungalows—a few car crashes, a few dead pedestrians, nothing I hadn't seen before. Like Great Falls and Helena, there had been fires here, with smoke still bleeding into the sky.

Like those two towns, the smell of death suggested this place would offer no life; it forced me to lather on VapoRub. I decided to find a bed for the night somewhere west of town, once I passed through the stench. There would be a habitable motel or a farmhouse, something with few or no corpses in the area. I would find a room and leave the door not only unlocked, but wide open. Prop it open with a chair, if necessary. It would be a long time before I put myself in a completely enclosed space again.

I worked the CB dial as I drove around a three-car wreck full of leaking, sagging corpses. I tried to stay unruffled, tried to strengthen the idea that I could defeat solitude before I went spectacularly bobo. I mean, of *course* I was seeing ghosts. I was living through the biggest tragedy in history. In such a situation, many people would have killed themselves by now. Others would have cowered in dark corners, or just sat at home and prayed to be rescued. A good number would have self-medicated to the point of numb apathy when the coyotes or bears tore into them. I had to cut myself some slack. I was no picture of strength, but at least right now I was *somewhat* balanced, wasn't I? More or less? I was exercising my rational internal monologue, the very faculty that had given me a career as a writer, complete with modest remuneration and sometimes-glowing reviews.

"Tenacity is a virtue," I told myself out loud. "Believe it."

But now—out of nowhere—I smelled whiskey again. It filled the Humvee cabin, nauseating me on the spot. I turned my head and looked left out the side window. I couldn't look right. Evan would be there in the passenger seat.

He's not there, don't put him there.

The whimpering started.

"Daddy..."

At last I looked but it wasn't Evan, it was Ronnie, holding her broken left thumb, whimpering in Evan's voice:

"Why did you hurt my thumb, Daddy?"

She gave a throaty moan and her expression flashed to evil. With her good hand, she reached across the cab and yanked at the steering wheel.

We plowed through the guard rail and into the ditch. Panicking, I stomped the brake pedal but hit the gas instead. The forest came up on me fast. I threw my arms up and screwed my eyes shut.

13

*N*OW I SEE RONNIE and me on a lush golf course. I'm hovering above us, an intimate bird's-eye view of my own life. We're laughing. Ronnie has just missed a gimme putt. A few feet behind us, I see Evan and Oliver. Evan is holding Oliver's hand. The two of them watch us with defeated looks on their faces, as if they've been trying to get through to us but they've failed and now they're all cried out.

I remember the real-life version of this round of golf, which didn't include Evan or Oliver. Ronnie and I are in Portugal half a year after our marriage-saving trip to New York. This is the last stop on a European odyssey. We've been to London and Paris, to Prague and Budapest. After Portugal, we plan to drive through Spain. We can afford it. Ronnie is a CPA and the novels are making money. We're recommitting to life, taking time off work, recovering what we've lost.

Oliver is of course dead, and Evan hasn't been born yet, but the two of them are now so close to us on the green that I can't believe we can't sense them.

"Look behind you!" I scream down at myself, but once the words are out the scene changes and we're at a table in a seafood restaurant in Malaga. Evan and Oliver are at the table behind us. They're in Ronnie's

My Only Friend, the End

line of view, but again, neither of us senses their presence. I remember this moment in the restaurant. I remember what I'm thinking—that the enjoyment of travel is wearing off. Yes, Ronnie and I are on much-improved terms with the world, but I'm also nagged by a growing feeling that we've been lapsing a little, trying too hard to escape the past—much like we'd been doing back when we decided to lash out in anger.

Because we've been seeing a shrink and going to group, I know enough to share this concern with Ronnie, right there at the table, between the lobster bisque and the main course. I tell her we've been lapsing, and she says:

"I know. I've been feeling that, too."

Behind me, Evan spoons soup into Oliver's mouth.

I say, "Maybe it's time to stop travelling."

Now she can't make eye contact.

"What's wrong?" I ask.

"I'm scared," she says.

"So am I."

"I'm scared of our house," she said.

"Then let's sell it."

"And I'm scared of my job and I'm scared of Great Falls. So maybe that's why we have to go back. We have to learn how to be okay in the place where it happened." She adds with a smile, "And we can do that, right? We can take that step?"

"We can," I tell her, and I truly believe it. We've come so far.

A waiter behind us drops his tray. It clangs to the floor and the version of me at the table turns to look—peering right through Evan and Oliver. Watching this from above, I sense wrongness in this; they deserve more than to be moved on from.

"Look at them!" I holler down. "Get out of your own heads and look!"

But the version of me at the table can't do this. The focus is on Ronnie, on how much I love her and on how stupidly destructive I'd been to blame her for Oliver's death.

I'm also thinking we should try for another child, but I'm afraid to tell her this; I might be moving too fast.

Our main courses arrive: tuna for her, paella for me. Once the waiter is gone, I say to her:

"I always thought Ebenezer Scrooge got a raw deal."

The non sequitur makes no sense—unless the version of me at the table can sense the real me watching from on high like the original Scrooge.

But Ronnie smiles at me as if we've just resumed a perfectly normal conversation. I continue:

"Ebenezer is nasty and cold-hearted, but he has certain qualities."

"Such as?" Ronnie says.

"Discipline. Practicality. Consistency."

Now I remember. The conversation was from the past, from the comfort of our living-room, curled up on the sofa a week before Christmas. We sipped eggnog and watched the annual airing of A Christmas Carol, with Alastair Sim. Oliver lay in his crib in a corner of the living room, sleeping.

"In fact," I tell Ronnie, "as a kid, I always kind of cheered for Ebenezer. The world never gave him the credit he deserved."

"That is so like you," Ronnie teases me, "to side with the bad guy."

Evan rises from his table, takes Oliver by the hand and leads the toddler to the exit.

"They're leaving!" I holler, but we can't hear me. "Wake up!"

Once Evan and Oliver are gone, Ronnie leans over the table and kisses me. I accept it eagerly, because after our post-Oliver trials we're treating intimacy as a salve—a returning home after a long, cold journey. Easing out of the kiss, Ronnie keeps her face close to mine, the better to prolong the tenderness. She says, "You want to know something?"

"What?" I say.

"I should have crashed you into a tree a long time ago. I hope you never wake up."

14

CONSCIOUSNESS RETURNED in bits and pieces. The first sense to stick with me was taste—iron on my tongue. Then a sense of smell, those unmistakable pines. But I couldn't yet move a muscle, not even my tongue, so I was stuck with the pines and the iron, the warmth of blood. When a stronger sense of touch arrived, I started choking on that blood.

I pitched forward in the seat, rapped my forehead on the spiderwebbed windshield, which now sat inches from my face, along with two splintered tree branches and a crushed dashboard. There was no trace of an airbag.

Despite a throbbing head and a fire just above my right hip, I felt relief—because Ronnie wasn't there. I shouldered open my door and spilled out onto the ground. The pain over my hip exploded. I grabbed it, felt around for an impaled object, but there was nothing there, just a burning band of oblique muscle. I looked up at the Humvee. The front end was wrapped around a spruce tree. The hood was accordioned. Radiator fluid dripped to the ground, soaked up by moss and pine needles. Behind the vehicle, gas leaked out of my back-up gasoline canisters, which had been ejected from the now-overturned trailer. Other items were strewn all over: water bottles, canned vegetables, clothes. A hiking boot was impossibly high up in a tree. One of my SKS rifles sat close to the trailer half unsheathed.

I spat out blood and worried the leaking gas canisters would ignite. With my tongue, I felt a deep, warm gash on the inside of my cheek. I managed to stand and grab the SKS from the trailer. There was no Ronnie in the tall grass, or in the Humvee, or out on the road, but I felt her nearby, watching.

A car sat in the ditch maybe a hundred yards up the road. I shambled toward it while keeping an eye out for my dead wife. When I reached the car, I tried to open the door with my bad hand. This sent a lightning bolt up my arm.

Something cracked in the woods. I stiffened, levelled the gun. The nighttime gloom served up no ghosts. I stared until my unblinking eyes started to water, then common sense prevailed. If Ronnie wanted to come, she would come. If she wanted me to see her, I would see her. And shooting an already dead woman was possibly the dumbest idea I'd ever had.

I got the car door open and was rewarded with the stench of death. A woman in a tank top and tight shorts sat behind the steering wheel. Around her neck was a now-dull glow-stick necklace, which raised in my mind images of dollar stores and children's birthday parties with grab-bag presents. I closed the door and walked back to the Humvee, where I filled a backpack with water, MREs and a bottle of codeine/caffeine pills. Then I crossed the highway and started down the hill toward Missoula. There was a trailer park close to the road. The trailers on the park's perimeter were burnt-out shells of fiberglass, but roughly half the other units looked untouched by fire. Judging from the number of parked cars and the smell in the air, a lot of people had been at home when the extinction hit. I staggered into the closest unburnt trailer, closed the door to a death odor in the bedroom, and eased myself onto the sofa in the living room.

VapoRub.

I won't sleep without VapoRub.

But I did sleep, because the codeine kicked in and the pain ebbed. And this time when I slept, I didn't dream.

• • •

When I woke up, my hip was stiff and my bad thumb throbbed. The first thing I did was look around for Ronnie.

My head felt worse than the worst hangover. I couldn't stay in the trailer. The death stench had deepened while I slept, a sour, gag-inducing thing. I dragged myself outside and checked parked cars for keys. None of them had any, so I opened trailer doors and checked walls for coat hooks and key hooks. I ended up with a Jeep Grand Cherokee with a full tank of gas and space in which to pack my undamaged provisions back at the Humvee crash site.

The movement involved in repacking my supplies helped to oil my joints and ease the stiffness in my side while I waited for a new round of codeine/caffeine to kick in. At the Humvee, along with food, water and guns, I salvaged my books on SUDC and the world's extinctions—and also three unruptured gasoline canisters from under the overturned trailer. The wise thing to do now: find a place in which to treat my wounds and recover. But after being stuck in the bunker, and after being crashed into a tree by an Evan-impersonating Ronnie, I needed one thing above everything else: to get as far away from Montana as fast as I could.

So I drove while gritting my teeth and begging the codeine to work. The pain redoubled, then grew fangs and gnawed at me. I stopped the vehicle and dug into my drug stash and swallowed two Percocets dry. So much for abstinence from heavy drugs; best-laid plans go poof once pain gets real. The Percocets took hold half an hour after that, and I drove through western Montana in a half-asleep, dry-mouthed fog.

Crossing into Idaho made me feel safer, like ghosts travelled only as far as the state line. At the town of Mullan, I considered stopping at a health clinic and figuring out how to treat my thumb and hip, but even there, even a hundred and fifty miles from the ghosts of Ronnie and Evan, I couldn't quite bring myself to stop. My body operated on a weirdly primal level, drawing oxygen, scanning the road for crashed cars, moving forward in a desperate, barely-awake quest to move ahead. Rational thought hit pause yet again. The only coherent thought that did flare was that it was a coup *not* to be thinking.

I tried not to look at Spokane, Washington, as I passed through it, but it was a bigger town, maybe two hundred thousand people; its many colors of death demanded attention. I peered down from the hillside interstate and saw smoke from still-burning fires, bodies on apartment balconies, one building that had exploded, sending the top floors a hundred feet in every direction. The ruin and sense of futility were deeper here, closer to the bone; they suggested that Seattle, far larger than Spokane, might be Hell itself.

To bypass as many gruesome sights as possible, I drove fast, forced myself to look at the highway's center line, swam deeply in a Percocet ocean. At the edge of town, the forest gave way to blazing high plains. Spokane was gone, but a new type of trouble started. The engine chugged twice and died. A fuel warning had no doubt been blinking at me, but in my current state I wasn't processing such things.

I stepped out of the Jeep and filled the gas tank with one of the canisters. My thumb was now completely numb. This did not strike me as a good sign. No feeling might mean no circulation, which led to images of me having to amputate my own digit, so I doubled back toward Spokane, toward an as-yet undefined self-treatment plan at one of the hotels just west of the ruined city.

I ended up at a Sleep in Style, a run-down motel with only three cars out front and a location upwind from the other buildings. Though the air was breathable, the Sleep in Style's lobby was littered with corpses. With the Percocet wearing off, I stepped carefully over a man still holding an iPad and grabbed some pre-magnet-card-era room keys from a wall rack behind the counter.

The room farthest from the lobby was an unoccupied double. I stocked it with water bottles and medical kits and gingerly pulled off my shirt to check myself in the mirror. My hip was blue. Which organs were in the area? Would there be internal bleeding? If surgery was needed, could I perform it? Of course I couldn't. I put the shirt back on and studied my thumb. There was a pebbly bump below the swollen knuckle, so yes, it was broken, but now I could bend the digit a little. The bulk of the bone was still in place. Maybe it would heal close to normal.

I gauze-wrapped the thumb and the rest of the hand so I would remember not to use it, then I popped another Perc—fast—before I could talk myself out of it. I moved food and clothes into the room, then sat in a plastic chair outside, where I used the rifle scope to scan the area for my dead wife. She was there, somewhere. She would always be there; that seemed to be the point of her. In the end she would have her way with me if I didn't devise a plan for her.

If I didn't preempt her.

After yet another pill, the concept of preemption gained a ton of credibility. While I turned it over in my mind, I literally started to drool—which made me laugh out loud.

"Ronnie! It's official! Your loving husband is cuckoo for Cocoa Puffs!"

The shouting made me pleasantly dizzy.

"Let's have a tete a tete!" I continued. "Come out come out wherever you are!"

I listened hard and a bird squawked in the distance.

I staggered to my feet, slung the rifle over my shoulder, stumbled out toward Spokane to draw her out.

Downtown was a good three miles away, but I could walk it—could've walked all the way to Seattle. I didn't need VapoRub, didn't have to look away from corpses and car crashes. The extinction wasn't so bad. It could be appreciated if it was looked at through the right kind of glasses. Since Ronnie wouldn't show herself, and since Percocet fired off glitter guns in my brain, I wore those glasses now.

Could I get used to this world? In the end?

You bet. How many disaster-film addicts, how many disaffected youths and recluses had daydreamed of this very scenario, of being the last person on Earth? For some people, this place would have been Shangri-La.

Here was the Sunrise Grocery, doors open to all the canned and packaged food you could ever want. Here was a strip mall with an open bar, a dollar store and a check-cashing joint that would never gouge anyone ever again. Ignore the upside-down Toyota with the rotting corpse reaching out the back window as if to grab the nearby shopping cart; such sights would eventually lose their power to shock.

Focus on good things, things created by rare circumstances reserved just for you. You could do what you want now, when you want to do it, and in the way you want to. Do it naked, or in garters and lace panties, if that's your thing. How would you react to the freedom? How would you take advantage?

The options would be endless if you could see the lack of human company not as the worst part of this new world, but as the best part. You could sunbathe, compose haiku, windsurf. You could drive wherever you wanted, read great books, eat ice-cream (maybe not eat ice-cream). If you missed intimacy, you could top up the gas generator and settle in front of your sixty-inch Sony Bravia KD for some scintillating hi-def porn. It wouldn't be like real sex with a real partner, but in the absence of alternatives you would have plenty of time to make peace with the concept of virtual eroticism.

And if you did still crave living, breathing company, why, you could make the most of your options and go find yourself a dog.

A dog. The two Jacks. The coyotes.

My Only Friend, the End

I started crying—on the spot—a keening, soul-wrenching bout of emoting, with no rays of light the pierce the darkness. I don't know how long it went on, but there was no self-consciousness attached to it, and when it ended I felt almost instantly, albeit shakily, better.

Because there were other dogs still alive out in the world. The Jacks couldn't be saved, but others could.

"Ronnie! Wife! I hope you don't want a dog because that's precisely what we're about to get!"

I pictured her standing in front of the Safeway—Ronnie smug and proud that she'd crashed me into that tree—so I levelled my gun and unloaded on her, blowing out the windows on the store.

"Ding dong, the witch is dead!"

The destruction was exquisite. The absolute power of a rifle, the crash of falling glass—why hadn't I discovered such simple delights earlier? I shot out windows on two other stores before I ran out of bullets. My heart pounded. My brow dripped cold sweat. I had to sit on a curb and gather myself.

Another dog? What if the new one dies, too?

If it did, it would be the end of everything.

But I couldn't let that stop me. Better to bond with man's best friend than with a homicidal ghost. I charged back to the motel, climbed into the Jeep, and drove to the nearest residential area, a suburban community with new houses and newly planted saplings.

I puttered down one of the streets with the windows down and my eyes darting in all directions.

"Car-rides! Treats! Walks! Come and get 'em!"

No dogs. This should have been easy. Suburbia was full of pets.

"Ronnie! You scare them all away?"

Some dogs were no doubt trapped inside houses, now dead after feeding on their masters and drinking from toilets. But others—the ones outside—some would be alive (though I hadn't seen any since leaving the bunker); some might even thrive in this new world.

I parked, got out of the truck and walked. None of the houses had caught fire. There weren't even any bodies in the street. The only sign that things weren't kosher was the string of overgrown lawns.

And the longer I went without finding a dog, the more I needed one—any dog: a big guard dog; a toy poodle; a blind, three-legged rescue dog; anything with a pulse and a need for human companionship.

But each time I turned a corner—crickets. Maybe they were hiding. Maybe they'd sensed I was schmacked on Percocet and were afraid of such unbalanced humanfolks. Or maybe the local dogs had eaten all the native street food and had lit out for new scrounging grounds in other parts of town.

In a nearby driveway sat a Dodge Durango with an open sunroof. I stopped, strung a blanket tightly over the front and back seats, then raided the house for dog bait. Five minutes later, I poured onto the blanket a bottle of barbecue sauce, a jar of Patak's Butter Chicken Simmer Sauce, two jars of Alphagetti, and some chickpeas as a *pièce de résistance*.

Guess what my dog's favorite breakfast is.
  Pooched eggs!

I cracked the side windows wide enough for aromas to escape but not wide enough for a large dog to fit through. That done, I rechecked the open gap on the sunroof—the dog's access point. A deck chair near the front bumper would help the canine leap from ground to chair to car hood. Said canine would smell the food, pounce through the sunroof, and fall into a trap. Unless it was a potent leaper, it would be stuck there until I came to free it.

Before I left the Durango, I placed a big bowl of water in the back of the vehicle and checked the angle of the summer sun. The vehicle was under a broad car port, would get shade throughout the day. With the windows and sunroof open, there would be no greenhouse effect. Anyway, I would come check the trap the next morning.

As I stood there and admired my work, my stomach started to cramp—not small, bad-diet cramps, but sharp, grab-your-guts spasms.

I doubled over, lurched back to the Jeep, waited for a pause between contractions, then sped back to the Sleep in Style, where I read the instructions on the Percocet. Three words jumped off the paper—"Take with food"—so I forced down some cold apple cobbler from an MRE and sat on the bed and held my guts, pleading with the pain to die down.

When it did, it took the opioid high with it. With a somewhat clear head, I told myself no more drugs, none, never, Percocet was a dangerous game. But my head and body aches gathered anew like waves curling toward the shore, where they broke and crashed with atomizing force. I held out as long as I could, then gobbled down the rest of the MRE (Salisbury steak, potatoes, peas) and took another Perc. After all, this was a temporary measure. I wouldn't succumb to hillbilly heroin. I knew the dangers, was strong-willed and level-headed. And addiction happened to other people, people with problems, weaker people. I wasn't weak. I was just in pain.

So I fell back into a senseless stupor, dry mouthed yet drooling, drowsy, clammy, sweaty and cold. No pain, no Ronnie ghosts—just me now willin' to be chillin'. I mean, fair was fair. Even at the end of the world, a guy was entitled to check out for a while.

15

OVER THE FOLLOWING DAYS, Ronnie refused to show up. This was cagey of her. A few things went bump in the night, and in the day, and I suspected they were her, but since I was zooming on Percocet, my fears were distant, unexplored territories. I soon stopped fretting over the fact I was being haunted.

I napped a lot. When I was awake, I was out of it. There were blackouts, gaps in the days. I daydreamed lucidly, stared out the window at small details that took on galactic significance: wiry smoke from a distant fire (a double-helix with a coded meaning that only just eluded me); blackbirds flying in and out of the shot-out storefront window of the Bed Bath & Beyond; growing grass (yes, I stared at growing grass and saw hungry roots, pulsing chlorophyll and *life*). I asked Ronnie what she thought about this, but she didn't answer, not that it mattered. Nothing could hurt me. Every little thing held meaning.

During this, the thumb mobility returned by degrees and the oblique-muscle bruise dissolved from purple to green and then to faded yellow. Other crash-related aches and pains also melted, and my concussion disappeared without leaving any residue.

In my less-blotto moments, I dunked my head in cold water and told myself to resume the hunt for survivors. But then I recalled the facts of the last month—the image of the satellites burning up in the sky over Great Falls. The satellite-controlling people were dead. The NASA people were dead. The people who hired the NASA people— dead. There was a pattern there, and the pattern was best addressed with more opioids.

But was Ronnie dead? Was the entity who'd crashed me into a tree—was she, in some warped, post-extinction way, physically alive?

The pills rendered the question moot. I amused myself without really trying. I loved the way the voice inside my head leapt with agility, pivoted, sprouted new wisdoms. I made up new words and used them in sentences ("millerite" comes to mind, though I forget the meaning). The more bizarre things got, the happier I was. At times, I heard a jolly James Earl Jones narrating gobbledygook poetry. And these were the more lucid moments, the times of glorious leisure. I told myself I was a good man— maybe not great, and certainly with flaws—but I wasn't *bad*. I'd done what I could with my life, and Ronnie—the real Ronnie, not the post-extinction imposter—could have done worse than me. Oliver and Evan could have had a worse father. I didn't have to guilt myself out over surviving.

On the third or fourth night of my Percocet binge, I lowered the dosage and turned back the clock to memories of me and Ronnie, to the times that followed our trip through Europe. (This was a good dosage because it kept ghosts at bay while I strolled down a foggy memory lane.) After the trip, Ronnie was nervous about being home, as was I, but we powered through it. We gave Oliver's clothes and toys away and painted his room a warm shade of yellow—then moved my office in there, because the room had no power over us. I was impressed by our bravery, especially Ronnie's, since she was resolute despite her fears. I wrote a new novel in that room—not a good novel, but a novel, and there was no trace of the ghost of Oliver in the subtext. Ring one up for the desire to live again.

On the fourth or fifth night on Percocet, I swam back to childhood. My sister and brothers on the trampoline, me in my bedroom reading, dad absent as usual but no one missing him, Then Mom in the kitchen making a late dinner after working all day, and me sitting down at the table to write a few jokes. The air smells like boiling rice. I tap my notebook with my pen. Mom pretends not to notice me, but she watches from the corner of her eye to see if I'll come up with anything. Just moments before this, she has told me to follow my dream and become a comedian.

"You can be anything you want, dear. Don't let anyone tell you different."

I told my Mom I wanna be an oyster fisherman when I grow up.
 She told me that was a shell-fish goal!

I wandered the motel room and talked to Mom and the others who weren't around—to everyone who'd deserted me.

"I know I wasn't perfect, but you didn't *all* have to die. I mean, you could have drawn lots or something to see who stuck around." I pulled open a drawer thinking there might be a Gideon Bible inside. It was disappointing not to find one, but I still had my make-believe audience: "You people give new meaning to the phrase 'I wish I were dead.'" This slayed me. I laughed and applauded myself. Then I saw myself in the mirror, me tottering and gaunt. I pulled off my shirt and flexed like a bodybuilder. In the mirror, I was Schwarzenegger's anorexic doppelganger.

Why was the big bodybuilder arrested?
 For shoplifting!

I laughed until I grew dizzy, me still there at the mirror, and soon my face and body became Ronnie's face and body, Ronnie on our wedding day, eager and nervous, so I turned the mirror around, put my shirt back on, and bowed to my audience. I told them the next show would be whenever.

Once I'd had enough of these little outbursts, I spent time imitating a sloth, eating cold canned food, growing stiff from inaction. My greatest exertions involved using the toilets in the motel's other rooms and throwing a lamp through the glass of the lobby vending machine in order to liberate a tantalizingly available Snickers bar.

And then there were the down moments—*very* down moments, with bad hallucinations (the Percocet version of cold, hard facts). In one dip into delirium, I saw myself in court, as a defendant. The judge was Ronnie, dispensing wisdom from an elevated bench. Judge Ronnie told me I'd had it all. I was white and male and born in a rich, free country—the trifecta of the world's luckiest birthrights—and yet I'd thrown these advantages away.

While African Americans fell into debt traps and ran from the police, while women worked for insulting pay and got groped by bosses, while immigrants picked tomatoes, refugees starved, students went into debt for unusable educations, I sat at a keyboard and made up stories and comedy-routine jokes that, in the big scheme of things, added as much value to the world as a Big Mac belch. Judge Ronnie informed me my novels' only real benefit was that they brought me a little money and an ounce of esteem. She told me to weigh that against the fact that for most of my adult life I'd hidden in my room, click-clacked away at a keyboard, and told the world outside to get bent.

"For avoiding meaningful contact with your fellow man," Judge Ronnie said, "for being too cowardly to leave the safety of your home office, for passing judgment on people you've never met, I sentence you to spend eternity alone in Spokane, Washington."

This was one of the milder hallucinations, one of the cogent ones. Others were weirder and worse. In one, I died and couldn't find my way back to the land of the living; I could only pound on a window through which I saw myself on the other side, at my computer, chuckling at some witty phrasing for a novel-in-progress or some witty one-liners that I'd never say out loud. And I dreamed this while being fully awake and aware I was sitting on a motel bed in Spokane. This was getting to be too much. I wanted to throw rotting heads of lettuce at myself and give myself the Vaudeville hook.

With time, the bizarreness grew too harsh to bear. The nosebleed highs and the grinding lows pulled me in too many directions. It was time to get off the Percocet, claw my way back to reality, deal with Ronnie if she really was out there—maybe even do something uncharacteristically reasonable and go look for survivors.

So I threw the rest of the Percocet pills onto the roof of the motel and spent two days taking in water, electrolytes and measured doses of healthy (albeit packaged) foods.

The withdrawal symptoms were mild: a little nausea, some jitters. The cobwebs took time to clear and the thumb was still tender, but it had a near-normal range of motion. The headaches were gone, but with my regained clarity came a need to confront, at last, the question I'd been avoiding for the last week.

Was I crazy?

Either Ronnie had crashed me into that tree or I had crashed me into that tree. Either or. The former option was unthinkable to anyone who had a working relationship with logic, but then I also wouldn't have tried to kill myself. An emotional truth is also a truth. I'd fought to escape the bunker, to get on the road to Seattle, to seek survivors. I'd kept a relatively even keel under the circumstances and hadn't thought about suicide since those first, out-of-whack days following the extinction. I wouldn't have harmed myself—I had to give myself at least that much credit.

Therefore, ghosts existed.

Or maybe there was a third possibility. Maybe the ghosts *were* there, physical things that could harm me, but their existence could not be rationally explained because they were products of the mysterious force that had murdered humanity. Like those atoms that affected other atoms miles away, the new world had its own incomprehensible phenomena. My lifelong method for understanding and solving problems—research followed by the test of action—was useless.

But my method was all I had. Logic and common sense couldn't be abandoned. Either Ronnie was real or I was nutty as a jar of Skippy.

Lovely choice.

I re-wrapped the thumb, reloaded the SKS, and drove out of town west toward Fairchild Air Force Base, a place whose military gadgets might aid me in my search for survivors.

Driving, I kept my head on a swivel. Why wouldn't she show herself? What was she waiting for? She could have easily pounced when I was drooling all over myself in that motel room.

Whatever she was doing, whatever she *was*, she had her reasons. My job now wasn't simple, but it was straightforward: hold onto the reins of reality with both hands and don't let go no matter how hard Ronnie bucked.

Even if a part of me still sensed my grip was slipping.

16

THE ACCESS GATE to Fairchild Air Force Base was open but a Jeep blocked the entrance. I had to park outside and enter the base on foot. This was an issue because the place was a small city, with over a hundred houses, a massive commissary, and a base fitness center. There was also a Burger King packed with deceased, Whopper-loving soldiers. Outside, stately decommissioned warplanes stood proudly on display. Every inch of the place was dead.

To get to the runway, I had to walk past dozens of corpses in uniform. Seeing them struck a low chord in me. If the deaths of Great Falls, Missoula and Spokane were a statement that everyone was gone, then the demise of yet another air-force base—Uncle Sam, protector of the nation, defender of the pure—felt like an exclamation point at the end of the sentence.

I found the base control tower and took the stairs up hoping to find an emergency power system. Maybe the computers would work. Maybe the radios would receive signals from Fairchild's still-alive military brethren halfway around the world. This idea hadn't occurred to me back at Malmstrom, but I didn't scold myself now for the oversight. In the first few days after the end of the world, one's ability to think useful thoughts tends to be compromised.

My Only Friend, the End

The control room had eight corpses (six in uniform, two in civvies). A circular bank of dusty computer screens sat in front of a whole lot of tinted windows that wouldn't open. I stepped from computer screen to computer screen, hit buttons and flipped switches to see if anything still had power. None of the hardware came to life—and even if it did, these machines looked inoperable for people like me who lacked high-level technical training. Still, there had to be a back-up system.

Militaries planned for contingencies. If I could find it, if I could keep my mind clear and do the right research, maybe I could coax some communication gear to life. After all, for a brief moment in time I had tamed a radio station transmitter out on the prairie. There was a success on the résumé.

In the end, everything in the tower refused to turn on. I descended the stairs and trudged toward the buildings closest to the runway. Fighter jets and transport planes sat in a perfectly straight line on the pad as if to say, "Don't blame us, we were standing at attention when this happened." The sun splashed off the sea of concrete with blinding brightness. I spent the next four hours moving through the nearby buildings, hitting switches on computers, seeking back-up batteries, often worrying I would open a door or turn a corner and come face to face with Ronnie.

I called out her name from time to time, sent out thought-waves in case she could read them, but she left me alone, let my jitters deepen while I sought salvation through technology. All the computers, the radios, all things electronic—they were as useful as the decaying soldiers on the floors. There weren't even any generators. Everything used electricity from overhead lines.

On the way back to the main gate, I told myself, *Fine, this was a long shot, don't get discouraged, just get to Seattle.* A little later: *Really? Not one single back-up generator?* Before I reached the street, I looked for a supply warehouse to replace the MREs that had been lost in the Humvee crash. During this, I passed a row of bungalows with big yards—officers' homes. None of them had caught fire, and only now did I realize nothing else at Fairchild AFB had burned down, either. That seemed positive at first, but I couldn't attach a meaning to it that would stretch the positivity out.

On a bench outside one of the bungalows sat a corpse in a neon-orange jogging shirt that was starting to slip down around his rotting shoulders. The man was sitting up straight, had defied gravity after dying. I saw him in profile, his upper and lower eyelids unclosed over a gap where the eye had once been. The rigid stillness of him reminded me of

Sean Vilmack back in the old Bijou, his mop of black hair and his fixed posture after he'd tried to hold my hand under the cover of darkness.

After that incident, I didn't see Sean again until school was back in, three weeks before he killed himself. I was at my locker digging around for my bio textbook when he walked up to me and stood at the edge of my peripheral vision. He waited for me to stop pretending I couldn't see him.

"I'm sorry," he said, which forced me to turn and face him. "I know you've been avoiding me. You don't have to."

"I haven't been avoiding you," I lied.

"I mean, it's okay, I surprised you. I should have found some other way to, like, tell you."

"I'm gonna be late for bio," I said.

"I just wanted to apologize. I'll leave you alone if that's what you want. Just say the word."

He awaited an answer, but that same stew of shame and anger boiled in my guts again. I couldn't speak, couldn't look him in the eyes. I was no longer the well-adjusted, totally with-it teenager that I'd assumed I was—I needed the awkwardness of the moment to leave me as soon as possible.

"The thing is," Sean said, "my dad's been sending me to this conversion therapy at the church. It's a nightmare. The minister is telling me all these really fucked-up things and my Dad says if I get kicked out of church he's gonna kick me out of the house. And my mom won't even look at me. She spends half the day crying."

I knew what he was doing: he'd come out to his parents and now, more than ever, he needed a friend. But the whole thing was just too big. Sean both impressed me and frightened me; he was brave beyond my understanding of the word, but I had no experience whatsoever with seismic change. I had rarely ever considered what it meant to be gay in Great Falls, Montana, probably because so few people my age ever admitted to it. There would be heavy challenges here, a need to take a stand. A need to accept consequences.

In the end, I told him, "Maybe you should give the therapy a little more time," then closed my locker and brushed past him as if I really was late for class.

I hated myself for the way I recalled this now—the cruel clarity of it—so I walked up to the corpse on the bench and nudged his shoulder. He spilled forward onto the ground and stopped looking like Sean.

You didn't kill him. His dad and his church killed him. Small-minded Montana did.
Maybe.
You were just a kid.
And maybe if I repeated this to myself often enough I'd be able to believe it again—just like I'd taught myself to believe it years earlier, right up until the day the world ended without me.

To chase the subject from my mind, I peeked inside the bungalow's living-room window: clean inside; conservative décor; wall portraits of a military man and woman with three children. The TV was unadventurously sized; there were no corpses on the broadloom, no pets.

Pets.

Rough-cut images blipped in my mind: a blanket, a jar of butter chicken sauce, a deck chair at the bumper of a Dodge Durango. The same bits and pieces had flashed during my Percocet binge, but as dreamlike images or homeless thought strands that were maybe part of some disconnected, unimportant whole. Now I recalled my setting of the dog trap in its entirety. I had probably killed man's best friend in an unspeakably cruel way.

I forgot about MREs—forgot about Sean and Ronnie and the reason I was at this army base—and sped back to Spokane.

• • •

It took me half an hour of cruising residential streets until I found my trap car. By the time I got there, I was bawling like a child, the type of sorrow that had consumed me when I was falling apart over the two Jacks in Great Falls.

I parked well back of the Durango, afraid to approach it and look inside. I sat behind the wheel a long while, still a mess, inwardly apologizing to a dead dog I hadn't yet met. The car looked the same as when I'd left it, and there was no movement on the street. These were good signs (maybe the dogs *had* lit out for different neighborhoods; maybe the trap car *was* empty), but in my heart I knew that wasn't true. There would be foam at the dog's mouth, dull, buggy eyes, rigor mortis, flies. I would have preferred to see every human corpse in the city of Spokane rather than approach the car and see that.

A magpie landed on the Durango's hood. The bird was fat and healthy, its white plumage burnished brown from having gorged on corpses. It paused a moment, scoped out the area, then hopped onto the edge of the open sunroof and down into the vehicle.

I launched myself out of the Jeep and ran to the Dodge flailing my arms, screaming at the bird. When I arrived there, the magpie squawked and careened off two windows before slipping out the sunroof and streaking away.

On the back seat of the car lay a barely-panting yellow Labrador, female. Her thick, purple tongue darted in and out of her mouth in time with each slight breath, and her eyes showed dull gray, but they registered my presence. The water bowl was empty and the bait food was gone, remnants of it dried into the blanket and car seats as well as the fur around her mouth.

Rather than help her, I stood there like a statue, with both hands on the half-down driver-side window.

"I'm sorry," I said stupidly, and somewhere the post-extinction Ronnie laughed. She had claimed me as a co-conspirator in the new world's crimes, had transformed me from victim to perpetrator.

I ran to the Jeep, grabbed a bottle of water, ran back, poured it into the empty water bowl. The dog didn't care. I held the bowl to her mouth, but she wouldn't drink, so I scooped some into my hand and dripped it onto her gums and tongue. After about a minute her head jerked, then the mouth closed and opened again and the tongue flicked in and out, licking the wetness from her snout.

"Good girl! Drink!"

For the next hour she whimpered and was too weak to stand but she grew more responsive to my voice, pricked up her ears, looked me in the eyes.

When she finally tried to lap water from my hand, I propped her into a sitting position and held the bottle under her snout. She drank with pitiful flicks of the tongue. Her eyes now showed a hint of keenness. She paused once between laps and licked my face. What a feeling. As low as the deepest low had been, this was elation.

Twice she choked and vomited out the water. Both times I waited a few seconds, then gave her more. Once she had her fill, she laid back on the seat and let out a heavy, contented sigh. I left her there and retrieved some MREs from the Jeep. I tore one open and handpicked some factory-formed chicken cubes, then held them to her snout. She sniffed and looked away. I poured the rest of the meal (chicken-lentil stew) into the bowl and left it on the floor in front of the seat. Then I sat back and ran my fingers through her food-matted fur. She gave me a satisfied look, a look of trust, canine faith in the preeminence of human beings. She closed her eyes, allowed herself to sleep.

For a long while she yelped and twitched in her sleep. I brought a blanket from the Jeep, settled in beside her, and stroked her hair. Her warmth felt good. The fact she was alive—I was no longer alone—was too large for words. I fell asleep with my hand on the back of her neck, afraid to lose contact.

17

I AWOKE TO THE SLURPING, snorting sounds of a famished dog attacking a bowl full of food. It was the middle of the night, but light from the moon gave me a view of her ravenous assault. She polished off the stew with a few succulent smacks of her tongue, then licked the bowl clean a second time, and re-licked it yet again for good measure.

I decided not to feed her more until the food had worked its way through her system. I gave her a hug and cried into the coarse guard hair on her neck—just couldn't corral my emotions—then I let her lick my face until it dripped saliva.

She had no collar.

"You'll need a name," I said. "What'll we call you?" The sound of my voice felt good, like a return to life after a long freeze. "Something resilient, strong, a woman who can escape Hell." I thought for a moment. "Anna? As in Karenina?"

She stared at me.

"You're right, things didn't turn out so well for her. Scarlett? As in O'Hara? Now there was a girl you knew would bounce back."

She sniffed the air, checked the bowl again.

"Then how about Flan? Flannie?" Flannery O'Connor, my favorite writer during my undergrad days. Wrote gothic stories about the south in the 1950s. Told the truth in ways that other writers didn't. Flannie O'Connor had rocked my world.

"Flannie it is."

I hugged her again and offered my face for another round of sloppy tongue-raking.

She wobbled while walking from the trap car to the Jeep. I lifted her into the back seat and asked her if she'd had enough of Spokane yet. She looked at me like *Just take care of me, okay?* so I said, "You're right, let's not dawdle, let's go find survivors!" I climbed into the driver seat and started us on the nighttime road toward Seattle.

Flannie slept while I drove. I was afraid to wake her, afraid she might *not* wake. There had been strange events in my life. I'd survived a flash-extinction while skydiving; before that, back in college, I'd fallen drunkenly from a second-floor balcony and had landed on a doorway awning, walking away without a scratch; there were times when I felt blessed and destined to live long and well. But if Flannie's recovery didn't take, I knew in my bones it would end me then and there, no resistance raised.

I kept the high beams on and navigated car wrecks with exaggerated care. At this slow crawl, the night played tricks on me. The cars against the guard rails, the flashing metallic auto paint in the brightness of my headlights—everything looked alive and pregnant with danger. A corpse behind the wheel of a Wonder Bread truck had blue eyes, like a dog in a photograph. I looked away and sped up a little to thirty, and things looked and felt normal again—until I saw the hitchhiker.

It was just a glimpse, a flash of a hoodie-wearing person on the shoulder holding out his or her thumb. The image didn't even register until I had sped past it. I slammed on the brakes and felt Flannie thump against the back of my seat.

I grabbed a flashlight from the glove compartment, scrambled out to the road, and pointed the light back at where I'd seen the hitchhiker. A wrecked car sat against the guard rail. In the Seattle direction, the road's painted lines trailed off into darkness.

I scanned the ditch along the road in both directions: tall grasses, sapling pines. At the tree line, no movement. I looked back toward Montana yet again.

"Ronnie!"

She didn't answer, so I walked toward the truck—and heard twigs snap on the other side of the road. I wheeled around, aimed the flashlight, and glimpsed the hoodied hitchhiker disappearing into the trees.

Either ghosts exist or I'm crazy.

Either or.

I climbed back in the truck, checked the bullet clip on the rifle, and watched the forest for a long while. Then I resumed driving.

Flannie had climbed up onto the back seat and was asleep again, her ribcage rising and falling with reassuring regularity.

Two miles up the road, Ronnie appeared again, another glimpse, too fast to I.D. her, but there was a pit-of-the-stomach knowledge it was her. I stopped, clambered out of the truck, and looked all around again, and for the second time, when I started back toward the truck, more twigs sounded and I saw her at the tree line.

This sighting lasted a little longer. The hoodie she wore was from our days together at Montana State University—MSU Bobcats.

I raised my rifle even though I knew I could never shoot her. She sauntered into the woods, disappeared.

Follow her? Run the other way?

I started into the woods, then checked myself, returned to the truck, and drove as fast as I safely could to Sprague, a farming hamlet with (no joke) the world's largest roadside spork. I parked under the hundred-foot monument to oddity and tried to wrap my mind around the meaning of Ronnie. Just thinking about her right now did not seem like a sound strategy for maintaining robust mental health. I needed a way around her.

Flannie yipped in her sleep. I reclined my seat, locked the doors, and put the keys in my pocket in case Ronnie teleported in and tried to grab them.

But of course I couldn't sleep; she made sure of that.

"If you have something to tell me," I said out loud, "then go ahead and say it."

Of course there was no response.

"In that case…"

I dug around in the Jeep and found my book on the Earth's five great extinctions.

Keeping my eyes on the page was impossible. I read half a sentence before looking up knowing Ronnie would be there, maybe with a knife at my throat. But she wasn't, and after five or six more false starts I managed to read a whole paragraph without conjuring ways in which she might pop by and kill me. I even retained a little of what I read. The second-most-recent mass extinction was the Triassic-Jurassic. It occurred 210 million years ago, killing half the world's species. Climate change and massive volcanic eruptions and possibly an asteroid made life a tad uncomfortable on Pangaea, the world's supercontinent.

I looked up. No Ronnie.

The Triassic-Jurassic extinction took ten thousand years to unfold. That was ten thousand years minus one second longer than what we'd had a month ago. Not exactly a solid comparable.

I looked around outside before moving on to the third extinction.

The Permian-Triassic:

Two-hundred and fifty million years ago, the world's largest extinction.

Killed ninety-six percent of marine species.

Seventy percent of land vertebrates.

Took millions of years to transpire.

I closed the book, looked around for Ronnie, then turned off the dome light.

"I'm closing my eyes," I said. "I'm going to sleep very soundly."

The moment I did close my eyes, I knew she was there in the cab with me. When I opened them again, she wasn't, so I closed them yet again, folded my arms over my chest, and tried to pretend I was in the most comfortable chair in the world.

In the darkness, I mused that maybe she'd been sent by little green men who right now were watching from above, laughing, placing bets on what I might do next. Ronnie was an extra-terrestrial avatar that the aliens threw at me for sport. Same with Evan back at the bunker. Maybe the little green men had other surprises in store. When they got bored with my reactions they would come down from space, zap me into particulate dust, and start harvesting my planet's resources.

"Goodnight, wife," I said without opening my eyes, and I did proceed to sleep, not much, but some, and upon waking I decided I'd won something important.

• • •

The next morning, Flannie was still weak, but she did her business in the roadside bushes without faltering. After that, she ate with a powerful hunger. She needed to be picked up and placed in the truck, but was alert and happy.

I talked to her all the way to Moses Lake, three wreck-impeded hours to the west. I told her about the real Ronnie, my wife, about her goodness, her beauty, our miraculous boys, our life in Great Falls. I told her how lucky I'd been—how lucky we all had been—and how if I had it to do over again, I would take part in life more instead of just observing and writing about it. I wouldn't be so judgmental because I would know that all people had problems and all people responded to challenges and adversity in their own unique ways. I would be more generous in my outlook, more of a citizen.

Flannie looked at me as if *What are you going on about?* but the talking was therapy. I told her about Great Falls, and about the thrill of skydiving and the rewarding parts of using Mike Stone as a can-do alter ego. I couldn't get the words out fast enough. More than once, I said, "Really, you had to be there," and I apologized for being a bit of a scatterbrain.

I can't seem to find my focus.

So tell Ford I'll need another one!

At one point I moved on to my other family—my mother and my sister and brother—and was surprised by how easy it was to start talking about them.

"We were distant, but we could rely on each other. You see, we were raised with this prairie reserve, this puritanical aversion to displays of emotion. But we loved each other. Does that make sense?"

It did, but it also sounded like a pat summation. In fact, my family was like professional wrestling without the chair throwing. Instead of getting violent, we allowed trivial slights to fester and metastasize into relationship killers. Calendar years passed during which brother hardly spoke to sister, or daughter resented mother, and always for reasons that (I suspected) most families would have seen as minor. In the early years, we were close (we were braver when we were younger), but time made us brittle and over-sensitive. We issued ourselves one-way tickets on a rocking, wobbling train of dysfunction that gained speed as we aged.

Over time I fell into the habit of blaming this on my father. He had some colorful anger issues and enjoyed batting the kids around when the world got him down. I know that left scars on us, but the violence rarely went beyond the odd open-handed smack, and most of the time he was so distant from us kids that a surprise clout or two wasn't the soul killer that it might otherwise have been. There didn't seem to be anything personal behind it—or anything personal about him at all—and when he finally exited the scene (my mother kicked him out and took up with the manager at the bank where she worked), there was a whiff of the anticlimactic.

And my siblings—as soon as he was old enough, Dale moved to Brussels and got lost in the bureaucracy of an EU agency. Joanie did IT security work and got married twice before relocating to Berlin and working for a biomass firm. She was angry before she left the States and angry afterwards and later she got back in touch with my father when no one else would. Whenever she and the rest of the family got together, we tended to be powered-down versions of normal people, hardly uttering a word, at least one of us with a drinking problem and all of us strangers afraid of igniting another childish spat. The whole family-troubles thing was more painful to analyze than it was to actually experience, and I think each of us understood this and was acutely confused by it, so we stayed apart, scattered like orphans, until a sense of decorum brought us back together every two years or so for Christmas or Thanksgiving or (worst of all) a funeral.

"So," I told Flannie, "when the extinction hit, Dad was long dead, Mom was in Arizona, Dale was in Belgium and Joanie was in Germany. I'm the only one who stuck around Montana."

Flannie gave a little whine.

"Don't care for family histories?"

Another whimper. Restless.

I stopped the car and eased her down to the ground. She did what she had to do, then waited for me to pick her up. We were in sync. On the road again, she wanted to hear me talk some more, but not about family—no, not that—so I gave her some unbridled optimism: I told her we would stick it out in this new world, she and I together, and we would find survivors whatever it took. No ghosts or alien avatars would be allowed to change that.

Let 'em try.

18

WE FOUND DOG FOOD in the town of George, Washington, at the Colonial Market, a stop-and-shop along the highway. After Flannie ate, she hobbled around the parking lot in lieu of a walk. She wasn't stable enough to join me while I checked out the town, so I lifted her back into the vehicle, parked it in the shade, and opened the windows.

There were maybe forty houses here, pleasant homes for canola farmers. I strode up and down streets trying to ignore bodies, looking for antennas on roofs. I peeked inside unlocked garages and stepped into the local community center, where women had been hanging wedding decorations when the extinction struck. One woman sat bent backward over a chair and still had the end of a streamer in her hand. The other end was attached to the ceiling. She looked like a Renaissance portrait—a dead Jerusalemite holding a beam of sunshine that would lift her to Heaven.

At Shree's Truck Stop, I climbed into two rigs and checked the ignitions for keys so I could listen to the CBs. There were no keys. One driver sat dead on the blistering pavement just outside his rig. He stared right at me and his decomposing face looked like it was laughing. I couldn't bring myself to go through his pockets to get the keys. Instead, I walked over to the 76 gas station next door to grab some food for the afternoon drive. The fact that I now had a four-legged companion in the truck had me feeling extravagant. I filled my basket with packaged apple turnovers, potato chips and Gummy Bears, three important food groups when you decide to junk it up at the end of the world. At the drink fridge, I grabbed some water. The contents of the open-faced sandwich fridge were caked with a uniformly gray fuzz that seemed to have migrated from the corpses on the floor. The smell was bad but bearable.

I grabbed some cash from my wallet, tossed it onto the front counter, and said to the withering stiff behind the register, "Keep the change, my friend."

Before I closed the wallet, I caught a glimpse of a card inside, my gym membership card. I stared at the photo on it, a me from before the fall, a me who had no idea. My pre-extinction cluelessness felt naïve. I grabbed the card and—*flick*—scissored it through the air without watching where it went.

Behind the gym card was my driver's license—more cluelessness. *Flick*. And behind that a debit card and a Costco card for the store in Bozeman—*flick, flick*. By the last of the flicks, a sense of loss had wormed its way into my mood like a fast-acting germ.

On the other side of the wallet, I pulled the cards out slowly, paused over each of them: two gas-station points cards, a MasterCard, my AAA card. There was also a prepaid Visa gift card I'd received as a rebate when buying a Christmas trip to Puerto Vallarta. I'd forgotten about it, had never used it. And I'd forgotten much of the trip, too, at an all-inclusive place where Ronnie and I sipped syrupy margaritas and made sandcastles with Evan.

Behind all the cards, in the last fold, were mini-portraits of Ronnie and Evan, all smiles and contentment. I ran my thumb over the shot of Ronnie, tried to feel her, to sense her like I could sense her ghost, but she was just a glossy image, wasn't real, never would be again. And she could be harmful, her there in my pocket, always available, calling out to me now that I'd discovered her. I flicked both photos away, dropped my wallet onto the counter, and turned and started toward the door.

Then promptly ran back, gathered up the photos, and slid them gingerly into my shirt pocket as if they were the most valuable things on Earth.

"I'm sorry," I said with a crack in my voice. "I won't ever do that again."

I walked out of the shop trying hard to keep it together. When I reached Flannie, she wagged her tail and licked my face. I couldn't return the love. I was empty—no hope there to drum up. Ghosts, gluey apple turnovers and yellow labs: this was as good as it would ever get in the new world. I couldn't even find an operable CB radio, and if I did find one, what was I going to do, raise Elvis?

Flannie lapped at my face, nudged me with her nose. *Get over yourself*, she said in her canine way. *We have to go back to surviving.*

"Just give me a minute," I told her. "This one'll take me a while."

• • •

I did get over it. What choice was there?

I drove back to the 76 station and grabbed all the water I could carry, then rummaged around the shelves for soap and Head & Shoulders. In the parking lot, I did my best to work the matted gunk out of Flannie's coat. She withstood the scrubbing and rinsing with slumped posture and a tight-mouthed frown.

When she was clean, I sniffed another unpleasant odor in the air: myself. I stripped down and worked the soap and shampoo into my own body. I scrubbed at my skin until the outer layer was gone and a fresh, stinging stratum took its place.

In the parking lot, I found a four-wheel-drive truck with a tow hitch (the Jeep didn't have one). After transferring my supplies to the truck's bed, I hit on a new idea. I walked back into the store, stepped over the half-kneeling, half-lying station attendant, and found the phone book under the counter. According to the book, the nearest hunting supply store was in Ephrata, twenty miles north of George. The nearest Washington Department of Fish and Wildlife regional office was in also in Ephrata, so back up the I-90 we drove.

"You're going to like this," I told Flannie.

Ephrata was bigger than George, maybe 10,000 corpses, a good number of them out on the streets looking spectacularly gross. Before hitting the hunting store, I trolled those streets trying (again) to ignore the bodies and searching (again) for radio antennas. I spotted one on the roof of a three-car garage attached to a McMansion. I had to kick in the locked door, but it was worth the effort, because the garage produced not only a portable ham radio but also a generator and two big fuel drums. I plugged the radio in to the generator and turned both on. The radio beeped and screeched, and when I worked the knobs I found no signs of life. But that wasn't unexpected; the main thing was that it worked. I turned it off, hauled it and the generator into the bed of the truck, then, after dithering over whether to load the fuel drums, drove to Johnson's Outfitters at the east end of town.

The flare guns were in a case behind the counter. Each gun came with a rack of six flares. I grabbed all four cases and put them in the bed of the truck. I could pick up more in Seattle or Tacoma.

The Washington Department of Fish and Wildlife regional office was hard to find, off the highway north of town. It was a long building with a parking lot full of cars out front. A woman had died at the glass doors to the lobby, so I had to drag her out of the way before walking in. This took both hands and made my injured thumb feel as if I'd slammed a car door on it.

Inside the building, the air was unusually foul. I put on a medical mask, found the offices, and started rifling through files. I sought anything relating to deer migration routes or road safety measures. After an hour of looking, I gave up. The information I needed must have been on the Department intranet. I considered bringing in the generator and firing up a computer, but the digital files were no doubt password protected.

As I left the office, I heard Flannie bark from the truck. I opened her door and she bounded down off the seat as if she'd never been weak. She jumped up on me, tried to lick me.

"Okay," I told her, "from now on, you go where I go."

I grabbed a flashlight from the truck, walked around back of the building and found the supply shack, a long Quonset hut with the door rolled halfway up. Flannie stuck by my side the whole way. We entered the hut and started poking around. There were parked department trucks, two boats, chainsaws, animal traps, baling wire. In the back, covered by a tarp, were two vacuum-powered fish tubes for stocking lakes with trout.

Under another tarp, I found what I wanted. I pulled the cracked, dried-out canvas off a trailer and a cloud of dust curled up into the air, making me cough. A flat-faced, twenty-inch disk sat on the trailer. It looked like an overgrown cosmetic mirror with a big battery and an unmanageable heft. The thing hadn't been used in years, probably didn't work. I hit the power switch and it started to hum. The lights on the control panel lit up.

"Sometimes," I said to Flannie, "you just have to believe in luck."

Flannie's expression said, *Is something good happening?*

I worked my way through the controls: power switch, volume switch, sound setting, record and play buttons. I lifted the disk off the ground and the thing was lighter than it looked, maybe 40 pounds.

"We'll have to put you back in the truck for this next part," I told Flannie.

She didn't like going in, but there was no choice. Once she was safely in the passenger seat with the windows rolled up, I returned to my new toy, chose "burglar alarm" on the control pad, stood behind the disk, and hit play.

A high-pitched whine blew right through me. I slapped off the power button and worried my eardrums were shredded.

After the ringing died down, I cleared my throat and spoke into the MP3 recorder:

"Honk if you aren't a corpse."

This time I covered my ears once I hit "play," and even through the protective layer of palms and fingers, my voice sounded with such volume and clarity that for a moment I actually worried someone might hear it.

I switched it off and ran outside to Flannie.

"We have ourselves the king of megaphones!"

The fish-and-wildlife people used the LRAD, or Long Range Acoustic Device, to scare deer away from the Interstate. Police departments used it to disperse mobs at street protests, which was how I'd first heard of them. The LRAD could carry messages for up to two miles—custom-made for companion-seeking survivors at the end of the world.

The Quonset hut had all the tools I needed to take the LRAD off the trailer and attach it to the Ram's tow hitch. The battery was unwieldy, but I managed to lift it onto the truck bed between the generator and the wheel well. I hoped it wouldn't slide around, but it didn't much matter. I would drive slowly.

One more thing to do before continuing on to Seattle. I drove around town and plucked real estate signs from lawns. When I had about twenty, I drove to the local Walmart and scooped four cans of red spray paint from the shelves. In the parking lot, I sprayed on the signs:

↑ *Survivor* ↑
↑ *Ch. 9 on C.B.* ↑

Flannie scratched behind her ear like fleas were holding a convention there.

"Need another rinse, girl?"

I found an irrigation canal and she attacked the water like she was made for it. Once she was in, I couldn't get her out—so I jumped in after her and splashed around until the fact that there were probably corpses upstream killed the fun.

Back on the road, I waited until we hit the Interstate before I propped my first realtor sign against the guard rail and recorded a message into the LRAD:

"I'm driving west on the Interstate. If you can hear me, make smoke. I'll come to you."

We drove slowly, about 20 miles an hour. The message repeated every 15 seconds. With the windows up, the volume was barely tolerable.

After half an hour and two more stops to plant realtor signs, I grabbed binoculars from my supplies and peered back down the road. There were no cars, no smoke on the horizon, but at least I was no longer blithely rolling down the road and possibly bypassing survivors.

"What do you think, girl? Are things looking up?"

Flannie's expression said, *Is it time for food?*

Once I reached Seattle, I could find a point high on a hill, on a building, maybe even up on the Space Needle. I could kick up my feet, uncork a bottle of something, let the LRAD attract the people like a stirring remix of Reveille. The LRAD's two-mile radius would get my message to a lot of people, some of them maybe even alive.

The next town on the I-90 was Ellensburg, about twice the size of Ephrata and twice as dead. The corpses there did not get me down—they couldn't be allowed to. The secret was to see them without thinking. I just had to remind myself they were no longer people. Seattle would be the payoff for all this roving investment, the target of all hopes. I stayed in Ellensburg just long enough to siphon gas from another truck and to upgrade my sunglasses to polarized aviator specs that looked hopelessly retro but that provided better protection. Flannie refrained from making Serpico jokes.

Thirty miles west of Ellensburg, the high-plains farms gave way to the pines of the Cascades. My map told me there were only a few more towns between here and Seattle, which meant salvation was nigh. I increased my speed to forty miles an hour, the fastest I could safely drive without being surprised by a wreck. I decided the faster pace wouldn't affect the quality of the LRAD message.

When the sun started to set, I pulled off the road at a motel west of the town of Cle Elum. The doors were key-card operated, so I tore open my chosen door with a crowbar. The breaking of the wood felt good. I was the boss here, a survivor of substance; little things like locks were trivial. The walk back to the truck, however, brought me down a notch. I tripped and fell, hurting my thumb more than at any time since I'd crushed it with Alvin Stinghold's hammer. I knelt there in the motel parking lot, massaged away the pain, told myself to get smart or end up having to amputate it.

Flannie barked—made me jump.

"Please, girl, not right in the ear."

I dusted myself off, took some toiletries and MREs into the motel room, then came back out to see Flannie still in the same spot, still looking off in the same direction. She barked again. I followed her gaze and saw a wisp of smoke breaching the tree tops maybe a mile away.

"Whoa!"

I scrambled to the truck, grabbed the binocs, and looked again. The smoke was gray, like a campfire, not deep black like the urban fires after the extinction.

"We did it!" I shouted, "we found them!" and I took off running down the road toward the smoke.

But while I ran, a dark thought came to mind: the smoke wasn't real; the smoke was Ronnie's doing, more teasing of the gullible lone survivor. I stopped running, then stopped moving altogether. For a brief moment, I wanted to dig a hole in the roadside ditch and crawl into it.

But I looked through the binocs again and the smoke was too real-seeming, too *there*. It couldn't be a mirage.

Then again: *That's exactly what she wants me to think…*

A wide, gray flake of ash wafted down through the air and landed on Flannie's snout. I touched it and it smudged. The little white blotch was real. The smoke was real. Flannie sneezed and licked her chops. *She* wasn't being haunted by ill-tempered dead wives. I charged toward the forest, started plowing through trees and tall grass.

But with evening falling, the forest was dark and full of fallen-branch obstacles. Moving through it was disorienting. If I kept this up, I'd get lost or injured, or maybe eaten by a bear. I stumbled forward for a few minutes, then gave in to common sense and trudged back to the Ram.

My Only Friend, the End

I aimed the LRAD at the smoke. On the control panel, I recorded a new message:

"I see you. Make more smoke in the morning and I'll come to you!"

The message ran while I sprinted to the motel and filled a backpack with food and water, a flashlight, a compass, everything I would need for a day's hike, plus extra food and water in case my fellow survivors needed it. This all got done with my heart beating at hummingbird pace.

Finished packing, I nearly lit out for the forest again, time of day be damned. Only then did I notice Flannie hiding under the bed, shaking because of the blaring LRAD message.

I stepped outside and closed the door behind me. Some rough math: 9:21 p.m. Night was falling fast. Sunrise would arrive in roughly eight hours—the longest eight hours of my life.

I drove the LRAD closer to the smoke (and farther away from Flannie) and kept my message playing on a loop. When I got back to the motel, Flannie wanted to roughhouse but settled for making herself at home on the pillows. I laid down on the other bed and told myself to eat something or tomorrow I would court a crash.

But I couldn't eat—too keyed up.

And there was no way in hell I was going to sleep.

19

THE NEXT MORNING, Flannie and I were out on the highway before sunrise. The LRAD battery had died around midnight, and in the darkness, even with the binoculars, I saw no stars in the clouded sky, no smoke in the distance, only the tops of roadside trees under a scattering fog. My heart sank. The survivors were gone or dead or summoned back to Sirius Six by my tormenting little green men, and with the LRAD battery dead I couldn't send another message. This was the way things went in the new world: tenuous hopes dashed by a shape-shifting reality.

But with the unfolding dawn came a clearer outline of the forest, more depth of vision. I paced nervously, twice started into the forest, twice came back, hoped daylight proper would bring a visual beacon.

And at last the smoke was there, the same place as yesterday. I whooped like a little boy and checked my compass, which told me to go in a north-by-northeast direction. I charged into the woods, past whipping branches, kept a close eye on my bearing. My rifle was in my good hand and my backpack was tied snugly in place.

The ground was a mat of parched grass. In many places the trees were thinly spaced. We were at the edge of a great mountain forest, not in the dense heart of it. I would reach the survivors in half an hour, an hour tops.

Without looking back, I said, "How we making out, girl? You keeping up?"

I listened. No sounds behind me.

"Flannie?"

I stopped and looked around.

"Flannie!"

Silence. A sinking feeling.

"Don't do this, please!"

A twig snapped somewhere among the trees. A moment later she skulked through those trees, ears pinned back, head low and sullen.

"What's a matter, girl? Come here."

She wouldn't approach. I raised the rifle, waited for a grizzly or a wolf to spring out of the woods behind her.

"What is it? Come here, girl, you'll be okay."

But she didn't trust me. I pulled a granola bar from my backpack. The sound of the wrapper got her moving in a tentative creep.

"Yummie," I said, "cranberries and cherries."

She nipped the bar out of my hand like a wild animal afraid of humans. She scurried back to a safe distance before she started to eat.

"What's out there? What'd you see?"

There was a choice: check out the area she'd come from or keep walking toward the smoke. I studied the compass and resumed thrashing through the trees toward the survivors. This time I heard Flannie following close behind me.

At a small clearing I scanned the treetops. The gray wisp of smoke was closer now, maybe a hundred yards away. Soon I would be able to smell it.

"Hello!" I hollered. "Can you hear me!"

No response. I thrashed through the trees. Fifty yards closer to the target, I called out again, and again there was no answer. Maybe the person was hurt, too weak to call out. Maybe there'd been an ATV accident, with the driver dying and the passenger being gravely injured. Or a hunting accident or a hiker whose companion had died and left him or her lost in the woods. Maybe the smoke signaler was a skydiver who'd jumped out of a plane just before the end ...

Flannie bounded ahead of me, into the trees. In a flash, she was out of sight.

"You smell something, girl?"

I picked up my pace, but so did she. The sounds of her leaping across the pine floor of the forest told me she was drawing farther away.

"Flannie, come back!"

But the sounds died. I didn't linger over this, because any second the smell of smoke would arrive, then I would hear firewood crackling, and see the campfire, and see people.

"Make noise so I can find you!"

I covered another fifty yards, which should have put me at the target. I called out again, then listened to the desolate breeze in the pines. Maybe I'd passed the spot, so I backtracked and saw a small clearing to the east. After beating back branches and scrambling out to the field, I looked all around. There was no smoke, no sound, save for the wind in the pines. Flannie was still gone.

"Anyone!"

Silence.

I checked the compass again. It was malfunctioning. Or I'd read it wrong. Maybe I'd underestimated the distance and the fire was farther ahead, with its smoke getting lost in a capricious breeze.

So I got moving again, calling out as I went (sometimes for survivors, sometimes for Flannie). I walked a good half hour, then doubled back, then mentally mapped a series of grids and marched out and back five times. My throat grew raw from shouting. I slumped down against a tree, soaked in sweat, wrung out, my voice gone. It was still only 10:04 in the morning.

Where were they? What was I doing wrong? And if I was doing things right, why weren't they responding?

Because the smoke signalers weren't people, they were Ronnie after all.

Meaning I was crazy.

No. There is no "either or." Not everything is a test of sanity.

But a few dark assertions took on the flavor of facts. There were no people left. I would spend the rest of my life chasing mirages. The endgame would be a drawn-out descent into harsher degrees of instability and, ultimately, too many toys in my attic.

I sent up a flare and called out in my failing voice, then expanded the grid and kept looking. My legs picked up welts and bruises from protruding deadwood and low-hanging branches. My feet ached. My voice made a dry, gravelly sound when I shouted. As day descended into dusk, I trudged back toward the road, beaten, famished, still alone, still no Flannie—but something made me stop and turn, do another pass. There had to be someone there. This wasn't faith or hope; it was need. If the forest was empty, part of me didn't want to go back to the road, or anywhere else, ever.

My Only Friend, the End

• • •

That night I slept in the grass against a tree trunk. In the darkness, I woke up swatting bugs and stared into the night. I shivered and wished Flannie were there. Three times my nostrils flared at the smell of smoke. When the breeze died down, voices rode distant waves. Car doors closed. Music played. I knew the sounds weren't there, they were a product of nighttime anxieties, and I knew Ronnie wasn't toying with me. There was simply nothing there.

I'd been *hoping* for smoke, had dreamed it up. Hope was turning me inside out—a cruel emotional trigger of delusions. Hope had created that flake of ash that had wafted out of the sky and landed so conveniently on Flannie's nose. But hope had been reigned in at the end, despite everything. I had, for whatever reason, corralled it and could now have this reality-based conversation with myself. In the future, hope would have to be avoided until it proved itself undeniably useful. It could not be allowed to hasten my destruction.

In the morning, there was a new day's energy and—despite everything—a new day's hope. I sent up another flare and made a half dozen more passes on my grid before my energy ebbed, then I took a southern bearing back toward the highway. It was over, that was all. Whatever I might or might not think about all this, I was done.

I kept unpleasant company with myself during the walk. I recalled family camping trips up in Alberta when I was a boy but couldn't remember much of what we'd done. There were twenty-pound northern pike and mosquitoes the size of black flies, but all interactions with Dale, Joanie and my parents were gone, bled away by time and trauma. The pre-extinction world was something out of a distant dream. I would lose more of it with each day that passed. Ronnie and Evan would fade like Dale and Joanie were fading.

I would forget Evan and Mike Stone and my writing routine. Also my mom in Scottsdale—books I'd read, and movies I'd seen. My childhood friends. The taste of Thai food and the sound of Ronnie's contented sigh when we snuggled on the sofa. The new world of lonely subsistence would become my only world. There would be no point to life beyond keeping myself going for another day, like an animal. Adopting a pet didn't ease that pain. Without humans, where was humanity? Everything good about me—everything any normal person lived for—would dry up like a snake's discarded skin. Sooner or later I would wear down and embrace defeat like an old friend and that would be that. Sole survivor goes out with a whimper, not a bang.

Flannie showed up at my side, nudged my hip as we walked. Her appearance was not something to be trusted without tactile reinforcement. I reached down and stroked the top of her head. It felt warm. I put the chance that she was actually standing there at fifty percent

"Okay, then," I croaked before bending down and hugging her until welling gratitude for her presence gave me strength. I held onto her until she squirmed out of my grasp.

"Don't ever do that again, okay?"

I blew my nose and stood up.

"And be ready, girl. I'm going to get more clingy by the day."

Walking again, I saw a glimpse of white in the trees up ahead—not just something white, but something bleached and right-angled, something manmade up in the branches. I picked up my pace, then stopped and looked through the binoculars. Paper. Just paper wedged in among the branches. I approached the tree without much thought. I plucked the paper from the flaking bark. It was a page from a book. It read:

"…the Triassic-Jurassic extinction. It occurred 210 million years ago and killed half the world's species…"

A shudder went through me. I snapped my rifle to a ready position and spun around.

"Ronnie!"

No answer.

I peered up ahead and saw more pages from my extinction book in other trees, and also torn pages all over the ground.

Flannie pinned her ears back again. She sensed Ronnie, and so did I. I even smelled her—a face cream she'd used.

I walked over and stepped past a jar of peanut butter, my back-up hiking boots, crushed MREs and dented cans of soup. The contents of two medical kits were scattered in the grass along with more shredded pages from my book. Closer to the truck, my back-up gas canisters had been drained and tossed into the tall grass beside the road. The doors to the vehicle were open, with the side windows smashed and my axe protruding from the spiderwebbed windshield. All four tires were slashed, and the LRAD was cracked and dented, hanging loosely from a hinge. Its control panel was pulverized. Only the LRAD battery remained undamaged, maybe left alone because it was useless without the now-broken sound plate.

But nothing was missing, not a single item. Whoever had done this had taken his or her time—or, from the looks of things, their time.

This made sense now. The smoke in the woods was a diversion meant to lure me away from the truck. Someone was messing with me.

But why? What could be gained from it?

That smoke was real after all.

I sent up a new flare, went to the truck and leaned on the horn. With failing vocal chords, I cried out, "Come out if you're watching! I only want to talk!"

An understatement if ever I'd made one.

Flannie was snout-deep in an MRE of pulled pork and pasta. I picked up another MRE and force-fed myself some cold stir-fry vegetables with noodles. Like all food since the extinction, it had no taste; it was just fuel. I honked the horn from time to time while eating and watched Flannie move on to another broken-open MRE—looked like chili con carne. To save her stomach from the spices and beans, I pulled the food away and tied her to the open passenger-side door with a promise she would thank me for it later.

Then it struck me; she'd seen whoever had done this. That was why she'd disappeared for so long.

So why had she returned in the end?

"What happened?" I asked her. "Did they do bad things to you?"

We waited by the car for an hour, sent up another flare, hit the horn again and again, but no one showed up. Still, the sense that someone was watching—maybe Ronnie, maybe someone else—was strong. I couldn't tamp it down.

In the end, the only thing to do was to walk back to Cle Elum, find another vehicle—this one a dusty half-ton—and start stocking it.

While I did that, I sought signs of human presence in town—a hand print on a dusty glass door, or fresh littering on the street, or handling of gas-station fuel tanks—but there was nothing. When filling my shopping cart at the pharmacy, I paused over the narcotics but didn't grab any. In rounding up clothes, I picked up walking shoes on top of hiking boots. When I had everything, or at least enough to get me to Seattle, I went back to the motel and cleaned and rewrapped my thumb, which was getting sore again.

During all this, a headache bloomed out of nowhere. My eyes narrowed to a squint. The warmth of the day felt like a blast furnace. I wore sunglasses—even inside the motel room—and downed ibuprofen and told myself the headache wouldn't last; I could chase it away if only I got some rest.

After feeding Flannie and forcing myself to eat a late dinner, I closed and locked the motel room door. The headache was with me while I lay atop the bed, an arm draped over my eyes. It was worse than other headaches, seemed to start not in the frontal lobe, but somewhere over and behind the ears, radiating forward. I told myself it would be cured by over-the-counter analgesics and the coming luxury of sleep.

But it's hard to fall asleep when you're all alone and listening hard for the sounds of life.

• • •

The next morning, I awoke without a headache, but the moment I sat up in bed, the pain poured in like molten lead, then swam around for a while, sloshing off the walls of my skull. I managed to stand, close the room's blackout drapes, and then lie right back down again. This earned me minor relief. Utter stillness in a pitch-black environment felt like the only thing that might get me from one minute to the next.

Flannie enjoyed the rest that followed. She curled up against me on the bed and moved only when I did. I slept for half the day, rising only to answer nature's call and to let Flannie outside to do likewise. Each time I stepped out, my freshly packed truck was in the same state in which I'd left it. No people. No ghosts. And each time I laid back down, it took a good long time to find respite from the cheese-grater behind my eyes. I resolved to go find stronger drugs tomorrow if this kept up.

• • •

The next day, the throbbing wasn't as bad, too mild for strong drugs but raw enough to keep me from trying to drive on a sun-bright summer day. After poking my head outside, I retreated to the room for more recuperation—and ended up spending four days there.

Four days so soon after the six days in Spokane. Each day I forced myself outside for brief reconnaissance in the murderous sunshine. There were no truck trashers or other signs of life, and no ghosts. No one came round to save me or torment me; no one made smoke. And all the rest in the dark put only the faintest dent in the cranial pain.

Percocet-flavored flashbacks started to flare. The days melded with the days back in Spokane, with nightmares of dead Ronnie rising from her computer and wagging her finger at me, and Sean Vilmack calling me a coward before diving off the gym roof with the panache of an Olympic springboard diver. It no longer took pharmaceuticals to scramble my eggs; just being in that dark room was enough.

After finally leaving the motel, I stopped the truck at the nearest gas station to fill up on water. The corpses inside were entering a new phase. The summer heat had drained them of liquids. A woman in the beverage aisle had a nut-brown mosquito net draped over her. Up close, the net was her skin, which hung loosely from her bones, shrouding her. Beside her on the floor sat two teeth and a bird's nest of hair.

Other corpses were likewise deflating and losing hair and teeth. The smell was no better or worse than in the days after the extinction, but medical masks and VapoRub were no longer needed. My nostrils had grown inured to the vapors of putrefaction.

On the road again, I pointed the half-ton toward Seattle and drove up to Snoqualmie Pass, three thousand feet above sea level, with cool, clean air and only a few crashes and corpses. A new thought flared in my mind: *This could be it—a place to settle if I can't find anyone.*

There was a ski lodge with nice chalets and clean lakes nearby. Winters would be long and snow-filled but not too cold. I could keep a garden in the summers, hunt for fresh meat, fish for trout. I could give up, accept solitude—get real about my prospects for the future.

I could do that very easily. It wouldn't take much talent, thought or energy.

The headache worsened. I asked myself where the closest LRAD might be, and the headache said, *Park. Nap.* I checked my map for the next town and the headache said, *What's the rush? Rest.* It drained me, this mental tug-of-war. Neither side budged an inch, and the edge of the Seattle urban sprawl was only thirty miles up the road.

I found realtor signs in the next towns, Riverbend and North Bend. There were more car wrecks here. I drove through the ditch rather than on the crash-filled four-lane blacktop. Each bounce and shake of the truck injected more fire behind my eyes.

I found an LRAD at the Issaquah Police Department. Why the police in the Washington State commuter belt needed an LRAD was beyond me, but the LRAD was only the tip of the military iceberg. The Issaquah force also had assault rifles, submachine guns, ammo cases full of flashbang grenades, no doubt purchased from the U.S. military after adventures in Iraq and Afghanistan. The LRAD itself was affixed to the top of an armored personnel carrier. Transplanting it to the truck's tow hitch emptied my last stores of energy and left me in a sweat-soaked state of near-collapse. I rested for an hour, then drove to the nearest drugstore to find meds to unplug the chainsaw in my head.

At a CVS there was a rack of pamphlets in the analgesics aisle: "Alternatives to opioid painkillers." I opened one and read.

Acetaminophen and ibuprofen. Not strong enough.

Cognitive Behavioral Therapy. Not a lot of shrinks available.

Hypnotherapy. Maybe Flannie could hypnotize me.

The big drugs were all locked in cabinets behind the high counter. I looked around for something to break open the doors. On a corkboard in the back office, I saw a list of marijuana shops. The closest one was just down the highway, so I backed away from the available opioids, drove the two miles, broke open cabinets and mulled over the choices: vaporizers, cookies, lollipops, tinctures, sub-lingual sprays, not to mention old-fashioned, smokable weed. I chose a little bottle with an eye-dropper, then squinted at the fine print on dosages.

Take it now, the headache said. *What are you waiting for?*

I pulled out the eyedropper, held it over my mouth.

That's it. Get it in you.

I hesitated, then screwed the dropper back into the bottle. I stared at the liquid dope a long while. How many days had it been since the extinction? About fifty. For at least fourteen of those days I'd been either drunk or zooming on Percocet.

So I loaded up on acetaminophen instead. I would stagger the doses with equally excessive doses of ibuprofen. With luck, my liver and kidneys would hold out until the head agonies ebbed.

Back out in the parking lot, I recorded a message into the LRAD—*I'll be at the Space Needle every day at noon*—and played it while I drove west. The CB's emergency contact channel blared static. Flannie nudged the closed passenger-side window with her nose.

"Can't open it," I told her. "The LRAD'll eat through my head."

And acetaminophen wasn't helping. Five minutes. Anything for five minutes without the ache behind my eyes. The only consolation was the weather. The sun dipped behind a band of thick clouds, which cooled everything down.

West of Issaquah, the devastation was absolute. This was no longer small-town America. Every intersection was a snarl. Every freeze-frame traffic jam ran twenty cars deep. I drove on sidewalks, over lawns and through fences, and more than once crunching corpses while looking away and talking loudly to myself to mask the sound of the crunch. Any right-thinking survivors would not be in town right now; they would have fled to a place with fresh air, plenty of supplies and no stench.

Unless they were too traumatized to move. Or were injured or disabled.

The LRAD message—*I'll be at the Space Needle every day at noon*—was unrealistic. The bridges into Seattle would be clogged. The air would be heavy with putrefaction. I stopped the car and recorded a new message—*Meet me at the Coastal Pharmacy in Issaquah at noon. If you can't get there, make smoke*—and spent the next hour driving around the periphery of town blaring it out.

So Issaquah got noon, while other bedroom communities—Sammamish, Klahanie, Carnation—got later daily timeslots. The next few days would be spent sending out the message and checking the meeting places. The plan seemed reasonable. The exurban neighborhoods had big houses and spacious yards. It was no longer hard to envision survivors holing up somewhere in these hills.

In that first day I made it to six satellites of Seattle despite the grinding headache. Flannie barked occasionally, each time making me grit my teeth and stop driving until the pain subsided. She grew more restless by the hour, and I didn't blame her. We were swimming in waters filled with death. There didn't seem to be much sense to it.

But there had to be.

There had to be an end to this.

By nightfall I was too drained to look for a bed. I parked at a random curb, turned off the LRAD, reclined my seat, and closed my eyes. While seeking relief through slumber, I heard Flannie jump into the back seat, exhale heavily, and settle in for the night. She did this slowly, protest through sluggishness. I worried that if I opened her door, she would run. I worried one of these days I would lose her forever.

20

I AWOKE IN THE NIGHT sensing a presence. I opened my eyes and saw a dim light across the highway, where the trees met the roadside grass. The hazy figure of Ronnie stood at the fringe of that light, stepping toward the yards of the closest houses.

There was no fear. Seeing her like this felt natural, even inevitable: Ronnie in jeans and baggy sweater. It was as if she'd tapped me on the shoulder and whispered while I slept, "Okay, let's get on with it."

I climbed groggily out of the truck and opened the back door. Flannie jumped down to join me.

Ronnie moved without urgency. I followed her. By the time I reached the yard the light dimmed and Ronnie faded from view, but this was no problem; my still-half-asleep brain knew on some instinctual level where to go. The yard bordered on a tumbling creek. Ronnie must have crossed that creek so I did too, stepping knee-high in freezing water and washing away the last bleary residue of sleep.

I pushed through trees on the other side of the creek, up a steep hill, stepped over fallen branches and clumps of dewy leaves before coming to a small clearing illuminated by another vague celestial spotlight. Ronnie stood in that clearing, at a baby-changing table. She was younger now, and now wearing a nightgown, Ronnie a new mother with her child. I recognized the child at first glance, even from a distance: Oliver, a few weeks old, gaily writhing and kicking on the table.

Ronnie was engrossed in changing his diaper. Oliver cooed as she tickled his stomach. She removed the old diaper and started dabbing his butt with Baby Wipes.

"Who's the pee-ey boy?" she said. "Who drinks it in and pees it right back out again?"

Oliver gave her a throaty gurgle and enjoyed a new round of tickling.

I watched this for a couple minutes, until the new diaper was on and she got him back into a jumpsuit decorated with a fun cartoon of the Liberty Bell. I'd bought him the suit while in Philadelphia on a book tour. Ronnie stood him up on the table, made him hop a little.

"Who's the hoppy boy..."

I could smell the baby powder. I could smell Oliver, that distinctive new-child smell that every parent knows. I wanted this to go on forever, but of course it wouldn't. At some point Ronnie would turn.

"What do you want?" I asked her, and the words had a breathless, shaky quality to them. She pretended not to hear anyway, made Oliver dance a little.

"Who's the king of the dance floor? Who's going to break the girls' hearts when he gets older?"

She laid him down again and kissed his stomach through the jumpsuit. Then she reached down to the rack under the table and grabbed something I couldn't see. When she brought the thing into view, I had to squint to make it out.

A syringe. She squeezed liquid into the air, then took hold of Oliver's foot, opened the toe flap on the jumpsuit, and injected him between the two biggest toes. With the needle still in him, she looked up at me with pupils as red as Satan's.

Flannie barked.

"I tried to make it look like SIDS." The voice was sonorous and male.

I ran, stumbling through the trees, slipping on dew-wet leaves. I was almost to the creek before I decided she wasn't following me, had never intended to. It took everything I had to turn around, walk back up the hill, and re-enter the celestially lit clearing.

She was still there. She had Oliver's jumpsuit off and was chewing on his entrails. Her face was sluiced with his blood. Her eyes remained satanically red.

Flannie barked again, but it sounded distant.

I managed to say, "I know what's real. You can't do this to me."

Ronnie laid the corpse of my little boy on the table and wiped her mouth with her sleeve.

"You can be with her again. With all of them. That's what you want, right?"

I wanted to tell her I would no longer talk with people who weren't there, but my throat constricted.

She picked up Oliver's corpse and looked for a good place to bite.

I stepped toward her as she bit into a rib. It crunched in her teeth. Oliver's head tilted in my direction. His dead eyes opened. My baby boy stared at me and smiled.

"If you want me dead," I said, "then you'll have to do better than this. You'll have to kill me."

As I walked back down the hill—slowly, settling my fear—I heard her call out, "Keep both hands on the wheel, dear!" and then laugh like the real Ronnie would never have laughed, with a wicked, over-the-top cackle.

Walking, I forced myself not to look back. My mind cycled through a host of possibilities: she was inches behind me with dead Oliver in her hands, and with Evan at her side, with Evan's mouth also dripping blood. Sean Vilmack was there, too, mangled from his jump off the gymnasium roof. He didn't speak, but his gaze burned a hole in me. To fray my nerves further, Flannie stayed close to my flank, barking the whole way. The volume of her baying made me feel like the Legions of Hell were closing in.

But I made it to the truck without wavering or looking back. When I did turn around and allow myself to peer down the street, Ronnie wasn't there, and neither were Evan or Sean.

I told myself I'd won this round against her, or it, or them. I was getting smarter, more grounded. There was less they could do to me—less I could do to myself.

But the image of my son's dangling intestines returned with a vengeance—and refused to leave. It would take more than a few minutes to purge all this nonsense from my mind.

21

THE NEXT THREE DAYS, Ronnie stayed away while I made my rounds through the leafy-green suburbs of Seattle. Each morning, I started things off by talking to her, or rather at her, knowing she could hear me even if she wasn't present. I made clear that I still knew a thing or two about my real wife (i.e. "You volunteered for Amnesty International" and "Your favorite drink back in school was Sex on the Beach"). These statements were designed to defeat untruths with truths, and because they received no responses or rebuttals, I told myself they were working. I got down to business.

I showed up in Issaquah at 12:00, in Klahanie at 1:00, and so on—and each time it was with a brittle sense of hope followed by an outsized crash of disappointment. The failures to find survivors grew harder to take, more personal. Each stop made me just a little less willing to forge ahead to the next place. It took all my energy to keep things moving.

The headache ranged from stinging to sapping. When the sun came out, the throbbing worsened. When it dipped behind clouds, there was only slight relief. But I pushed on. In Sammamish, I came across a library, a chance to gather more books on SUDC and the world's extinctions. I parked at the library doors but just sat in the truck gaping at the building. The head hurt too much to consider reading, but something deeper was also at play. As much as I couldn't pore over the pages of a book now, I also saw no value in reading books later, when the pain was gone. I saw no value in reading anything, possibly ever again. What was the point? My old ways of doing things were useless, were only taking up energy.

After three days of trolling, the LRAD message sounded like fingers on a chalkboard. Near sunset on the third day, I stopped at a snarled intersection in Redmond and turned it off. Then, after firing off a flare that I knew no one would see, I stood outside the truck, ate an MRE, and told myself I would no longer be troubled by ghosts—period. Maybe things were still slipping away, but Ronnie and Evan wouldn't be the ones to end me. There would be no more clouding of the issue.

I had stopped at this intersection in Redmond because there was no way to drive through it: dozens of bodies in cars, one of them draped halfway out a window; at least ten bodies on the sidewalks, including a woman with two small children and a man still holding a bird cage with a dead parrot inside.

It's a Norwegian Blue! It's pining for the fjords!

A few days ago, a classic line from Monty Python might have produced at least an attempt to chuckle away the horrific. Today, it was a throwaway soundbite from an expired history. I tried to figure out which traffic lights had been red and which had been green when the extinction hit. It was a tough call; it looked as if everyone had driven into the intersection at the same time.

I checked my map for the location of Joint Base Lewis-McChord. Why exactly was the U.S. military still an object of faith? It wasn't, really; it was habit and false hope, neither of which were getting me anywhere. I crumpled the map and tossed it in the general direction of the Norwegian Blue, then drove around the jammed Interstate and made my way to the Newport Yacht Club on the eastern shore of Lake Washington. This was between the burbs to the east and central Seattle to the west. The I-90 bridge over the lake was clogged with a freeze-frame of chaotic traffic. I'd been right earlier: there was no way to get to the Space Needle, at least by road.

And the smell. So much for being used to the stench of death. Even on the lake's less-populated eastern shore, the pong of decay was multiples worse than anything in Spokane or Great Falls. The stench downtown would be strong enough to melt steel, but Seattle had to be checked out. What other options were there? I slathered on VapoRub and apologized to Flannie, who whimpered because she knew we were moving deeper into the heart of darkness, then I looked around the yacht club's docks for a boat with gunwales thick enough to support the LRAD.

There were six docks with maybe fifty boats each, mainly smaller yachts and speedboats. Only a handful of boats had corpses. One of them was an old nineteen-footer with a Seattle Seahawks awning and a key in the ignition. The body at the stern was reaching out to (I guessed) unmoor the boat. I pumped the throttle twice and turned the key and the engine roared to life. While it warmed up, I held my breath, grabbed the corpse by the pant legs, and pulled it over the transom, into the water. That done, I untied the rope and steered the boat in close to shore, where I could re-dock it and load the LRAD and its battery without having to walk too far.

Flannie watched all this from the safety of the truck. When I had the LRAD screwed onto the starboard gunwale, I called for her to come, but she pinned her ears back and stayed put.

"I know," I said, "but look at it this way: there are no corpses out on the water."

With more coaxing, she crept toward the boat but still wouldn't hop in. I took the choice away from her by picking her up and setting her in the passenger seat, where she cowered as if she'd been scolded for peeing on the carpet.

Before we got out onto the open water I hollered, in case Ronnie was listening, "You bought me the world's ugliest sweater for Christmas! You couldn't keep a straight face while you watched me put it on!"

Once the boat was moving, I turned on the LRAD. Like the previous LRAD messages, the newly recorded message presupposed survivors wanted to be found: *If you're alive, make smoke. I'll find you.* The volume of the message drilled a hole in my aching head, but I couldn't skimp on decibels. This was the best chance so far to reach survivors, the most people I could troll within a short period of time.

Lake Washington ran roughly twenty miles north to south. We trolled the eastern shore for five hours, up to the boat-choked bay in Bellevue and down along the shore of Mercer Island, which kept downtown Seattle out of view. When the heart of the city became visible, at the far western shore, it was shrouded in a distant haze of heat and lingering smoke. It was also dead, much of it charred. I wouldn't reach downtown until tomorrow. I worried about what I might do once I stood there in person, in the heart of a major city, alone among smoke and ruin.

To escape such thoughts, I fired off flares, watched them climb and arc, imagined people miles away seeing them and weeping with joy.

"You bought me skydiving lessons for my birthday."

A few minutes later: "I saw you crying in your car after the bouncers at the Smokehouse broke my nose."

In the narrow canals of Newport Shores, every lakeside house had a mini-dock and a yacht out back. I saw a pug feeding on a gardener's femur, and a woman in a backyard hammock that rocked ever-so-gently in the breeze, as if catching some z's. In Medina, the walls of a fire-gutted mansion had fallen away to reveal a thirty-foot dinosaur skeleton, a wealthy person's idea of foyer art. Somewhere around here was Bill Gates' smart house, maybe Bill Gates himself.

For the first hour of the trip, I forced myself to look for smoke through the binoculars. For the second hour, the binocs hung down around my neck. For the third and fourth hours, they sat ignored in the seat behind Flannie. While my last bits of energy bled away, I visualized Evan sneaking into the kitchen for cookies on Saturday mornings, then saw my father palm-smacking my brother Dale because for some reason Dale annoyed him more than the rest of us did, which made Dale sullen and withdrawn. When the sun started to set, I headed back to the Newport Yacht Club with a dryness in my mouth and throat that felt like death spreading from my head down into my chest.

Before I pulled in and docked the boat, I gave brief consideration to gunning the throttle and plowing the craft into one of the many boats drifting aimlessly along the shore.

That would have simplified things. It would have cut to the chase.

Just like my dead wife wanted.

• • •

The next morning, I forced myself out of the truck, siphoned gas into the boat's tank, and pointed the nineteen-footer toward downtown Seattle. I'd barely slept. The headache was torture. The constant trickle of pain made me clench my teeth and cry—but despite this I managed to stay away from heavy drugs. The ache may have butchered my sleep and clouded my thoughts, but at least it was real. Reality had to be guarded.

I said out loud, "I saw you thumbing through my SUDC book when you thought I wasn't home."

To reach central Seattle, I had to pilot the boat past the north shore of Mercer Island and into Union Bay, a verdant shoreline marked by the University of Washington on the right and blocked-up dual bridges on the left. The route narrowed into a canal that was eerily silent between blasts of the LRAD message. Rudderless boats nudged the banks. One of them was a small fishing boat that looked like Sean Vilmack's father's boat: maybe 15 feet long, flat bottom so it could run up shallow rivers. I flashed back to the three of us on the water of Lake Elwell, our minnow-baited hooks submerged at walleye depth. It was two months before Sean would try to hold my hand, and Sean's dad decided to impress us with a joke.

"There's this little homo—a real flamer, limp wrist, lisp, the works. He walks into a bar, orders three double bourbons, slams them back, and says to the big football player on the stool next to him, 'You think you're tough? Gays are the toughest guys in the world.'

"The football player looks him over and says, 'How do you figure that, Dorothy?'"

"'It's easy,' says the fag. 'Who else is able to take eight inches up the caboose without flinching?'"

We all laughed. Sean laughed hardest of all, doubled over in the boat because it was such a killer joke. I paused over this memory—Sean working so hard at it, avoiding eye contact—and bang, now my mind flashed on the look of Evan at the lip of his grave waiting to be buried, Evan unnaturally small, a mini mannequin, and nothing would ever change that image or make it into something less than what it was, so I aimed the boat toward the shore, jammed the throttle full-forward, and took comfort in the wind on my face and the fact that soon I would hit a dockside boat and be beyond pain just like Evan and Sean were, right where I should have been all along.

While steaming toward the shore, I considered the post-extinction Ronnie's take on the matter:

Good for you! It's high time!

Her cheerfulness was a blast of cold water hitting a foundering drunk. It couldn't be accepted, couldn't be the last thing I heard. I turned hard starboard, narrowly missed hitting a moored sailboat, and the canal opened up into Portage Bay, a formally picturesque arm of the lake, with floating houses, more yacht clubs and plenty of dead people to remind me there was no reason for me to be doing any of this.

But this still wasn't central Seattle. That came after a left around the next corner. The view, once I made that turn, was precisely as I'd expected: scorched buildings, aimlessly floating boats, a concentrated stench. A number of floating houses had escaped the fires. A Ride the Ducks amphibious landing craft sat in the water close to its ramp, full of still-seated tourists. The skyscrapers of downtown, maybe a half mile to the south, had escaped the blazes that had hollowed out so many of the buildings closer to me. When I pointed the boat south, the LRAD's message rode the wind and echoed back at me. The sound must have reached the whole of downtown. Hooray for that. No survivor in his right mind would have stayed here.

My headache migrated down my spine toward my stomach. I wanted to drill a hole in my skull, pull out the tentacling source of the disease, and toss it in the water. Instead, I docked at the Museum of History and led Flannie on a quest for dope, opiates, Death-in-a-Package, anything to end the throb and dissolve this metropolitan perdition.

The grass on the boulevards was a foot high. The smashed traffic was thicker, with a thicker coat of dust. The wilted people looked less like people. And the silence, the utter silence—no wind in the trees, no birds in the sky. A din of explosions would have sounded softer than this. Flannie had been right to fear the boat. We should never have come here.

A sign advertised a Bartell Drugs two blocks from the boat, across a six-lane road packed with freeze-frame traffic.

But when I reached the store, it was boarded up. This caused the pain in my head to explode anew. I pounded on the wooden door, asked it *why*, acted like there were no other drugstores in town. There were no survivors, no relief from the headache, *no anything of value*.

But what there *was*, right in front of me the moment I turned around, was another Episcopal Church. This one was an old granite building with big double doors and a proud, angular height that had no right to pretend toward glory.

"You have got to be kidding."

I charged across the street, tried both doorknobs, but the doors were locked.

"Open up!" I tore a picket from the church's character fence, used it to whack at the doorknobs. I was going to storm inside and bash everything to bits. God had no business advertising here. I was so onto him. He'd told us he'd created everything good in this world but had said everything bad was created by nature. He'd ordered us to judge him as good but had invoked divine privilege when we pointed out the bad. He'd created evil, so much evil, and then turned around and said, "Don't bog down on such things; just trust me, even though you can't understand me."

And he was still doing that, even though one look at this world proved he was a psychopath, a serial killer. Therefore, I was going to—with much sound and fury—knock the holiness out of his precious, sacred house of worship, and let him, in all his glorious omniscience, strike me dead if he didn't like it.

But I couldn't get in. The iron door hinges looked like something off a moated castle. I briefly considered getting some cloth and alcohol and lobbing Molotov cocktails in through the windows, but even in my tangled state, this struck me as taking things too far. My head throbbed even worse. The world around me lurched and shifted. I staggered down the street in search of a drugstore.

And found one on the very next block. The glass doors were unlocked and the shelves heaved with cures. By now I was an old hand at finding drugs in a drugstore. In the locked cabinets behind the high counter were Tramadol and Endocet and Percocet. Demerol and Dilaudid and Fentora. I tore open a bottle of Vicodin and washed down four pills with a peach electrolyte drink from the shelf, then slumped down against a cabinet and closed my eyes while Flannie nudged me with her nose.

"Can't do it, girl. Can't take any more of this."

She nudged me again.

"I'm done. You're on your own now."

It felt good to give up—not to kill myself, just to refuse to sustain my own life further. A weight was lifted. I breathed easily now, waited for the Vicodin to carry me to a better place—and to solidify that journey's destination I popped four more pills. I grew conscious of a throbbing in my hands, both of them, the good thumb as well as the bad one. I held my hands up for inspection, a dying man's random curiosity. On my bad hand, the bandage was torn and stained like smoker's teeth. On the good hand, the fingernails were half-black and jagged, bracketed by a web of shallow nicks and hangnails. The skin was cracked, reminded me of my drywalling days before I wrote my first novel. Farther up on the fingers, splotchy redness portended a developing rash. I needed cream, something antibiotic, something from one of the aisles in this store.

Yes, God was dead and the world was a nightmare, but my mind travelled all the way from the first steps of suicide to the concept of restorative hand cream. People were ridiculous. They jumped around without sustaining purpose.

In the end, they didn't matter.

Flannie nudged me again, then circled a few times, sniffed the linoleum, and laid down with a restless thump. I tuned my ears to the silence of the store. The calm persisted for a long, beautiful time before something creaked an aisle or two over. Neither Flannie nor I paid any attention to it. We were done looking for signs of life in this realm of death, or at least I was. Curiosity was for suckers.

The creaking continued, closer now, sounded like footsteps. There was no surprise when Ronnie appeared at the end of the aisle wearing the blouse and skirt she'd had on when she died, the clothes I'd buried her in.

I didn't bother speaking to her. She approached me slowly, without emotion. When she arrived up close, she squatted down on her haunches, then sat cross-legged on the floor, all the while just looking at me. Her eyes, so warm and inviting in life, so evil that night in Issaquah, were cold and diagnostic.

Flannie whimpered, nudged me with her nose again, tried to get me moving. I was only barely conscious of her.

Ronnie said, "You're not curious about what I want?"

Flannie barked again, started to paw at me.

"Being mad at God," Ronnie said, "is foolish."

Not if he deserves it.

"How can you be mad at him if you don't believe in him?"

Same way you could pray to him right after he killed our boy.

"Maybe he's testing you."

By killing everyone? Typical.

"These thoughts you're having—you're acting like you think he can hear you."

The voice of reason. Her penchant for switching guises was growing boring, so I closed my eyes and ordered myself to switch gears, move on to something else—anything else.

"What were you going to do if you found survivors?"

The question was louder and clearer than anything else she'd said.

"Would finding people have made that much difference to you?"

Why couldn't I shut her up? What was wrong with me?

"And what I don't understand is: you want her and the kids back, but on your terms only—your terms that no longer apply. This whole thing—trolling for survivors, wanting to burn down churches—everything you do is a pathetic form of negotiation."

That was a good way of putting it.

"A negotiation you can't win. You tried to adapt—*anyone* would, it's natural—but you failed, and you know you failed, so now, *finally*, you're coming around, right? So I have to say: good for you. Let's just stop all the theatrics and get on with it, shall we?"

Ever-so-gently, she pulled the bottle of Vicodin from my bandaged left hand. She was careful not to touch the thumb, not to hurt it. A smile formed on her lips, a smile I recognized from tender moments with the real Ronnie, a look of easy, unquestioned love.

Peering deeply into my eyes, she unscrewed the bottle, gently tapped out one pill, and held it out.

I opened my mouth and allowed her to place the pill on my tongue. Then she gently lifted my chin and watched while I closed my mouth and swallowed the pill dry.

We repeated this six times, six pills on top of the eight I'd taken earlier. We were on the seventh pill when Flannie leapt and knocked the bottle from her hand. The pills scattered over the commercial linoleum flooring. Ronnie calmly plucked them up one by one and resumed the feeding.

With sixteen pills inside me and one more being held out, Ronnie gave me a new smile, this one with glee in it, just a trace, but enough to snap me out of it. I slapped her hand away, struggled to my knees, and drove two fingers down my throat.

While I heaved up the Vicodin, I heard Ronnie say, "It's my fault. I gave you too much time to think about it. I coddled you. Next time we'll just dive right in."

Flannie licked my face and whimpered.

"I almost feel sorry for you," Ronnie said. She turned to leave as if she would hail a cab and carry on with some run-of-the-mill errand.

"Wait," I said, and she stopped and pivoted.

There was hope in her eyes.

I told her, "You lost your virginity when you were fifteen. He was twenty-seven. He hurt you."

Her expression morphed to exasperation. She turned and marched out of the store.

I staggered to my feet, returned to the pharmacy counter, and tried to catch my breath. After a minute to steady myself, I grabbed another electrolyte drink from a shelf, and when I was reasonably sure I could keep it down, I plucked up an almond energy bar from the counter and unwrapped it with shaking hands.

Walking out of the store, I forced the energy into me.

22

I HIKED DOWNTOWN, used the Space Needle as a beacon. On the way, I started to feel exposed without my guns, which were in the truck on the far shore of Lake Washington.

Flannie looked at me like, *Let's not do this*. I told her it was the best of bad options.

Options that required firearms. Since I'd decided to live, the uncertainty of the new world became a threat again. If Ronnie could keep showing up, who else could? *What* else could? The parameters of this reality had not been spelled out, so any trouble my addled mind could dream up was both logical and possible.

I found a pawn shop and rummaged through its second-hand weapons, ending up with a 9 mm Smith & Wesson. The bullets sat in a drawer a few feet away.

Since my binoculars were back at the boat, I poked through the pawn shop shelves until I found a pair, then continued on toward the Space Needle, with Flannie sticking close to me and whining from time to time. The parking lot at the tower base showed us more dead traffic, more decaying pedestrians, two Ducks vehicles full of sagging tourists.

"It doesn't mean everyone's dead," I said to Flannie, and thought, *Who are you trying to convince, the dog or yourself?*

I found the entrance to the Space Needle's open-air stairs and started climbing. The observation deck had to be more than five hundred feet up, a daunting distance. I climbed roughly twenty stories, lungs aching, the breeze gathering. Flannie hated every second of this, took the stairs gingerly, with whimpers of protest. I remembered my flare gun was with my first pair of binoculars back in the boat.

Somewhere during the ascent, the Vicodin still in my stomach kicked in, evicting the pain from my head and thumb. I kept my eyes on the stairs, didn't look down at Seattle, was too afraid of what I would see. After thirty stories, I grew light-headed, had to sit and rest. This I did with my eyes screwed shut and with my back hard against the metal cage encircling the stairs. When I stood again to resume the climb, a bout of dizziness nearly knocked me over.

Flannie stayed close, only climbed when I climbed. She seemed on the verge of turning and heading back down, even though this far up—how high were we, three hundred feet?—there was no corpse odor.

The smell returned once I neared the door to the revolving restaurant. The door was locked and I had no tools, only the gun. In the movies, shooting open a door is splashy simplicity; in reality, it takes four bullets and is attended by a fear of ricocheting metal fragments.

Inside the restaurant, I scanned the litany of corpses and got up the courage to peer out the window at Seattle. To the south, fires still burned among the skyscrapers. Far beyond that, Mount Rainier overlooked everything with imposing indifference. To the west, a cruise ship sat docked in Elliott Bay, awaiting a voyage. Other ships and boats lay scattered across the water. To the north were mounds of greenery. Nothing moved.

I raised the binoculars and looked more closely in all directions: random boats on the waterway into downtown, the empty Washington Huskies' stadium, corpse-littered boulevards. My boat was still at Lake Union Park where I'd left it. In the greener areas, the verdancy would one day blot out all signs of civilization, and there weren't many of those now. No vehicles crawled the streets. No rooftops were spray-painted with "S.O.S." Life existed as an article of faith only, a product of a battered faculty for hope.

I found the restaurant kitchen and searched the sliding stainless-steel doors for something to drink. It struck me I was absolutely zooming on Vicodin. Once I came down and the headache returned, it would be hard to get over the things I'd seen here—or the things I hadn't seen. Maybe it would be impossible.

Flannie nudged me with her nose, gave me another hopeful look.

No, it was a look of need.

"You're thirsty, aren't you?"

One of the kitchen fridges was stocked with bottled water. I poured some into a mixing bowl. While Flannie lapped it up, I stepped back out to the restaurant and peered through the binoculars at the roads leading south out of town. There were two Interstates: one hugging the shoreline and five elevated lanes farther east. Both roads were clogged with impassable jams. The downtown streets were likewise blocked. The only way out was the way I'd arrived, by boat and suburban road.

I started back toward the kitchen to round up Flannie. Before I got there, I heard two pleading words from behind me:

"Jump, Daddy."

Evan's voice.

I turned and saw Ronnie standing in the posture of a shy little boy. She shifted from foot to foot, needed to pee. Her face was scrunched up in overwrought distress.

"Shoot holes in the windows, Daddy, and jump just like Sean Vilmack jumped."

I raised the gun and pointed it at her. She started to laugh in her own voice, in the real Ronnie's voice, with unselfconscious volume, and kept laughing until I lowered the weapon.

She said, "You'll never be rid of me."

"Maybe not," I said, "but I won't forget who you really were."

She paused to think that over, then shrugged. "So what now? I liked marmalade but not honey? I was a Capricorn?"

"We won't be talking anymore," I said, and I pocketed the gun and fetched Flannie from the kitchen. While leading my dog down the Space Needle's outside stairs, I resisted the urge to say, *And you were a Pisces, wife, not a Capricorn. Nice try.*

23

I WAS IN THE BOAT halfway to the Newport docks when my Vicodin high petered out and the headache stormed back.

I popped two more pills, and once on shore I staggered into the closest house and cut a straight line for the basement, where I found a corpse-free bedroom with posters of K-pop groups on the walls. There was only one small window. This I stuffed up with a blanket before crawling into the unmade bed to sleep.

But sleep wouldn't come. The new round of drugs barely dented the pain. I drifted in and out of hallucinations. I was back in the Space Needle restaurant. Ronnie jumped through the window and while falling screamed back up at me to save her. I was under the 100-foot spork in Sprague again. Evan and Oliver were in the truck with me. They engaged in a spirited thumb war until Oliver fell down dead in the seat, followed seconds later by Evan—then they both sprang to life and resumed the war…

When morning arrived, I dragged myself to my feet, pulled down the window blanket, and squinted outside. Dense cloud cover gave the day an ashen dullness, which would be good for the headache, but there was another issue now. My vision grew blurred. The things in the yard outside the window lacked edges and detail.

My Only Friend, the End

Flannie barked. The volume of it punched a hole in my head and made me check an impulse to swat her, actually swat her. She had curled up at the foot of the bed to sleep. Now she wanted outside.

When we got there, she barked again, then fell into a spasm of snarling and yowling. Across the street, another yellow lab, a mirror image of Flannie, stared back at her. The intruder dog had been chewing on a shin bone of a mostly eaten United States Postal Service employee. The dog's mane was rusted with weeks' worth of corpse meals. I squeezed the trigger on my gun, and the volume of the shot sent me to the ground holding my head and begging for mercy.

Flannie whined and licked my face and this time I did swat her, with a gust of anger that seemed to come from outside me, with someone else pulling the strings. She yelped and ran in little circles before coming to a stop a good distance away.

The guilt that now flooded in was beyond all proportion. I sobbed, spluttered apologies, tried to approach her, but she leapt away, kept her distance, tail between her legs. I approached again, and again she backed off. In the end, I won her back with an open can of organic lentil-vegetable soup, but still she wouldn't let me touch her. Her eyes accused me in a way that no human's ever had.

So I gave her space. After forcing down canned orange slices, a handful of almonds and more Vicodin, I coaxed Flannie into the bed of the truck, climbed into the cab, and got us moving east toward Issaquah. While driving I worked myself over. Things would get worse before they got better. Flannie would leave me and I would deserve it. I would be alone again, and finding another dog for company wouldn't fix anything because Flannie would still be out there, herself alone, growing feral, forgetting who she'd been.

I watched her closely in the rearview mirror, nearly crashed the truck in doing so. I'd left the LRAD on the boat, hadn't had the strength to lift it back onto the tow hitch. On the seat beside me sat my new gun but it looked oddly out of place, like a skipping rope or a blender.

The suburbs looked different now. I'd spent three days trolling these streets but now I couldn't remember which roads led where. This confusion—the insomnia, blurred vision, mood swings—my post-concussion issues were entering a dark new stage that I suspected might kill me if I didn't address them.

But knowing this didn't help. The concept of rest and recovery was an invitation to the bed-ridden horrors of Spokane and Cle Elum. I had to keep moving—but keep moving where? Where was life if it wasn't within the whole of the Pacific Northwest? The world was a wasteland. To move would be to do so for the sake of movement itself. What was the point in it beyond trying to escape creeping lunacy?

There were no bright answers to the question, so I just drove—and watched Flannie in the rearview mirror—and some length of time later I sensed Ronnie in the seat beside me—sensed her before I looked over and saw her there, Ronnie still dressed in her death clothes, her white blouse that had become her funeral shroud.

She said, "So can we, like, finally wrap things up?"

Despite my promise to shut her out, I found myself saying, "You loved me. You can't change that."

"And it's enough to carry you?"

"It'll have to be," I said.

"Stop the car," she commanded, "or I'll stop it for you."

I firmed up my grip on the steering wheel—so she reached as if to grab it. That made me flinch and nearly crash us into a parked car.

She laughed.

"I cheated on you, you know."

"Of course you did."

"Two weeks before Oliver died. Mark Christian. You were in your office working on your novel, I was in the living room blowing him. He was so much better than you in the sack. I mean, the guy had *zero* hang-ups."

I stared at her now. She looked so calm that I almost believed her.

"A part of you always knew this. Not that it matters. It's time. Stop the car."

I gave the engine more gas.

"And Mark Christian wasn't the first. There were two others, earlier. I went to them because you were in your own little world, always writing, always making me wait."

I plucked the gun off the console and aimed it at her.

"Are we going through *that* charade again?"

"You laughed at Mark Christian," I said. "You used to say if his head got any bigger he'd able to rent out space on it."

"Since when do you have to like the guy you're screwing? In a way, it helped that I didn't like him. It kept things simple."

My Only Friend, the End

I looked away from her, ahead at the road. There were two crashed cars and a corpse of a child pinned under a mountain bike.

"You want to know what Mark used to call you? He had a real good nickname, something I think you'll appreciate."

I screwed my eyes shut and pulled the trigger. The sound of the blast tore through my skull and rattled the stem. I slammed on the brakes, poured myself out of the truck and fell hard to the pavement. My body felt too heavy to raise, but somehow I made it to my feet and ran-stumbled down the street.

Ronnie's disembodied voice followed me:

"I take no pleasure in this. I just want you to stop putting yourself through these things."

Still lurching, I fired two shots in the general direction of the voice. One of the bullets hit a taxi door; the other slapped into a house's vinyl siding. After this, the voice stopped.

I looked around and saw a blurred suburban hill town, which I would later come to know was called Renton, home to hundreds of Boeing employees. I waited a moment, heard only my own pounding heart, my rasping breath. This gave me hope that in this altered world I had somehow wounded or exorcised this ghost. I squeezed off two more rounds toward where I'd last heard her, and they were likewise followed by silence.

I dropped the gun and crumpled to the ground. A distant part of my mind grew conscious of Flannie hopping out of the bed of the truck and faltering on the ground, weak on her feet, injured after I'd slammed on the brakes. Long minutes passed and Flannie wouldn't come to me, still didn't trust me. My headache raged and my sight recovered to a point where I could make out the shapes and colors of some things but not all. I tried to stand, but my drugged-up, post-Space Needle legs were jelly. I staggered and landed hard on my side.

And now, all at once, Flannie began snarling and barking.

She sprinted down the street, over a fence and into a back yard. The ensuing silence was followed by the ferocious sounds of animal combat.

The din didn't last long; it ended with a series of sharp dog yelps.

"Flannie!"

I struggled to stand, managed a few choppy steps toward the fence. I was caught halfway between the truck and the fence when the blurred outline of an animal—something of Flannie's color but twice her size—leapt over the fence and crept silkily toward me.

There was coolness in the animal's approach, an inborn poise. I redirected toward the truck and started running. The cougar did likewise, pouncing on me when I was still a good forty feet from safety.

While the beast mauled me, I fired off three rounds. The bullets either missed or had no effect. She slashed me with her claws. Her teeth closed around my neck and pressure built up in my chest. My mouth gulped like a fish. I jammed my gun into her ribs again, pulled the trigger and heard only a *click*, so I dropped the gun and tried to gouge her eyes out.

The cougar kept up the grip. The weight against my anoxic brain built toward an explosion—until out of nowhere, the pressure lifted; the cat climbed off me.

I rolled onto all fours, choked and coughed, fought for wind. My vision was vividly clear now, processing details in HD: the blood dripping from my nose; the little rocks in the asphalt; the cougar, just five feet away, belly round and overfed. She watched me, looked ready to pounce if I showed her too much life.

I kept still a long time. She snarled once, then just watched with executioner's eyes.

I gained my feet slowly and backpedaled unstably toward the truck, my eyes on the cat the whole way. She snarled, showed me her teeth, but there was no urgency there. Still moving backward, I bumped into the grill of a half-ton truck parked at the curb. The sound awakened the cat's instincts. She leapt again.

I ducked and a claw raked the top of my head but the cat overshot me. While she righted herself for another lunge, I opened the truck door, scrambled on top of the corpse in the driver seat, and slammed the door behind me.

The cat leapt at the side window, bounced off it, then skulked close to the door, keeping tabs. I climbed off the corpse and looked at it. It had the same nut-brown mosquito netting for skin that I'd seen on other corpses, but the eyes were sunken and the jaw slack and there were no longer any liquids to speak of. The jeans and jacket were too big for what was left of him. He was a dried patch of crusted remains.

I tried to start the engine, but the battery was dead. The heat in the cab blazed. I couldn't stay there. I was leaking and fading fast. One moment I was looking out at the cat, the next I saw houses and trees swimming in the sky above me. A flap of nose-skin hung loosely in my

My Only Friend, the End

left eye's line of vision. I reached up and plucked it off; the skin portion of it was attached to a gristly shred of nose cartilage.

I struggled out of my shirt, wrapped it around my head to stanch at least some of the flow. My truck and medical supplies were a good twenty feet away—no way to reach them. I ordered myself to stay awake, cracked opened the passenger door to let some greenhouse heat escape. The cougar pricked up her ears but stayed on the other side of the truck, so I settled in to wait her out.

And naturally, not long after this, Ronnie appeared in the distance, leaning against a mailbox, watching me with curiosity, as if waiting for me to do as I'd promised and take out the garbage.

She looked ready to watch me all day, if it came to that.

• • •

As dusk approached, the cougar stirred from her spot beside the truck. She yawned and stretched extravagantly before sauntering down the middle of the road for a full block. Without looking back, she turned right and darted over a fence between two houses.

During the cat's stay outside the truck, Ronnie had appeared off and on in different locations: leaning against a mailbox, sitting on the front steps of a house, crouching just behind the cougar. Each time I saw her she had a sly look for me, or a shrug that said, *This is some mess, huh?* One time she started whistling the tune to Inner Circle's *Sweat*—our song— and then broke into laughter that echoed down the desolate street.

And now Ronnie was gone and the cougar was gone. I spilled out of the truck and lurched toward my Ford. I fell twice, and both times it took a wobbly false start before I could stand. My muscles had lost their link to my brain. My balance cut in and out. The blurred vision seemed to grow out of a wooziness that made me want to stop moving and close my eyes, but I managed to heave myself into the truck, get it started, and drive toward the fence and hedge that Flannie had jumped over. On the way, I sideswiped a parked Camry, corrected my angle, and bounded up the curb and over the lawn to the fence.

A high hedge blocked off the house's back yard. That forced me out of the truck again. With leaden arms I parted the branches of a maple tree, leaned over the hedge, and squinted through the dusky daylight into the yard.

Flannie lay in a pool of blood. Her tongue dangled and her eyes were open. I sagged to the ground with my back to the fence, then wept for a long while until it morphed into distant-sounding humming. My thoughts grew elusive, fickle, reduced to snapshot images that flared like fireworks. Everything had a color and a carnival-like sound. The coldness of the now-falling night arrived as pin-prick streaks of electricity. The cracked dryness in my throat was a jumble of accordion notes. My fever whirled, eddies at the base of tall falls that I could reach out and touch.

Where is the marmalade, where are the scones
Where are your fingers, where are your toes.

The world was light as air, and this was the only state of being I could ever possibly want to be in.

I gave up what was left of me and stayed there against the hedge. I checked out.

24

DURING THIS LATEST time-out from reality my mind viewed a new array of astral projections:

Me standing in line at my bank in Great Falls.

Me sitting on the edge of the bed, watching Ronnie do her morning stretches on a yoga mat by the window.

And watching a gentle tide lap at Evan's toes in Playa del Carmen.

But the memory files soon gave way to events that were more current, with sharper detail:

Me hitting the gas pedal before crashing the Humvee into a tree outside Missoula.

Me gripping a sledgehammer and knocking the LRAD off the truck's tow hitch outside Cle Elum.

And slamming shut the steel-plate door to Alvin Stinghold's bunker.

The images swirled. Consciousness leaked in slowly: moisture on my lips, a waft of fresh air, an interlude of pleasant darkness followed by a glimpse of another episode I was seeing for the first time:

Me setting a fire in the Cle Elum woods.

This last image was still with me when I opened my eyes. I was back in the truck. The wetness at my lips was from Ronnie dabbing a moist cloth at the corners of my mouth. She watched me with compassionate eyes—nurse's eyes. I didn't reach for my gun. She was different now, explicable. She held a water bottle to my lips, waited for me to sip.

"That help?" she asked softly.

I tried to ask how long I'd been unconscious, but my mouth produced a pitiful *mohh* sound.

She responded anyway. "I'm not really sure." Her voice sounded vaguely male, almost like my own.

"You didn't crash me into that tree."

She shook her head.

"You didn't do any of it."

"I'm sorry," she said, and she meant it: she was sorry because I was sorry.

I grasped for the first time that in a way she'd always been straight with me, had always taken her cues from me, even when she was feeding me Vicodin in the drugstore. Another image came back to me now: me placing the pills in my mouth myself.

"Did you really sleep with Mark Christian?"

She shushed me with a finger to her lips, then, after a short pause, said, "You know I can't answer that."

She smiled, and I saw the real Ronnie there, the woman I'd loved, present and connecting. I closed my eyes a moment and swallowed hard. When I opened them again I was alone in the truck with a water bottle in my hand.

Right where it had been all along.

25

WHILE I SET ABOUT mending my broken body, I drilled myself on some hard, essential truths:

There were no more people.

I was alone.

I would always be alone.

And I would never know why.

Accept it. Don't bury it or deflect it. It has to be lived with.

There was no longer room for negotiations with reality. I couldn't need things that weren't within my power to obtain. Desires would have to be managed, and decisions based on things observed and experienced.

No more longing for Ronnie or Evan.

No more thinking back to old times or flogging myself over my failures with Sean Vilmack.

The past ran a dangerous con. It lured me in with promises of meaning, but all it could really tell me was how much had been lost.

It was cunning. The past smiled innocently while it loaded its gun. I had to destroy it before it destroyed me.

But the present—the present demanded respect, because it was where everything was and it offered passage to other presents of the future. The present was the place to invest energy and emotion: being part of it meant more than merely striving to avoid death. Survival on its own would be incomplete. I would truly live—whatever that turned out to mean—only if I forged a connection with whatever was left on earth, and every day was thankful for the opportunity to do so. I would have to be engaged, forward-thinking, disciplined. That's how I would keep the ghosts at bay and stay off the train to Crazy Town.

Repeat it to yourself:
You are alone.
You will always be alone.
You can learn to live with that.

The injuries from the mauling were treatable after a barely conscious trip to the local CVS. Semi-occlusive bandages closed the deepest gashes, and daily doses of antibiotic pills and slatherings of ointments staved off infection. The nose missed a teardrop-shaped divot of cartilage and would hurt for a long time, but the nasal passages were intact.

My headache treatment schedule came from athlete concussion protocols. As long as pain lingered or sensitivity to light arose, I rested in semi-darkness, ate only healthy foods and didn't overprescribe analgesics (sticking to safe doses of ibuprofen and acetaminophen rather than opiates or stomach-turning NSAIDs, no matter what). To keep my mind active, after the first two days I tried to read books from the house that I'd chosen as my recovery ward. But reading hurt my eyes, so I played games of chess against myself with the curtains closed, and little by little the headaches and sensitivity to light abated.

After eight days of rest, I was able to read without pain (*Alone with My Thoughts*, same book about the Oregon hermit that I'd read in Great Falls; this copy I liberated from the Renton library). But though I reread the book without cranial aches, I couldn't concentrate. Thought clips lasted at most a minute before dissolving. Nothing got retained.

On the tenth day, I took my first extended walk around the neighborhood. The foliage was lush and green, the air pregnant with rain. Back home, the leaves would soon start to change colors. Here, things would stay alive. I could get used to the place. But the next morning I paid for the walk—a delayed headache that sent me back to idle darkness for three more days.

Once I could walk without sunglasses or headaches (after seventeen days), I started climbing the steeper hills in Renton, just a few minutes each morning, to rebuild cardio and test the threshold for symptoms.

During the hill climbs I ignored Renton's many gruesome post-extinction sights. I told myself, whenever I saw a decaying dog leashed to a rail outside a grocery store, that Flannie was dead but that she couldn't have been saved and I had to let her go. Which inevitably led to:

Stop thinking of the past.

Regret will only eat you up.

Practicality instead. Present-time tasks—real things. Find a place to live—a place to come to rest, where I could be healthy, sane and productive.

Why did that last one matter? Productive? What did it even mean beyond finding a way to occupy my time?

The concept felt like a yardstick by which I could measure myself in the new world, a way of quantifying progress, but it raised an obvious question:

What could I produce?

There was no easy answer, but I did have time to come up with one. I didn't need to pressure myself. Instead, I invested most of my thoughts in the first order of business: deciding where to set down roots. My new home would have to satisfy certain requirements: weather, water, soil quality, proximity of supplies. After research at the Renton library, I narrowed my focus to temperate coastal locations, and then narrowed it further to the most fertile region of North America, the Salinas Valley of California, the "salad bowl of America." The place seemed ideal. Salinas checked all the boxes and had the added bonus of being only a couple days' drive from Renton. It was also fitting, in a way. Even after the end of the world, people were still moving to California.

I was strong enough to leave Renton on September 3rd, seventy-nine days after the world had ended without me. I'd gone seven days in a row without a headache and could walk the local hills for forty minutes at a brisk, sweat-breaking pace without growing dizzy or exhausted. Even my broken thumb felt better. I stopped bandaging it and realized it had now become second nature to favor it when using the hand.

Pace was essential. Do things without bogging down in interior monologue. Get moving and ignore the inner child. Inertia invited reflection. Reflection invited the past.

The distance to Salinas: roughly nine-hundred miles. By the map, the fastest route was south down the I-5 through Tacoma and Olympia. Because of car-crash traffic jams, I took backroads wherever I could. There was no LRAD on this trip, no CB radio, no investing of false hope in a trip to Joint Base Lewis-McChord. I was now a one-man society. The things I needed to earn could not be earned at dead military bases.

Driving, I listened to CDs from the glove compartment: Pink and Drake and Harry Styles. Whether I cared for the music or not, I committed the lyrics to memory and tried to sing along. This attempt to enjoy my own company at first made me feel ridiculous, like I was belting out *Shiny Happy People* at a funeral, but with repetition and sheer force of will I taught myself to accept moments of genuine joy—and to truly believe that maybe I *could* tame my own mind.

A clogged road east of Tacoma forced me to ditch the truck and claim an old station wagon parked at the far end of the jam. This was no problem. I had filled a sixty-liter hiking backpack with provisions in anticipation of such switches. I walked through this and other dead traffic jams without pausing much over the bodies. The only corpses I looked at closely were in the cars and trucks I wanted to drive. All told, I changed vehicles five times before I reached Medford, Oregon.

I needed to calm down at this point. There were heart palpitations and hot flashes of adrenaline because I felt so damn alive—so fiercely in search of a future—for the first time since the world had ended without me. There was a desire to drive all the way to Mexico just because Mexico was there to be driven to—so I bled the excess energy away by slowing down and stopping for two days at a mall south of Medford, where I slept on a store-display Posturepedic and read a book about nuclear power plants (to confirm that the plant on the California coast wouldn't have blown up after everyone died).

After that, I became better at keeping my emotions in check. The road opened up. By the time I crossed into the Golden State, I was driving a BMW and had an old CD collection that included Tom Waits, Lady Gaga and even some Burl Ives Christmas tracks (the individual artist didn't matter; I sang anything and everything until fatigue shut me down). One day later (five days into the road trip), I buzzed past Mount Shasta, out of the northern California mountains, and into the edge of an unbroken agricultural expanse that would stretch east of Salinas all the way to Mexico. Normally fed by water from northern dams, the crops here, outside Redding, California, were brown and dead. The heat had something to do with it. The temperature in Redding was ninety-eight degrees, forcing me to sleep on a roll-away bed outside a motel room.

Sleep came easy.
All thoughts were tame.

• • •

Moving again, I avoided the urban sprawl of central California, but not without spending good chunks of three days walking. On a country road outside Dixon, California, a jackknifed semitrailer blocked the entire road and forced me to hike under the blazing sun to a farmhouse a mile away. This I did with Bruno Mars blasting out of a JBL Flip speaker dangling from my backpack.

Outside Stockton, just a hundred and thirty miles from Salinas, my Kia got a flat tire and had no spare, so down another dirt road I walked—singing out loud—to four different houses with a dozen corpses and six parked vehicles that had no findable keys. No matter. I couldn't be disappointed if the word "disappointment" was banished from my lexicon.

Obstacles can slow you down but they can't stop you.
Only you can stop you.

Closer to Salinas, arid mountains smoothed out into bucolic rolling hills and then into the farmland that would become my new home. The temperature outside my car dropped from eighty-six to sixty-two degrees in a half hour of driving. A blessedly fair autumn after a feverish summer. This was the place, the perfect, ocean-kissed climate for crops of artichoke and broccoli and celery. Cauliflower and spinach. Lettuce, potatoes, endives, peppers and a dozen more. Some of these crops were even still growing (the lettuce and spinach) despite a lack of irrigation. The manicured green of the fields looked more alive than the amber grain crops outside Great Falls had ever looked, and when I rolled down the window in order to smell the air while driving, I tasted a hint of a saltwater breeze wafting in from the Pacific.

The ocean, as the saying went, was the cradle of life.

26

I WAS CAREFUL not to get too far ahead of myself.
Stay focused. Stay real.
To overdo a thing is to undo it.

A house couldn't be chosen until I found a cluster of big box stores to serve as my future supply depot. I drove the fringes of town. Salinas was maybe twice the size of Great Falls, a hundred thousand corpses, maybe one fifty, most of them now more bone than flesh. The airport, on the southeastern edge of the urban area, was a sooty husk of a building, though only two planes had caught fire. The produce warehouses and packing businesses to the south smelled worse than the town itself, with uncountable tons of produce still generating a stomach-churning odor.

The largest concentration of big-box stores sat on the north-western fringe of town, far away from this. It was perfect: Home Depot, Walmart, Costco and Dollar Tree. Also Dick's Sporting Goods. All the stores bordered celery and strawberry fields, all within walking distance of one another (and all absolutely littered with bone-rack corpses). There was even a California Welcome Center, with lots of local maps and pamphlets to help guide me around the area once I was settled in. I took the discovery of the pamphlets as a harbinger of good things to come.

This was everything I'd envisioned back in Renton. The stores were here, the roads weren't clogged, and that hint of fresh Pacific Ocean air felt alive, an easterly crawl of cool, rich O_2 that right now carried a trace of corpse-and-dead-crop odor but that in a matter of months would offer scents of springtime renewal.

I slept that night in a motel near the big box stores. Outside, a pack of dogs loitered near the lobby. There were six of them: three mutts, one boxer, a German shepherd and a collie. Seeing them of course led to thoughts of the two Jacks and Flannie, but I cut off all dark musings before they could spawn emotional infections. These dogs here looked confused to see a living human, attracted yet repelled, no longer pets but not yet truly wild. I whistled loudly and the collie loped toward me but the pack leader, the German Shepherd, snarled and sprayed saliva. The collie stopped and whined. I made sure the motel room door was closed before I climbed into bed. I also told myself not to ruin things by fretting over Flannie and the two Jacks.

But erasing the past wasn't easy. My mind went back to the days following the cougar mauling—days in which I couldn't quite suppress the guilt that came with having left Flannie dead in that back yard. This led to guilt now, so I tried to chase the whole subject away by rereading *Alone with My Thoughts*.

Third time on the book.

Maybe this chronicle about an extreme loner held a vital recipe for living on my own. Maybe I'd missed the message earlier.

So what did I have here? I had a hermit spending twenty-four solitary years in the wilderness without going crazy. I had him actually enjoying his rough and lonesome life. But was he born with that orientation or had he learned it somewhere along the way?

He seemed to have been born with it—was just wired differently from the rest of us. Most people needed to be with other people; a very few others needed desperately to escape them—and the escapers weren't afflicted by childhood trauma or intellectual deficiencies or off-kilter ideology; they just preferred their own company. Could I learn to do that? Maybe I could, if I worked at it.

But there was no blueprint. The hermit was in no way noble or principled, and he offered no recipe, no behavioral routine that could be emulated. I found myself thinking *People do need people*, and then chasing that thought with *It's dangerous to need a thing you can't have*.

I tossed the book in the garbage and told myself to stick with the plan, be a pioneer, choose life. If the hermit couldn't help me, then I would just have to help myself.

The best thing about disappointment and failure was that they inevitably became part of the past and therefore were not allowed to harm me. They could always be moved on from.

• • •

First thing the next morning, I drove out to the farms closest to the big box stores. There were six houses within walking distance. Two were mansions on estate-like grounds; four were 1950s bungalows built on small parcels with modest barns. Most of the machinery must have been out among the crops.

I ruled out the mansions straight away. Too much upkeep. Of the four remaining houses, one was falling apart and smelled like dog. Two of the places had newer roofs and solid window frames. Both received their water from aquifers via well pumps that looked new and operable. Both came with big bedrooms, comfortable sofas, newer appliances and no real luxury indulgences. Neither of them had solar panels.

Of these two houses, one had two corpses inside, the other had five (including two that ruined the living-room broadloom). I chose the one with the two corpses, in part because of the lower number of bodies and in part because it was the closest house to the edge of town. Walmart and Costco were visible from the bedroom windows, while the west-facing living room showed me strawberry fields as far as the eyes could see. That would be soothing for a Montana boy like me, a prairie-like uniformity once I cleared away a flatbed truck that sullied the view; the truck was accompanied by stacks of produce boxes and nine or ten dead pickers in various unflattering poses.

The house closest to me was the one with the five corpses, a four-minute walk through the strawberries. The only real drawback in the house with the two corpses, apart from the absence of solar panels and the dead pickers in the field out front, was the lack of natural light (the windows were small).

So this would be it, home, my personal Strawberry Fields Forever. I didn't stand outside the house and get poetic or satisfied over the fabulousness of it all. Sentimentality was a cousin to reflection, potentially as dangerous and therefore barred. I dragged the two almost-disassembled corpses out to the yard, started opening windows, and noticed two living-room wall portraits of a happy, sun-blessed couple and their teenage daughter. The sight of the family stung a little, so I removed the portraits, then changed my mind, put them back up, and drove to the big box stores to gather bleach and cleaning supplies, a generator and fuel, and some food. Later in the day I let my hair down a little by grabbing a bottle of Coke from a gas station. Once I got the generator going, a nice, fridge-cooled glucose fizz would taste like nectar of the gods.

• • •

It took two days of cleaning, two days of shopping after that and three more days of arranging and assembling to get the main things up and running. Now I had power and running water, a cold fridge, an oven for warm meals, heat in the winter, air-con in the summer. The living room got a new TV and stereo. The master bedroom got a new mattress (a corpse had decomposed into the old one), and the backyard got a shiny new gas barbecue, a deck made of tire-rubber tiles and an outdoor recliner that you could melt into like bubbling cheese on rye. I celebrated with a hot meal of packaged Dal Tadka and ran a mental checklist of the things still left to do.

Useful things. Reasonable things.

I would have to learn how to maintain the backyard septic tank, and how to install and use solar panels, and how to switch over a portion of the strawberry field to grow fresh veggies. I would have to drive the three or four miles to the coast and learn how to catch saltwater fish.

But none of these things were urgent. I could tackle them at my leisure. The time for being productive in another way—in a way that would carry me through over the long term—was fast approaching.

No. If I thought about it honestly, the time had already arrived— but I'd been too busy to notice.

So what could I now produce that would occupy my mind and body and keep Ronnie and Evan at bay?

Crickets.

This would have been easier had there been zombies coming in through the windows or a kraken rising out of the sea to step on me. A lethal external threat would have reduced life to a series of basic instincts, with no time for fretting over ways of taming inner weaknesses.

But the conditions were the conditions. I was safe and sound in Strawberry Fields Forever—a wonderful place, all things considered. The pace would now slow and idle thoughts would soon threaten unless I managed to stay disciplined and ward them off.

The gods would be angry if I dithered, so I decided to act. I would fend off idleness—at least for now—by doing the only thing I knew how to do.

27

WRITING A BOOK after the end of the world didn't strike me as peculiar or self-absorbed. True, no one would ever publish or read the work, but that wasn't the point. I would compose a novel-length story about the new world, infuse it with honesty and (most importantly) generosity of spirit—no, more than that, with positivity, acceptance and optimism—and when I finished it, I would print it out, stick it in a drawer, then write another one, and so on. One day when I was old and unable to compose fiction, I would look back on what I'd produced and feel proud that I'd stared down adversity and excelled under the most challenging of conditions. I had kept on keeping on.

But what to write? After you've buried your family, conjured up ghosts and nearly offed yourself, you couldn't then start penning novel number nine in the Mike Stone series. The new novel would have to be personal, reflective of the world I lived in, and of my place in it.

My life in general would have to be that way. Writing was just one element of a larger whole. I needed a schedule for my waking hours, a way of ensuring I would be productive not only when I was working, but when I was living, too. So before I sat down to pound out a novel I drew up such a timetable.

7:15—8:00: wake up, shower, breakfast.
8:00—12:00: work on the novel with a morning-fresh mind.
12:00—12:30: lunch—never skip it, just like Mom used to say.
12:30—5:00: staying-alive work—daily household chores, solar-panel installation, gardening, repairs, cleaning, sundry drudgeries.
5:00—6:00: dinner—always cook a decent meal; do not eat another cold MRE so long as you live, so help you God.
6:00—8:00: trips to town for supplies and research materials—food and bottled water, generator gas, gardening tools, library stops, whatever else.
8:00—11:00: leisure time—reading books, watching movies, chilling to music, counting the stars.
11:00: bedtime—read until nodding off.

The four morning hours of writing would also apply to Saturdays and Sundays, but those hours would kick in at whatever time I woke up (weekend sleep-ins struck me as a warranted extravagance that might support mental health). The schedule could be broken only in the case of illness or injury. There would be no alcohol allowed at any time, and no drugs, because it was well established where those two things led. Junk food would be a Saturday night thing, as would movie watching (the first priorities would be the Coen brothers, something deliciously careless, like *The Big Lebowski*). Both Saturday and Sunday would include flexible travel hours, time to tool around town and check out the local hood, journey to the beaches and the coastal towns, maybe do some fishing, or hiking, or whatever struck my fancy. I wouldn't be puritanical about doing work; I'd just stay busy, appreciate my time, keep Ronnie and Evan out of the picture. This rolling stone would gather no moss; my wandering soul would not be pinned down.

And this new way of living would start with the very next sunrise, in roughly fourteen hours' time.

• • •

I couldn't sleep that night—too many plans in my head. For breakfast I ate organic raisin bran in wondrously cold UHT milk, then, to prevent interruptions while I worked, I popped outside to top off the gas in the generator. After that, I retreated to the house's second bedroom, which I'd converted to a home office with a desk and computer from OfficeMax.

The sound of the computer turning on was uplifting. The opening of Microsoft Word felt like going home. But now that I was all set up, now that the stage of productivity had been set, I had no idea what to write. I stared at the blinking cursor on Microsoft Word, at the white page with gray background, and it looked unbelievably daunting.

What do you call a neighborhood full of idle novelists?
 A writer's block!

How had I ever done this before?

Being blocked was foreign territory. Writing had always been an act of faith, a knowledge that words would come. But then I'd always had Mike Stone to fall back on, had always allowed him to guide me.

So I considered plunking Mike Stone into this story, right in the middle of a post-extinction setting. But there aren't a lot of mysteries to solve for a detective who's the last man on Earth, so Mike Stone was out, of no use. What other writing subjects were there? The most obvious thing was me—this, here, a writer who tries to save himself by writing. But that exercise would have led too easily to reflection on the past. Besides, I didn't want to hear *my* voice, I wanted to hear *the* voice, the voice that would help pull me through.

So I sat there four straight hours and stared at the screen. I upbraided myself for letting my mind flash on Ronnie, Evan and Great Falls, and I grew frustrated enough to consider tossing the computer out the window (then chastised myself for the unacceptable lapse into emotional excess). I broke once from this "work" to make coffee, but the caffeine didn't help. Nothing helped. I turned the computer off at noon, ate lunch, then drove into town to round up solar panels.

The next morning, I was back at the computer before eight. Things didn't go any better, but since I was on a schedule, and since the schedule could change only as a result of illness or injury, I again stared at the cursor until lunchtime.

On the third day I could stand it no longer; I typed a single sentence just to see words on the screen:

Detective Michael Anthony Stone was not a fan of the end of the world.
The choice made itself. I had to write.

Mike Stone went to an afternoon Mets game on the day of the extinction. He sat behind home plate nine rows up, poised to bite into a very mustardy hotdog when everyone around him keeled over.

Ronnie would have disapproved of this glibness, but I struck her from my mind because of course she wasn't allowed to be there. And anyway, the extinction itself had been glib. Some people were having sex when it happened. Others were on the toilet, or pulling on their pants, one leg dressed and one leg bare, or furtively picking their noses while other people pretended not to see.

Somewhere in the world, a movie director probably yelled "Action!" a split second before everyone cratered. Bad humor was part of the package.

Mike Stone was bigger than this anyway. He would adapt to the post-extinction world because he was smarter than me, and stronger, and better in the end. This novel would be about how he responded to the death of humanity. He would teach me things I'd been too weak or afraid to learn myself, things I could use in the new world. He was, I now understood, not only right for this new book; he was perfect for it.

So I wrote. And the hours flew by like minutes. I missed my twelve o'clock deadline for lunch. Tomorrow, I told myself, I would set an alarm and snap myself out of the writing trance at the appointed time.

The schedule could not be compromised.

Rules were made to be followed.

28

For the next two weeks, I wrote a thousand words a day before noon, then erected solar panels, read library books about water pumps and septic tanks and drove around gathering up late-season veggies. I relaxed in the evenings by listening to Bob Marley, Bobby McFerrin and other musical merchants of positivity. On the weekends, I drove to the docks in Monterey Bay and caught enough rockfish to fill my freezer. Life was as I'd strived to make it—busy, productive, future-oriented—but a sense of something not quite right was also taking root. The slight buzz of my computer began to sound louder day by day, until it etched grooves on my brain. The sound of the fridge compressor bloomed into a rumbling industrial system. The generator behind the shed outside—instant headache. Every mechanical sound was magnified a thousand-fold. Relief could be found only by going outside, far from the generator, to a place where there was only the Pacific breeze and a chorus of birdsong.

I identified the problem when I was lying in bed one morning and I cleared my throat; the minor action sounded like the Enola Gay's payload hitting Hiroshima.

The issue wasn't the volume of the sounds, but the silence *around* those sounds. Silence was an affliction—a producer of jarring absences. Because I made so little noise at most times in the day, certain sounds stepped in to overcompensate for the nothingness. Even the voice inside me when I wrote, it had gone from a confident old friend to a shrill and harried nag, injecting the spaces between my usual thoughts with vague, dissonant clatter.

Only music helped, only fluid audio, so I drove to the Walmart and picked up a hundred more CDs: rock, blues, classical, music I liked and music I hated (1990s heavy metal was *so* the opposite of silence). I would play it when I was inside the house, when I was driving and when I was writing. There would still be the voice inside my head, I would still be able to focus and function, but I would no longer be alone.

This helped, but only for a few days. My ears started to hurt and the voice in my head grew louder. If I turned the music up, the voice responded in kind. When I sought relief in the sounds of nature outside my house, I heard the generator's low rumble, sometimes even after I turned it off.

Evenings were the worst. While lying in bed, trying to sleep, I allowed a disturbing new habit to form. The room had a clock radio with a projector that beamed the time onto the ceiling in red, right-angled numerals. I watched those numerals in the darkness, couldn't not watch them, and after a while the numbers turned into letters. "2:14" became "HIS." "3:45" became "SHE." The numbers could be read forward or backward and could be flipped. "4:37" became "HEL" and "6:16" was "GIG" or "Girl In Garlic" or "Gigantic Incendiary Gargoyle."

There were a million more and I couldn't get enough of them. I did sleep, off and on, but never for more than an hour at a time, never without the number-words being the last thing on my mind before I drifted off.

This state of affairs qualified as an incipient illness and/or injury. Maybe it would usher in a relapse of post-concussion syndrome—or maybe this was a relapse, though the new headaches were mild—so I temporarily revised my daily schedule to make me busier, put me on the move more, load my senses with undemanding but rewarding sights and sounds as well as work, any tasks that might take me away from internal monologue. Lord knew, there were plenty of tasks to carry out in the post-extinction world.

I started with a job I'd been putting off. I moved the strawberry pickers out of the field across the road from my living-room window. I commanded myself not to be squeamish about it, tossing what was left of the workers onto a trailer and dumping them in the back yard of the neighbors' house with the five corpses.

That done, I went home and sat on my living room sofa to take in the new view. Now, apart from the two trucks and the strawberry boxes still in sight, there was no visual sign that anything was wrong in the world.

I felt better, like this was an achievement.

But that truck *was* still there. It reminded me of the bodies, so I retrieved diesel fuel from town, boosted the battery, and drove the thing out of frame.

This time when I sat on my living room sofa, it might as well have been a normal, sun-drenched Sunday back before the end of the world. My fridge purred softly. The voice in my head was warm and friendly. No noises threatened.

To solidify this state of affairs, I cleaned up the country road between my house and the Walmart, which was also an eyesore, with four cars visible from the bedroom and home-office windows.

I gassed up the tanks of all four, boosted two of the batteries, and drove the vehicles and their corpses around front of the Chuck E. Cheese's next to the Walmart—finally get that impossibly cheerful mouse back for tormenting me with his rote gleefulness at Evan's birthday parties.

Now, no matter where I stood in my house, there were no signs of the extinction.

I slept soundly that night, no numbers-to-words fixations, and when I awoke in the morning, I was so afraid I might lose this re-earned state of grace that I moved the dead cars out of the T-intersection where the crops bordered the Salinas city limits. I couldn't *see* these wrecks from my house, but I did have to drive past them to get to town, so they needed to go.

And they were easy moves—simple gas fill-ups and battery boosts. Now I could go all the way to Walmart before having to encounter the end of the world.

This claiming of my little slice of town was rocket fuel to my sense of self-worth. The feeling of accomplishment made me want to find other ways to improve the neighborhood. But what other ways? The area around the house was all clear now, but I still hadn't seen much of the town of Salinas itself (outskirts and big-box stores aside). I jogged out to the truck, popped open the glove compartment, and scooped out the pamphlets I'd picked up at the California Welcome Center.

My Only Friend, the End

The state tourism office wanted me to see the Monterey Zoo, the Mazda Raceway, a thing called The Farm. There were also pamphlets for the Old Town, Toro County Park and Tatum's Garden.

And the National Steinbeck Center.

I paused over that one.

They gave John Steinbeck a museum? I recalled the Chinamen and Polacks and Wops of *Cannery Row* and wondered if colleges still had places for such dated voices on their reading lists. Maybe—if the author was respected enough to get a museum. It was no small feat, a writer being celebrated with an entire building. Even in the U.K., where culture was less disposable than in the States, even the ghost of one of their favorite sons, Charles Dickens, had to make do with a modest townhouse in London.

This called for a writerly pilgrimage. Steinbeck had been one of my favorites back in school, a guru for my youthful anti-establishment leanings. *In Dubious Battle, The Grapes of Wrath, Travels with Charley*— he had corroborated my belief that for every good, honest person in the world there was an equally soulless sociopath willing and able to step on a throat. In the pantheon of Great American Writers, I ranked Steinbeck in the second tier, below Faulkner, Flannery O'Connor and Eudora Welty, but above Henry James and Fitzgerald.

There was also a pamphlet for a thing called Steinbeck House, a stately old Queen Anne Victorian where Steinbeck had once lived. These days it was a Steinbeck-themed restaurant done up in 1930s style.

So the writerly pilgrimage. Glean some inspiration for the Mike Stone work in progress.

The museum was on Main Street, in the heart of town. The building, when I got there, was true to the picture on the pamphlet, a real museum, solid and proud of its purpose. Inside, the corpses could be counted on two hands, and that included a man behind the cash register and a woman with a National Steinbeck Center nametag reading "Gladys." This was good; the bodies were fast and easy to remove, the smell was livable, and the light was good even without electricity.

I moved slowly through the exhibits, read everything, felt instantly younger and more capable. I developed a twitch in my eyelid, accompanied by a strangely nervous energy, as if I would have to give a speech or a reading here. There were life-size statues of Steinbeck, a crossword puzzle with Steinbeck clues, a section devoted to his Nobel Prize. They even had

Rocinante, his camper from *Travels With Charley*. I recalled parts of that book that some back in Montana would have called "communist," and I thought back to my young-man discoveries of the *Cannery Row* boys, of Tom Joad and the concept of social justice. I recalled where I was when I first read *Of Mice and Men* (in my high-school library, my feet up on the table; I read the whole thing in one sitting). But those memories weren't allowed, so I chided myself for indulging in them and decided this pilgrimage could not be allowed to serve as a kind of literary contravention of my very-clear rules for the new world.

Then I encountered some problems that needed fixing. The rows of first-edition covers of Steinbeck's novels were in the wrong order. *The Pastures of Heaven* came before *The Red Pony*, not after. I had to tear the covers out of their case (they were glued to the back of the cabinet) and put them back in the right order.

Doing this did not strike me as "productive," but I couldn't help myself. I proceeded to spend the rest of the day in the museum. My eyelid twitch worsened. I left only when the sun started to set and the exhibit panels became too hard to read.

On the way out, I found yet another deviation from the almost-but-not-quite-verboten History of Before. Steinbeck had always written his first drafts long-hand, in pencil, on yellow notepads. Some of those notepads and pencils were on display, but the pencils were wrong; they were hexagonal, while Steinbeck had only ever used finger-friendly *round* pencils (this fact was written right there on the wall above the hexagonal pencils). I confiscated the offending graphite and exited through the gift shop, miffed that the keepers of Steinbeck's legacy allowed such egregious inconsistency.

The night passed without numerical word associations, and without headaches or unsettling thoughts. The next morning after breakfast, I drove right back and resumed the pencil hunt—in case I'd missed any. But the remaining pencils were fine, so I left the museum and drove two blocks west to see what Steinbeck House was like.

Outside, the house was an example of well-preserved history, with steep steps to a covered veranda under a corner-facing cupola that crowned and fronted the house's many quaint Victorian-era rooms. The grass out front was burnt-brown and dead, but that seemed somehow preferable to being overgrown, perhaps because lawns in Great Falls had tended to look like burnt straw. The place could easily have been a rooming house back in the day. Maybe it was.

Inside, everything was true to the Depression era: deep-crimson carpets and wallpaper, rich oak wainscoting, flowered tablecloths in the restaurant. Since the extinction had occurred late-morning on a Friday, there were no corpses in the dining room. A rope at the base of the stairs cordoned off the upper level.

I pulled it down and listened to my footsteps creak as I climbed the nearly vertical stairs. It was strange. Only my right foot made the stairs creak, only the odd-numbered steps. When I reached the top, I felt compelled to go back down and climb the stairs again, this time with my left foot hitting the odd-numbered steps. I sighed in relief when the expected foot produced the expected number of creaks.

I found Steinbeck's writing room straight away. It was small, with an antique single bed, a dresser with a wash basin and a simple wooden chair. On one wall was a mass-reproduced watercolor of a Mona Lisa holding a cat in her lap—a bit of harmless kitsch that maybe someone had put there as a joke. This room also had a feel to it that couldn't be described. It was as if Steinbeck was there with me, and not in a ghost-of-Ronnie way, but in a benevolent-muse way. I knew then and there I would finish writing my novel in that room. I would drive from Strawberry Fields to Steinbeck House every morning, subtract the seven or eight minutes of travel time from the writing portion of the daily schedule, stick to the overall plan. It made sense. The drive would get me out of the house in the a.m., show me the town, a little weather, make things closer to normal.

That was the grail here: normalcy. Consistency. Consulting only those elements of the past that might help me claim the future.

I walked downstairs with measured care, with each foot causing two stairs to creak, then I moved through the kitchen, found one corpse, dragged it outside, and doused the place with enough bleach and Mr. Muscle to kill all germs within a five-mile radius.

On the way home, there was a traffic jam a block from Steinbeck House. I tried to drive past it but couldn't help myself; I stopped and spent two hours removing the six cars from the road and the four pedestrian-corpses from the nearby sidewalks. (The cars got gassed up and/or boosted and driven around the corner; the corpses got dragged behind bushes, out of sight.)

At home, I couldn't sit still. I found chores to do, topped up the generator, went up a ladder in the dark to hammer the rain gutters flush to the roof. But even after all this, before I could drift off to sleep my numbers associations kicked in. "11:11" became a screaming "IIII." "12:12" became "ISIS." The numbers didn't have to form proper words. "12:22" was "ISSS" or "SSSI" or "Serious Soporific String-theory Internalized." I nodded off at about "4:15"—"hIS"—and when I woke up again it was "7:07," which of course was "LOL." This reminded me of my first calculator, which I'd received when I was seven or eight years old. Back then, everyone in class knew that "71077345" was "SHELLOIL."

29

I WAS TOO GROGGY to eat breakfast. I drove to Walmart to pick up yellow notepads, round pencils and a pencil sharpener—things I hadn't used since childhood. At Steinbeck House, I walked around opening windows in rooms and found another body upstairs. This annoyed me; it meant more cleaning before I could get to the important stuff.

I didn't sit down at the writing table until 9:34. I was well awake now, but the daily schedule had been compromised. To get my four hours of writing in, I would have to push everything else back.

This was the last time I would bend the schedule. After today, there would be slavish fidelity to the plan, no excuses or dispensations.

Mike Stone was happy to see me, even if we now communicated by notepad and pencil, which slowed composition to a crawl. When I had re-met his acquaintance two weeks earlier, he'd decided very shortly after humanity dropped dead that he would figure out why the extinction had happened. That was a tall order, yes, but for Mike Stone there would be no crying or fiddling with an AM shower radio or getting plastered and giving up while the fires raged and the floodwaters rose. He wouldn't mess around with radio-station transmitters out on the prairie. He would get moving and figure things out.

My Only Friend, the End

So twelve hours after the end of the world, Mike Stone drove into the parking lot of the medical examiner's office in Morristown, New Jersey. Not only had he escaped the sea of corpses in Manhattan, he'd also concocted a plan to see if extinction corpses looked internally different from pre-extinction bodies.

Like me, Mike Stone had no medical training. Unlike me, he wouldn't let that stop him. If SUDC (and by extension SUDE) had a neurological cause, then maybe the brains of the dead were discolored or fried or bruised. If not, okay, the only thing Mike might lose was his lunch—thanks to the grisly task of sawing into skulls and sloshing around inside.

That was how far I got before I put pencil to paper at Steinbeck House. Mike Stone had to dig out only one brain, not two, because there was already a pre-extinction brain in the medical examiner's scale pan, ready for viewing. For the extinction brain, he cut into the dead pathologist who was conveniently draped over the brain-free corpse, still holding an electric saw powered by the morgue's still-functioning backup generator.

It was gory work but Mike Stone kept his lunch down and powered through it (pun somewhat intended). But both brains looked and felt the same. They were similar weights and hard to hold without using two hands. Mike Stone cleaned himself up and walked back out to the car.

Now I developed the thread. Instead of hanging around New Jersey and hoping to be rescued, instead of being overwhelmed by the tragedy of it all, he packed a car full of provisions and drove down the east coast with an LRAD in tow and a collection of flare guns in the passenger seat (this idea came to him much faster than it had come to me). He quickly deduced that a) he was all alone in the world, and b) he would now have to create a new one-man civilization in order to survive without going bonkers.

Mike Stone arrived at this stage of his journey within the space of four days, without injury, without going doolally and conjuring ghosts and trying to do himself in. I wished I'd started writing about him back when I was locking myself in bunkers and playing mental Whac-a-Mole with Ronnie and Evan.

He thought hard about the world that was gone and the world that should replace it. He took stock of political systems and economic and social systems, pondered the rules, the types of freedom. This was important, because no matter how many people were left, there had to be rules. Some things had to be out of bounds. A type of constitution would have to be drawn up in case he wavered or grew lazy (as if).

He didn't dally over this. He capably concluded that manmade systems and structures were powerless against the virus of human nature and that people forgot and ignored their own histories, repeating the same problems with predictable regularity. What they needed now—what he needed—was to build things up without influences of past weakness, with a kind of newfound purity.

I had to stop writing there. I'd sailed past the already-revised writing deadline by twelve minutes, which felt unforgivable, but I'd also filled thirteen notepad pages in the space of four hours. My fingers hurt, and my handwriting was nearly illegible, but the pages were there. It was time to make good on the rest of the daily schedule. Rigor had to be restored. Man did not live on fiction alone.

• • •

Driving home, I saw the same six dogs that had been roaming outside my motel room when I'd first arrived in town. Again, the dogs looked both drawn to me and frightened. Alpha, the German Shepherd, snarled and growled. The capacity for redomestication struck me as dubious at best. But the notion that they would grow feral was unacceptable, a challenge to the idea that the new world could be made livable.

I called the dogs over, tried to sound friendly, and the collie started toward me but was interrupted by Alpha's growling.

"Don't be afraid," I hollered, but the collie cocked his head as if I were a bizarre curiosity. The other dogs crept toward me ready to attack, so I buzzed up the window and drove toward Strawberry Fields. The twitch in my eyelid returned—or had been there all along but I only noticed it now. Maybe it had something to do with my cougar-mauled nose. Maybe the damaged nerves in that part of the face were acting up.

After all my plans and promises to myself, when I got home I ignored the rest of the daily schedule. This was not a conscious decision; it was an organically grown deviation, with no second thoughts. I gobbled down cold rockfish from the fridge, then turned on loud music and looked around for tasks to fulfill.

But despite the blaring tunes, silence invaded my thoughts. The house felt like someone else's, like I was a squatter, which of course I was. I found myself running out to the truck and driving back downtown to look for the pack of dogs, to get myself a companion, much like I'd done while high on Percocet in Spokane.

But the dogs were gone. I drove around a little, called out to them, but they remained elusive—playing hard to get.

In the course of the driving I found it harder to look at the cars on the road and the bodies on the sidewalks—harder to accept their presence. There was only one thing for it: they had to go.

I removed the sidewalk bodies first—every body between Steinbeck House and the big-box stores on the western edge of town (one full mile and twenty-eight bodies). The cars were a bigger task. There had to be fifty of them, including a city transit bus and various service vehicles. The bus was particularly vexing: all that death in one neatly contained package. But the thing would be hard to move, so I started on the cars instead, and almost all of them needed both a boost and gas. Only six cars got relocated before the evening chill settled in and fatigue drove me home.

The house at Strawberry Fields was cold, though the thermostat was set at seventy to combat the autumn nip. I chose to power through the discomfort, like Mike Stone would have done. Mind over matter. I ate, took a somewhat frenetic shower, went to bed, and slept for an hour before turning "11:06" into "GOII," and "11:07" into "LOII" and "IIOL."

Come morning I still felt drained. I ate cereal standing up at the fridge and dropped the bowl in the sink a little too hard. It broke loudly, made me jump, but I left it where it was. I had work to do.

There were no dogs anywhere between the Home Depot and Steinbeck House. The dead cars still cried out to be moved (that bus looked even more daunting today), but the morning hours were for the novel, so I tried not to look at the vehicles while driving and soon found myself climbing the creaking stairs at Steinbeck House (two creaks per foot) to get to Mike Stone.

I was at the top of the stairs when I heard a dog bark outside.

Yes!

I ran back down and peered out the kitchen window. There they were, all six dogs, at the same intersection I'd moved the cars out of. I studied the collie a moment. Despite his mess of tangled, matted hair, there was a kind of lightness in his bearing that the other dogs all seemed to lack.

I rummaged through the kitchen cupboards and pulled out a dozen cans of tuna, three of which I opened and portioned out into bowls. The dogs were still at the intersection when I opened the side door and stepped out. I whistled loudly and all the dogs' ears perked up.

"Puppies! Lookie-lookie! Comestibles!"

I crept closer to the intersection than was wise, set one of the bowls on the dead grass and retreated to the doorway.

The dogs all hesitated, then one of the smaller mutts sprinted toward the food, with Alpha hot on her heels.

I placed the second bowl halfway between the first bowl and the house, and the dogs sorted themselves into two tuna-seeking groups, snapping at each other, renewing or revising orders of dominance. The collie was in the group farthest from me, looked unable to claim any fish—wasn't mean enough.

"Here boy!" I called, and held out the third bowl. One of the smaller mutts began creeping toward me, but stopped short of the food, afraid.

"Come on, fella, it's chicken of the sea, get some."

The collie started toward me. I backpedaled into the kitchen, left the door open and called out again.

The next thirty seconds brought silence. Then I heard the patter of approaching dogs. The boxer poked her head around the kitchen doorway.

"Attagirl. Check it out—delicious non-human meat."

I placed the tuna on the floor tiles and stepped back. The boxer entered warily, inched toward the bowl, followed by the collie.

I opened another can and put it outside. The boxer followed me. When she was on the other side of the door, I closed it.

"Let's make a deal," I told the collie. "If you don't like it here, I'll let you go. But first you have to give me a chance."

I reached out to pet him but he snapped and snarled, so I opened another can and put it on the floor. He wouldn't go for it.

"Come on, guy. We've pretty much exhausted my dog-whispering talents."

After much deliberation, he slinked toward the food and began eating. While he emptied the bowl, I cleared the air:

"We're gonna call you Charley, okay? Like Johnny S.'s dog—like *Travels with Charley*. In case you haven't read it, Johnny and Charley travelled around the country in a camper, looked for the real America.

They liked some of what they saw but didn't like other things. You and I will do some travelling later, maybe next spring, if the spirit moves us."

He finished eating and looked at me while licking his lips.

"Just how many corpses have you eaten, anyway?"

He cocked his head at me.

"Not that I'm passing judgment."

A memory flashed of the cougar clamping down on my neck. Best to take things slow.

"Hop on a sofa or something," I said. "I've got work to do."

I climbed the stairs carefully (two creaks per foot), sharpened a new pencil, and flipped open the notepad of yellow paper.

But words wouldn't come.

Again.

I sat there and thought—hard—as if effort was all it took. The result was predictable.

Writers block.

Lovely.

Backtrack. Where's your starting point?

Mike Stone had driven from Morristown, New Jersey, to Albermale Sound, Virginia, to begin his new life. But what would that life entail? *That* was the problem. He wasn't one to sit around and soak up easily obtainable comforts. He needed a purpose, just like I needed a purpose. But unlike me, he wasn't a writer; he couldn't fall back on the idea of working on a novel.

What could he do?

It took forty minutes of tortured thought to realize just how lost at sea Mike Stone was, how rudderless.

I jotted onto the notepad, *How to Create a One-Man Civilization*.

But Mike Stone's new world was both too big and too empty, had had too much removed from it, so I tried to reduce the problem to something manageable. Who was the bad guy in this story? Every story needed a bad guy, even if he or she or it came in the form of a circumstance, or the weather, or a part of the main character himself, a flaw from within.

Yes! A good writer asks the hard questions!

But Mike Stone's problems started where exactly? They didn't start in Morristown, New Jersey. They didn't even start with the extinction. They started before that.

I knew where they began: everything started to fall apart for him in novel number three.

In the first novel in the Mike Stone series, he was a fresh tough guy supremely confident in his abilities, a true archetype of the genre. In novel number two, he became an overbaked antihero, but at least he knew what he wanted and was determined to go out and get it.

But that changed starting in novel number three, which was a strained overcompensation for the hardboiled sins of novel number two. In book three, while Ronnie and I took our first, tentative steps back toward normal life, Mike Stone softened, became a kind of crime-solving pop psychologist. He travelled to Rio to rescue a waif of a boy who lived in a garbage dump. Gangsters had put the child there, made him collect bottles, various metals, and other detritus of value. Mike Stone tracked the boy down, freed him and his fellow child slaves, and reunited him with his parents. Of course, he also made the criminals pay.

But the crimes weren't only punished, they were analyzed in great detail, pored over like entries in a psychology textbook. Mike Stone even started hugging people in novel number three. Unforgivable. Not surprisingly, that was where my sales started to flag, the beginning of a trend that at the time I hoped was temporary but that turned out to be long and steady.

That was because in novels number four through eight Mike Stone played things safe. Conflicts were easily solved, the storytelling language was trite, and the characters rarely broke a sweat. Every new novel had less life and energy than the book the preceded it. Each time I sat down to write, I was a little less engaged. At one point I cut back my daily novel-writing hours and started keeping a file of one-liners just because dumb puns were more fun to be around than earnest storytelling. A little voice inside my head (okay, *the* voice inside my head) told me this was okay. I had a new child in my life and a renewed relationship with my wife. Risks and bold moves couldn't happen. They'd have to wait for later, when the boy had safely outgrown childhood and the wife was appropriately revered to the point where she could never, ever, question my commitment to her again.

Poor Mike Stone. I had turned my perfectly adequate tough guy into Doctor Phil.

That's why he now sat there on the page like a coffee stain. I labored at ideas for setting him in motion, tore myself in a thousand directions, but ultimately decided the problem would not be solved. Sometimes you just have to admit you're a hack who can't be trusted to write so much as a grocery list.

My Only Friend, the End

So maybe it was over, maybe I would never write again. If so, what would I do then?

Walking downstairs, I passed Charley without looking at him. I was too damned miserable. But:

Even if I couldn't write, I would still have to be engaged and useful. Those were the rules and they gave me comfort because in the absence of writing there was something important I could do.

I could go outside and take back more of my new city.

I could move more dead traffic off the street.

30

I RETURNED TO THE JAM I'd been working on the night before. Driving the length of West Market Street, I counted fourteen cars, eighteen trucks, two delivery vans, one electrical maintenance truck and that one city bus. Thirty-six vehicles. The sooner I made them go away, the sooner I could start the next task. The more tasks I completed, the more productive I would be.

Instead of filling gas tanks and boosting batteries, I found a garage with a tow truck. It took an hour to figure out how to use it, then I practiced on a Volkswagen parked outside the garage, towed the thing onto the street out front. After that, I drove back to the jam and started moving the cars rather than the trucks—rather than that big, daunting bus—towed them into store parking lots and onto side streets. A few of the bodies looked like Ronnie. One of them looked like Oliver. I forced such images out of my mind. The cars went fast. At this rate, I *could* clean up all the roads around Home Depot and Walmart. This whole town could be what I wanted it to be. I had all the time in the world to achieve this.

On the seventh car of the day, a Chrysler Something-or-other, I tore open the driver-side door, shoved a spindly corpse over to the passenger seat, and leaned in to check the transmission gear.

My Only Friend, the End

A CB radio receiver hung from the dash. Seeing it gave me a fright, like a tarantula had just ambled by. I pushed the talk bar and said into the mic, "Nice try! There's no one out there to talk to!" then dropped the mic and climbed out of the car and moved it and three others before hunger and dusk forced me to suspend the vehicle relocation program for the evening.

• • •

Before going home, I peeled back to Steinbeck House and opened the kitchen door. There was dog feces on the tiled kitchen floor. Charley lay stretched out on the hallway carpet. He looked comfortable.

"You can roam around outside if you want to," I told him. "I'm going to be busy a while."

I opened another can of tuna, placed it outside the kitchen door, and left the door open while I went home for the night.

Back at Strawberry Fields, I filled the generator with gas and told myself the house was just a house, it had no business tormenting me. This strategy worked. My tenacity worked. I stepped inside the place and everything felt safe and the way it was supposed to be—until I saw an overhead light hanging from the kitchen ceiling. Its moth-eaten electrical wires held it at eye level, low enough to zap me if I touched them. This made me angry, because unforeseen repair tasks could only stand in the way of the real priorities, so I left the light hanging where it was. I ate a can of beans at the sink, dropped the can and spoon onto the broken cereal bowl over the drain, then poured myself into bed for the night.

The ceiling numbers were there. I unplugged the clock radio, laid back and screwed my eyes shut, but the numbers were still there, pulsing blood red in my mind's eye. I laid awake the whole night, and when morning came, I took a deliberately long shower in order to push through this nonsense. Then I stepped into the home office and printed out all the writing I'd done before moving my writing space to John Steinbeck's room.

After that, I rounded up some candles, hopped in the truck, and sped back toward Steinbeck House.

On the way, I passed the side street where I'd moved the Chrysler with the CB.

The car sent out a strong thought-wave. I stopped the truck, reversed until I was close to the car, then just sat behind the wheel and stared at it.

This thing was a problem. It needed addressing—exorcising. I grabbed my booster cables and popped the car's hood.

I let the car battery charge for a minute before turning on the CB. I turned up the volume. Static. Found the emergency channel. Static. I pushed the talk bar and said, "Temptation is the root of bad things!"

I released the talk bar and moved to turn off the radio.

But a kind of murmur sounded, something low and electronic. It sent a shiver through me. I turned up the volume. The sound was a new kind of static, maybe a weather anomaly—but the morning sky was clear and calm. I adjusted the dial, played around the fringes of the signal.

Muffled music, something Middle Eastern.

Or something approximating music.

There was a pattern to it, something non-random, something produced.

I slapped at the dial, turned the thing off.

Then I sat still for a long, terrified moment before grabbing a pipe wrench from the truck and bashing both the radio and the mic to pieces.

• • •

Back at Steinbeck House, I raced past Charley and up the stairs and set up the candles before sitting at the desk. I sharpened a pencil without pausing to catch my breath.

Once again I scribbled on a notepad, *How to Create a One-Man Civilization.*

It couldn't be that hard. Mike Stone was smart. He had time, he had a goal, and there was no one standing in his way.

But he wouldn't do it, wouldn't move an inch. I held my breath and put my ear to the page, but I could have sworn I heard him laughing. My alter ego was mocking me.

I crumpled the page and tossed it at the wall. My gaze landed on Charley in the doorway, Charley with hope in his eyes. He was hungry, but I had bigger problems. I leaned back in the chair and breathed deeply, tried to stay calm. I locked eyes with Mona Lisa—her with that cat in her lap. She smirked. I exploded out of the chair, tore the painting from the wall, and launched it through the window. Shattered glass flew everywhere.

I looked out the window at the painting on the sidewalk below. She smiled up at me.

"Cheesy, mass-produced Motel 6 kitsch!"

My Only Friend, the End

I stepped over Charley and drove like a fiend to the National Steinbeck Museum. There, I pored over the wall photos. The writing-room shots showed Johnny S.—no, not Johnny S., they showed *John Steinbeck*, American man of letters—in a Spartan bedroom, with a blackboard on one wall and manuscript pages taped to another. There was no art of any kind. It was a workspace, plain, too honest for adornments.

A few photos showed Steinbeck at a typewriter, which he used after completing first drafts longhand. I knew where that typewriter was. It was in Rocinante, his camper, on the kitchen table.

But when I got to Rocinante, it was locked—although I didn't remember closing the door—so I found an in-case-of-fire ax and cleaved open the door with two satisfyingly fierce swings. Inside, there was a ribbon in the typewriter. I hit a key, and a faint "p" showed on the page in the carriage. I tucked the machine under my arm and carefully closed what was left of the door behind me before I scampered away.

At OfficeMax, I scavenged ten rolls of Scotch tape and a blackboard. A blast down the painting-supplies aisle at Home Depot produced a wallpaper scraper.

Back at Steinbeck House again, I scraped off stubborn flowered wallpaper with jaw-clenching resolve and taped up my fifty manuscript pages: thirty-nine typewritten pages from the house and the thirteen notepad pages from here at Steinbeck House.

That done, I nailed up the blackboard. How I would use it was not yet clear, but fidelity to the original writing space was vital. Details could not be omitted just because their purpose was not yet apparent.

When the room was finished, I stood back and looked at the room. I told myself it was good, minutiae mattered, productivity did not abide imprecision.

And the room responded with silence—but an acceptable silence, not the affliction of recent days. The room offered a truce.

This could not be wasted. I scurried to the chair, took up my round pencil and readied the notepad.

And words came to me in Mike Stone's voice. Not sentences—simple, confident nouns.

Justice. Laws. Charity.

Themes in the books. Things Mike Stone had stood for.

Thai food. Brake sensors. Farmers' markets.

Details that made life better. I kept going:

Pizza slices. Welcome in the new world.

Delta blues. Vital.

Artistic graffiti. Calorie-count labelling. Books. Teachers. People who refrain from using "impact" as a verb. People who vote.

Yes.

Small businesses. Local newspapers. Honest politicians.

It went on and on. When I looked up from the pad again, an hour had passed and I had seven pages jammed full of things that Mike Stone had liked. The list made sense as a jumping-off spot, a way of defining the future by excluding negative elements of the past. Mike Stone would know how to synthesize this information. He would make something out of it, something better than I could make. That was his job.

But he still wasn't finished counting up old-world virtues.

Free weights. Cormac McCarthy books. Road trips. Halloween decorations. Christmas dinners. Philanthropy. Political activism. Kids' baseball games. Fair mortgages.

I laughed while I wrote. This was the best writing day of my life—the best *day* of my life. The only problem was it would have to end, sooner or later, and I would have nowhere to go from this thrilling apex except down.

So I made the executive decision to pull back on my own terms. Like a man of bravery, I finished the page I was working on, rose from the table and went back, yet again, to the frozen traffic on West Market Street. This made sense because the writing would be there the next time I sat down. There was a direction now, a flow. I'd earned that flow.

Plus, *I* was in control, not Mike Stone. *I* would not be a prisoner to success. *I* would maintain my equilibrium. Temperance was needed. Temperance was one of the four Platonic virtues.

But on West Market Street, the city bus sat there like a beached whale. Its bloated presence grew more toxic by the second, a mocking challenge to my desire to recreate the world.

Stick with the plan, I told myself: *cars first, trucks second, bus last*. But how many times had I driven past that bus? How many people were inside? I could spend the rest of the day clearing the cars one by one or I could remove the towering oak with one fell swoop—a big, beautiful breakthrough, just like writing again after the inertia at Steinbeck House.

But the bus wouldn't start. It was a hybrid vehicle that ran on lithium batteries and diesel. I siphoned diesel fuel out of a stalled truck in a nearby parking lot and charged the battery for ten minutes, but

My Only Friend, the End

the engine wouldn't turn over. The dashboard lights wouldn't even come on. I studied and re-studied the controls and indicators. It was just a vehicle—this wasn't rocket science—so what was I doing wrong?

The nine or ten corpses on the bus didn't lift a finger to help. This was the first time I'd paused to really look at them. They were well-settled in a state of skeletal disinterest—preferred things just the way they were.

"Freeloaders," I told them, then tried the key again, then climbed out of the bus before the failure could grow larger and engulf me.

I moved the rest of the cars and some of the trucks that day, two dozen vehicles, and went back to Strawberry Fields without thinking about much of anything apart from Mike Stone's list.

Live theater. Concussion protocols. Athletes who give back. Organic farming. Whistleblowers. Ombudsmen. Social movements. Stevia…

The CB radio message nagged at me, but I found that if I thought fast, if I stayed mentally agile and engaged, I could tamp it down and keep moving along that one road toward the future.

But that didn't stop the house's silence from starting up again, this time with an underlying Ronnie soundtrack—the sound of her humming a song from the hallway. It reminded me of Ghost-Ronnie eating Ghost-Oliver's intestines and it made me want to pour cement in my ears. I stayed in the house all of five minutes before grabbing a bottle of water and escaping back out to the truck, where I spent the night with the window rolled halfway down. The frigid nighttime air made me shiver. I hardly slept—again—but at least the sound of the breeze kept Ronnie away.

31

THE NEXT MORNING, I got back to Steinbeck House well before dawn. In the still-dark kitchen Charley was splayed out on the cold tile. I gave him some water, lit a few candles, opened a new can of tuna. I also told him that if he knew what had happened to my last dogs, he'd steer clear of me.

Charley looked hopeful despite the statement.

Upstairs, I lit the candles and picked up where I'd left off yesterday: *Debt forgiveness. Playoff baseball. Wikipedia. Independent cinema. People who support independent cinema. Incognito browsing. Free shipping.*

Five more pages in less than an hour, roughly three-hundred new items, including *A list of things I hadn't known were good.* During the writing, Charley appeared in the doorway, whined a little. Apparently he needed a master's affection. The canine loyalty had not been hard to earn. Was that why I wanted a dog? Because dogs were easy marks? If so, what did it say about me? Maybe my problems right now stemmed from a propensity to settle for easy solutions.

Citizen journalism. Co-existing religions. Brown rice. Wheat beer. Game reserves. Coffee shops instead of social networking. Coffee in general. E-books.

My Only Friend, the End

At noon, I skipped lunch and drove back to the bus, but it still wouldn't start. I asked it why it was messing with me, warned it I would *not* be messed with. I punched the dash buttons, broke off some plastic switches. I tried to tear the steering wheel off, but the wheel shivered and held firm, which made me clench my jaw and pull even harder.

Calm down. You're smarter than a bus.

I stepped out onto the street and tried to study the beast without emotion.

Think. Use your head.

Tow the thing.

Go find a bus tow truck. But spend time reading manuals and learning how to use it? That felt cumbersome—too slow. Immediate measures were required, and I had all sorts of measures at my disposal—a whole planet full. Unequivocal force could be brought to bear.

I made sure the bus was in neutral, then drove to a truck stop off the 101, checked out the parked semi-trailer trucks.

Mountain bikes. Telephone opt-out lists. Due process.

One truck was a fire-engine-red, dual-exhaust behemoth with a flat grill and steel bumper. It was custom-made for shoving a stubborn city bus off a road—preferably off a cliff. The driver was on the ground outside the door, keys poking out of a now-loose-fitting jeans pocket. He looked like the truck-driver corpse outside the gas station in George, Washington. I'd been too squeamish to fish through his pockets for his keys. This time there was no hesitation. I grabbed the keys, climbed up into the cab, and sought the ignition.

And saw another CB radio, which looked bright in the dull light.

"No!" I shouted at it, "no more of that!" I drove the key into the ignition, hit the clutch and brought the engine to life.

Success.

First gear was right where it should have been. I stomped the gas and let out the clutch. The engine croaked and stalled. I tried a second time, got the same result, then paused to check the dashboard gauges.

The oil was at sixty. Maybe it needed to climb higher. I recalled something about airbrakes requiring time to build to a certain pressure. Fine. Let the thing idle a minute.

But get away from that CB. While the rig warmed up, I climbed out and dragged six different bodies under six different semi-trucks, got them somewhat out of sight, then crossed to the convenience store and guzzled a bottle of water, spilling a good portion of it on my shirt.

Back behind the wheel, I stomped the clutch, jammed the gearshift into first and stalled the truck again.

It took me two more tries to get the monster moving. The engine then whined out at high rpms. Fourth gear was as high as I could go. Fine. I needed power, not speed. I crawled all the way back to West Market Street, pulled up behind the bus and —without stopping— tried to push it off the road.

Metal scraped against metal. The semi's engine howled. The bus shook and bounced, then crept forward.

Yes!

No waffling. No passivity. No giving in.

I gave it more gas. Something in the cylinders grated. Smoke billowed from the engine. The bus scratched forward, then something snapped and it moved faster unimpeded.

But I'd forgotten to fix the steering wheel in place. The bus veered left, careened off a concrete divider and shuddered to a stop. I gunned the gas. The back of the bus crumpled a little, but the bus moved no farther. The air was purple, smelled like a Bangkok traffic jam.

I put the rig in neutral and climbed down to inspect the damage. Where the bus had plowed into the divider, the front driver-side wheel was bent at a forty-degree angle. Now the thing not only couldn't be driven, it also couldn't be towed.

I climbed back into the semi cab and cried like a baby, tearing the CB mic off its cord for good measure. Then I backed up, jammed the gearshift into first, and drove to the El Pollo Loco parking lot across the street. On the way, I pulverized two sedans with fourth-gear malice.

This bus would not defeat me—it just couldn't. I could out-duel an inanimate object. In the El Pollo Loco office I found a phone book, which showed me where the welding-supply warehouses were. I drove to one of them and checked out the welding vehicles. They wouldn't do; the beds were too small to carry much acetylene. But one truck in the yard had a nice, low trailer, and it started with the first turn of the key. I kissed the steering wheel—planted one right on the grimy plastic—then got out and started rolling acetylene tanks toward the trailer.

Some of the bigger tanks weighed more than I did. I left them alone, focused on the small ones, maybe eighty pounds each. The trailer accepted twelve bottles before the suspension bowed and strained. I drove those bottles back to the bus and hefted them, one by one, up the bus steps and rolled them down the aisle.

It took nine trips and more than one hundred bottles before the bus was sufficiently packed with acetylene. By that time, my muscles ached, I had blisters on both hands, it was past nine in the evening, and I hadn't eaten since breakfast.

I sat in the welding truck to catch my breath. Soon I struggled to keep my eyes open. I licked salt from the corners of my mouth, a mixture of sweat and tears. I was hollow, with a kind of diffuse disconnectedness that made me think of Ronnie lying dead at her computer in Great Falls. I squeezed my bad thumb in order to override that memory. The thumb refused to cry out, so I punched it with my good hand, producing a jolt of pain that felt bracing and right, and there were no more thoughts of Ronnie.

I ran to my truck, grabbed a jerry can and went back to the bus, where I sprinkled the corpses and acetylene bottles with diesel fuel. For a fuse, I ran a simple trail of gas from the bus to a spot in the middle of the street about twenty yards away. Then I lit the gas and ran like hell to the El Pollo Loco.

By the time I got inside, the bus interior was ablaze. I crouched at the window, ready to duck when the first bottle exploded. But there were no blasts. The fire went on for two full minutes, then for three more before I decided the bottles were fireproof. I stood up, worked stiffness out of my knees, called myself a fool.

Hasty. Sloppy. Thoughtless.

While I reached for the ceiling in an exhausted, full-body stretch, the first bottle exploded—or, rather, took off. It blew through a bus window and streaked toward me like an airborne submarine missile. I ducked, and it shattered the El Pollo Loco window before crashing into the food-prep area, where it spewed fire, painting the kitchen white-orange.

I scrambled out the front doors and ran. I was almost to the side of the building when two more bottles went off, this time in place, tearing away the bus's roof. A fourth bottle burst and sailed up and out of the open space like a cumbersome firework. It thudded into the roof of a roadside house, embedding itself there, pouring fire down into the attic.

I stopped looking back while I sprinted into the darkness, north through a dilapidated storage company's yard, tripping over crates and pallets, then out to the railroad tracks, to a safe-seeming distance. There,

I sat on a rail, caught my breath, and watched the show without feeling much of anything. I wasn't relieved or satisfied or appalled by the fruits of my labor. There just didn't seem to be any meaning. In meaning's place: head-to-toe fatigue and pangs of thirst and hunger—but no desire to address them.

I don't remember falling asleep, but I do recall lying there on the rocks beside the railroad track, hearing the popping and whizzing of the acetylene bottles. This aspect of things felt good and right. The blasts brought life—or at least a crashing, colorful imitation of it—to a city where everything else was dead.

32

WHEN I WOKE UP the next morning, smoke filled the sky and the whole neighborhood burned. The storage company, the auto-body shop next door, another place that sold gas pizza ovens—everything along West Market Street was alight. I walked up the tracks and where there were breaks in the smoke I could see to the south side of the road. The houses and apartment buildings all burned. Nothing close to the bus had been spared.

For a brief moment I thought, *That'll be a lot to clean up*, then I saw Alpha, the German Shepherd leader of Charley's pack. He limped down the middle of West Market Street toward the charred remains of the bus. His left hind leg dangled from his body like a loose strap. He moved in faltering arcs, stopping and starting, looked all around him, couldn't choose a direction. In the end, he sat down and yelped weakly. He looked toward the bus and panted, fighting to catch his breath.

I approached him slowly. He saw me but didn't care I was there. I reached out and stroked the fur over his ribs. The fur had the feel of Flannie's coat: wiry and warm. His head bobbled a little. He whined, then he eased himself down onto his side and resumed panting.

My Only Friend, the End

The light left his eyes bit by bit. He watched me right until the end, hopefully at least somewhat comforted by my presence.

I peered east down Market Street, at the bus, at all the cars I'd moved off the road. Beyond them, there were dozens more unmoved vehicles on the 101. Beyond those, out of view, there were hundreds more, thousands. Worldwide: millions.

I looked at the bodies I'd dragged behind hedges and under parked cars. Legs poked out from under those cars like bones half-buried by a dog. I couldn't remember moving many of the bodies; they all blended together, a fog of frenzied city cleaning. The whole scene looked like something out of a video game.

I stepped away from Alpha, sat on the curb, and buried my head in my hands. When the tears came, they weren't something to be defeated or powered through. They were to be respected like an elder who had something important to say.

These things I'd been doing weren't normal.

Nothing worked.

Everything backfired.

And I'd run out of tools to fix even the smallest of problems.

This last truth kept me seated at the curb for a good long time, until the biggest piece of honesty arrived:

"I just want you back," I said out loud. "Is that so terrible?"

After a minute I sensed her there, next to me on the curb. I still had my head in my hands; it felt cinderblock heavy. I was afraid to look at her, and I think she sensed this because she let the pregnant silence last for an excruciating length of time.

"I don't think it's terrible," she said, "but I wouldn't know. I've never gone through something like this."

My head still in my hands, I said, "Tell me how to get you back."

"We've already been through this. You can't have me in the way that you want me."

I looked at her. She was wearing a pantsuit and had a poised appearance that had always made me feel a little stronger whenever something got me down.

"I'll take what I can get," I said. "Just tell me what to do."

"You already know what to do."

"No, I don't."

"I think you do," she said simply.

"Then why haven't I been doing it? Why have I been doing this instead?" I pointed out at the devastation surrounding us.

"I can't answer those questions for you."

"But you can help me," I said, "by being with me."

"I can't be with you in the way that you—"

"Be with me anyway. It's the only way I'll make it."

She picked at a thread on her jacket. "If I do, then you'd have to do something for me first."

For the tiniest fleck of time I recalled that not long ago she'd wanted me to kill myself.

"Anything," I said. "Just tell me."

"You'll have to prove you're not crazy."

"Is that all?" I said with a sad laugh.

"Otherwise, we'll just go round in circles."

"Then it becomes a question of how," I said. "I need rules—a kind of road map."

"No," she said, "you don't need all that. It's not as complicated as you think. Everything is a matter of actions. You just have to stop doing crazy things."

That's easier said than done. But the way she looked at me—poised and self-assured—I knew I had no choice but to trust her. I was too afraid not to—afraid she'd leave.

"I've been trying all along," I said, "not to do crazy things."

"The difference this time," she told me, "is that now you won't be doing it alone."

33

SHE WASN'T CARING or nurturing. She couldn't be. There were no attempts to go over old times. We didn't make plans for times to come. We were together again. That was enough. For the moment, it was everything.

We walked around the fires until we found a truck that had both keys and gas, a big Honda behind the bay doors of a U-Haul outlet. We left West Market and drove toward Strawberry Fields. I told her some of the things I was sorry for: for leaving her at her computer when I found her dead, for burying her in someone else's grave, for being judgmental of people, superior, for wasting time that could have been spent making more human connections. I rolled out a real laundry list of sorrys.

She didn't absolve me of my sins; she only listened, because listening was all she could really do.

At Strawberry Fields, the silence couldn't touch me now that I had her. While showing her the kitchen, I gulped down two bottles of water and she reminded me to eat something. After I did that, we stopped talking. We went to bed and laid on the covers, then just looked at each other. Apart from seeing her face, I could smell her—not a cream or a perfume, just her. During this, I nodded off and ended

My Only Friend, the End

up sleeping for a full day. When I woke and didn't see her, I felt panic start to rise. But she hadn't left me. I found her in the living room looking at the wall photo of the family who'd lived in Strawberry Fields before I arrived.

"The mother and daughter were in the house when I got here," I told her.

"Where are they now?"

"In the neighbor's back yard."

"The father?"

I shook my head.

Ronnie looked at the picture again. "It would be nice if they could at least be together."

"A lot of things would be nice," I said, and she nodded in agreement.

I showered and ate, and she was waiting for me in the truck when I was ready to go do what we now had to do.

At the truck stop off the 101, we climbed into a Peterbilt cab, where I turned on the CB and started blipping through channels.

It was there again, the same scratching, wavy sound from earlier.

"It's some kind of code," Ronnie said.

"It was louder the last time, but it's clearer now."

Ronnie leaned close to the radio. "Is that metal scraping on metal?"

"It sounds like some kind of code—something like Morse."

But then the blipping sounded like dolphins. This wasn't how salvation was supposed to announce itself. I considered the obvious possibility that this was a post-humanity trick of the ears.

"I'm still crazy," I said. "I'm creating sounds."

"Maybe," she said.

"So what do I do now?"

"What would Mike Stone do?" Ronnie asked, and I knew the question was a test.

"I don't care what he'd do."

"You're sure about that?"

"Mike Stone is gone," I told her. "He died in the fire."

Her smile said she liked the answer.

On the way to the Cesar Chavez branch of the Salinas Public Library, we stopped at Steinbeck House, where we picked up Charley but stayed away from the creaky stairs and the writing room. Then, at the library, the books told me that, depending on weather and topography, CB signals could travel roughly one to two miles per foot of antenna. That gave me a radius of up to six miles if the message had come from a vehicle. That distance would take me outside the city of Salinas in all directions.

We traded our Honda for a truck with a tow hitch and a CB radio, then we drove to the Salinas Police Station. They had no LRADs (at least none that I could find), and neither did the police stations in Seaside or Monterey. The closest LRAD was in Carmel-by-the-Sea, a rich beach community that had about as much need for a crowd-dispersal weapon as Issaquah, Washington.

To get flare guns, I drove to Fisherman's Wharf in Monterey and boarded the biggest yacht on the theory that it would have the strongest flares. From that yacht and two others, I rounded up four flare guns and forty-eight cartridges.

Charley was alert and clingy during all this, always close, guarded, not like the independent poodle in *Travels With Charley*. This was good. I wasn't Johnny S., and he wasn't Charley.

"He'll need a new name," I told Ronnie.

"Yes, but not a literary name."

"No, the opposite of literary."

"How about 'Rex' or 'Fido'—something clearly unoriginal?"

"How about 'Dog,'?" I said.

"'Dog?'"

"What's more unoriginal than that?"

Dog took the name change in stride by licking my hand.

I recorded a message on the LRAD—*Go to channel nine on the radio; I'll check it every hour*—and for the next two days we trolled the Salinas streets and the roads outside town and played it at low volume, listening hard to the signal on the CB. The signal was strongest in the city center, so we went street by street at a crawl. It grew louder in some places, cut out completely in others. The downtown buildings skewed the reception, made it impossible to get a fix.

On the third day of searching, we entered stores and offices that might have had radios: a sporting goods store, the post office, the police station again. After finding only dust and corpses, we drove a mile south to *The Salinas Californian* (reporters scanned emergency channels to get a jump on breaking news). After that, we hit the places with the most trucks: truck stops, the airport and the veggie warehouses at the south end of town. The last stops were at each of the town's seven radio stations.

Everything at all these places was dead. None of the post-extinction dust had been disturbed.

We never did find the signal's source. The sounds on the CB were real, but they refused to accept classification.

I sensed Ronnie watching closely for my reaction to this fact.

"No big deal," I told her, and that was how I felt. No real hope had been attached to the investigation. I'd sought the source of the signal because it was the sane thing to do. Now we could get down to the business that really mattered. We could start building a new life together.

But first Ronnie wanted to grill me regarding my intentions.

"Will you ignore new signals in the future?"

"No."

"Will you make a point of checking for signals from time to time?"

"If I forget," I said, "you can remind me."

"No, I can't. You'll have to be able to remind yourself."

"I can," I said. "I'll be all right from now on."

And I would stay away from Steinbeck House and I wouldn't move around any more cars. I would embark on no foolish missions to fix the unfixable.

By now, most of the fires along West Market Street had burned out. A few continued to blaze, and black smoke still filled the sky, but I had a sound idea of how much of the city would be lost. I wouldn't have to relocate to another town.

Embarking on this new life with Ronnie involved preparing for winter, which was fast approaching. Salinas almost never got snow, but the autumn mornings were chill, which made a good heating system essential. I'd already taught myself how to feed a home furnace with condensed natural gas, so now I rounded up a compatible motor and heat exchanger in case of emergency. I also laid in tools and parts for the water heater and two extra generators.

On the fifth or six morning with Ronnie, I walked into the kitchen and saw Evan at the table eating cereal. Evan wearing soccer kit. Evan focused on his Cheerios just like he'd been focused on his ice-cream cone in Alvin Stinghold's bunker.

"Can we play soccer?" he asked as if we'd never been apart.

I looked at Ronnie, too afraid to ask what I wanted to ask.

She answered anyway. "He's all you get. Oliver was gone before this happened."

"Can we, Daddy?"

"Let's do it," I told Evan, and after I ate we played soccer in the back yard, with the morning fog lifting and the wetness of the grass causing me to slip and slide and whoop and scream.

After that, I drove my wife and son to Monterey and showed them my fishing spot at the docks. Evan wanted to swim, so after casting for fish we drove a couple miles north, away from the corpses, and swam. Evan charged into the water like he was dying of thirst. I followed, tearing off my clothes as I went. Ronnie stayed on shore and screamed, "You'll freeze to death! You're both crazy!"

She was right. We lasted maybe three minutes in the water and then spent the rest of the afternoon at home wrapped in warm blankets, drinking hot chocolate and watching *Shark Tale*, Evan's favorite movie.

As the days passed, we completed more of our staying-alive tasks and found ourselves with more leisure time. During the days, we taught Evan how to read and exercised and concocted sumptuous, sophisticated meals. In the evenings, when Evan was in bed, Ronnie and I grabbed a flashlight and strolled along the frigid nighttime country roads and talked. We covered a lot of ground—the past, the present, and even now the future—and in brief moments when the clouds parted, we looked up and saw the same stars that we'd seen in Montana.

During one night walk I raised a point that had been bothering me since we'd started this new journey together.

"I'm growing older," I said.

"That's how life works," Ronnie said. "Hold the light steady or I'll end up in the ditch."

I steadied the flashlight. "But you're not getting older. You never will. And neither will Evan. He'll be four years old for the rest of my life."

"Would you prefer we grow old?"

"Of course I would."

"Would you prefer we grow old?" she asked again in the exact same tone.

I missed a beat before saying, "Yes. I would prefer you grow old."

"Ah. Of course, you would." A pause before she asked a third time, "Would you prefer we grow old?"

I didn't answer. I waited until she broke the silence, something about me being right; if she and Evan didn't age, this thing might become hard to maintain. She looked at me with innocent eyes. She had no clue she'd been repeating herself.

A hiccup. A bug in the machine. I couldn't fix this. I didn't know how the machine worked.

"Are you all right?" she asked.

I had to be. There was no choice. "I'll take what I can get."

She smiled.

A few days later at lunch, Evan sat down at the kitchen table and glanced at his food and gave me a child's I-won't-eat-that look.

"What's a matter," I asked him.

"I can't *stand* rockfish."

"You love rockfish," I told him. "It's your favorite meal here."

"I *always* hated rockfish. I always hate *all* fish. It's oogy."

Ronnie was at the table. "What's he doing?" I asked her. "Why's he saying this?"

"Evan?" Ronnie said. "Honey? Please eat the food your father prepared for you."

Evan folded his arms and sulked.

"Please, honey?"

"But I hate it."

"That's not the point," Ronnie said.

"No," I said, "it *is* the point. This is maybe the only child in the history of children who loves fish."

"Actually," Ronnie said, "he hates it. It's prawns he loves. Shellfish. That's as close as he gets."

"See!" Evan said.

He ended up getting peanut butter and jam for lunch.

Later that evening, it was raining too hard for a walk. Ronnie and I sat in front of the tube and half-watched *Casablanca*. I asked her why she'd taken Evan's side at lunch.

"I didn't take his side. I took the side of the truth."

"But you know he loves fish. We went to Red Lobster almost every week and suffered through those awful, salty biscuits because he wanted fish so badly."

"We didn't go to Red Lobster," she said. "You're misremembering this."

The next day, she started to glitch like an image on a frozen computer screen, a split-second pause in mid-sentence before continuing as if nothing had happened.

This could be ignored no longer. I told her, "You just froze."

"What do you mean?"

I explained it to her, and she listened to me like an earnest psychologist hearing out a frazzled patient. Then she said, "Are you feeling okay?"

I sensed where this was going, so I pushed the subject away, said something about feeling tired.

"Well, no wonder. You're always working on something. You never slow down. You should get some rest."

The next evening, we watched another movie, *Forrest Gump*, her favorite, and she laughed in all the right places, cried when crying was called for, and stayed in the moment without any further glitches.

The following morning, Evan wasn't in the kitchen when I got there. But Ronnie was, sitting at the table, waiting.

"Where is he?" I asked her.

"Where's who?" she replied.

"Evan. Where's Evan?"

She furrowed her brow and looked to the ceiling. "Oh. I bet he'll be here soon."

He walked in shortly after that and the rest of the day was normal, but I couldn't pretend this wasn't happening. Ronnie and I drove to town to fill a truck-bed tank with generator gas. She looked out the window and hummed *Sweet Dreams* by the Eurhythmics, one of her favorite songs.

"Where did we meet?" I asked her.

"Excuse me?"

"Just humor me, it's kind of a quiz."

"A quiz why?"

"I'll tell you when we're finished," I said. "Come on, it'll be fun. Just tell me where we met."

"We met in Bozeman, in college."

"What did I study?"

"Are you serious?" she said. "You majored in How to Become a Modern-Day Ernest Hemingway."

That was how she'd liked to introduce me to other students—as "a budding Ernest Hemingway." It sounded great to me back then and I was relieved to hear her say it to me now, but it wasn't enough.

"And what did you study?" I asked.

"I studied?"

"We were in college. That's where we met. You studied something."

She looked to the sky, drummed her chin with her fingers. "Oh, you're right. If I was there, I must have studied."

My Only Friend, the End

Okay. She'll forget things unless I help her remember them.

"Finance and accounting!" she blurted, then doubled over and laughed because she'd just pulled one over on me. "Are you really afraid I'll start forgetting things? Like some kind of—" She glitched again, then and there; she was gone three full seconds before reappearing and finishing her sentence: "—Wi-Fi signal?"

I raced home and found Evan in the garden. He was digging for worms with his bare hands. He didn't notice me, looked right through me when I stood in front of him. Despite a hollowness in my stomach, I said, "Hey, Bud, wanna play some soccer?"

"Why?" he said, eyes on the dirt.

"We haven't played in a while. It'll be fun. I'll go in net."

"Soccer's stupid," he said. "I only like hockey."

Which he'd never played or, to my knowledge, even seen on TV.

I took Ronnie into the house and asked her if any part of her knew what was going on here.

"Of course I know," she said. "Nothing here surprises me."

"It's you and Evan, you're starting to cut out."

"Maybe," she said.

"Maybe? That's all you can say about it?"

"It's not like we're the ones who are doing it."

"But you should at least care," I said. "You should at least help me stop it or slow it down. That's why you're here. That part of you *has to* survive."

"You really think we have that ability?"

The answer to the question was two-fold: Yes, I'd hoped she had the ability, but no, the deepest part of me knew we were living on borrowed time.

"One day you'll be gone altogether, won't you?"

"Maybe," she said. "Or maybe we'll still be here but we'll be different. We'll fade slowly. Or maybe we'll become too much like us, like home videos you've seen too many times. You'll predict our every move, maybe even arrange and direct our actions. But I wouldn't recommend it."

Her saying this was less painful than the way in which she said it: without feeling.

I said, "You've known this all along."

She shrugged. "What can I say? How can I change anything for you?"

Yes, she was leaving me, or vice versa, and it was a leaving that couldn't be stopped.

"I'll take what I can get," I reminded her.

"I think it's pretty clear you've already taken it."

"It's happening too fast."

"No it's time for you to let go."

I stared at her. My Ronnie was saying this.

"You said you would stay with me. You said we could do this."

"I will stay if you want, but will it be any good? How long do you think you can keep this up?"

I nearly said, *For the rest of my life*, but that would have raised the question, *How long is that?*

Ronnie put a hand on my shoulder, like a friend or a mentor, not like a wife. "You've done what you can, but maybe this is inevitable."

"If I don't have you," I said, "I might as well be dead."

"If you really believed that, you would have killed yourself by now."

Dog came bounding into the house. He was head-to-toe mud. Right behind him stood Evan, equally filthy, out of breath.

"I'm finished!" Evan said. "Now we can go play golf!"

"There's a silver lining," Ronnie said.

I couldn't tear my eyes away from Evan. He needed so badly to play with me.

"At least you're no longer blowing up Salinas. At least we're having this talk. You know what that says?"

Still watching Evan, I understood. The need in his eyes wasn't his; it was mine. And it was okay it was there. It wasn't weakness. It was just sadness, natural and needed. It served a purpose.

"It tells me," Ronnie said, "that you have a chance to be okay. You've always had that chance. So why don't you do that? Why don't you go be by yourself now?"

She sat and drummed the table with her fingers.

"Dad?" Evan said.

"I don't think so," I said. "There's not going to be any more soccer."

"Awwww."

I turned to Ronnie. I wanted to hold her, to kiss her. I wanted that more than anything, but of course that wouldn't happen.

"I won't ever let you go."

"I know," she said. "Now go be well. Before you change your mind."

I didn't go, not right then. I needed to stay with her a while longer. I did that. I hung on as long as I could without losing the meaning of our conversation. And I tried to commit every second of it to memory.

34

THE NEXT MORNING, I woke early, walked into the kitchen alone, and ate breakfast. Then I drove to Steinbeck House, chipped the glass shards out of the paneless window frame, and measured the wood. At Mikkelson's Custom Glass on West Rossi Street, I cut a 30" by 38" replacement and found some frame nails and window putty.

The new piece fit perfectly in the century-old frame. The putty was nice and malleable. I spent as much time cleaning up the old pane as I did installing the new one.

When I was finished, I crossed to the doorway and took stock of my writing room, the pages on the wall, my jagged cursive on the yellow notepad pages by the typewriter. I pulled the pages off the wall (was careful not to tear them) and gathered them into a neat, single pile on the desk.

There were seventy-three pages in all, maybe 15,000 words, about one fourth of them my laundry list of free-association nouns. I sharpened a pencil and placed it on top of the pile of pages. The crumpled pages on the floor went in the trash can. The candles stayed where they were: one on the dresser, one beside the typewriter.

When I left the room, I eased the door closed behind me and walked down the stairs without caring which foot caused which stair to creak.

My Only Friend, the End

Dog nudged my hand as we walked from kitchen to truck. I stopped and patted his head, then massaged his neck and chin despite the corpse stains still in his fur.

Back at Strawberry Fields that afternoon, I cleaned the kitchen sink and retacked the dangling light to the ceiling. Later, I changed the sheets on the bed, rinsed out the shower, and vacuumed and mopped the floors—then packed a travel bag with clothes, turned off everything that needed turning off and moved perishables from the fridge to the garbage can outside. I didn't forget to top up the generator before turning it off, too.

One more thing to do before leaving town. I drove to Walmart, picked up a Fujifilm Instax camera and a dozen packs of self-developing photo sheets. Then I returned to the house and snapped a single shot of it from the front yard. I didn't wait for the chemical reactions to produce an image. I tossed the still-wet photo through the truck's open window, onto the dash, and walked around to the other side and climbed in behind the wheel.

I still had some gathering to do before hitting the road, but this was the last I would ever see of the house.

It surprised me a little to know I would miss the place.

35

SOUTH OF SALINAS, the bracing coastal temperatures gave way to warmer September air. Crops of strawberries and celery yielded to carrots, peppers and tomatoes. Most of the vegetables were dead, but south of King City I filled a pillowcase with miraculously alive red potatoes. After that, I didn't stop again until I passed Bakersfield and reached Cooper Field. This was where Mickey, my skydiving instructor, had learned how to jump. There was no one alive here, but the office did have a nice map of United States Parachute Association Member Drop Zones. In the parking lot outside, I baked a couple potatoes and heated up some packaged veggie tikka masala on a Coleman stove.

The potatoes were good, and the tranquil autumn fields looked like a moody photo spread in *National Geographic*. I snapped a few shots of my own, tried to capture the way the sun and shade mingled on the crop leaves. In doing that, I lost track of time—and eventually decided to spend the night there.

There would be no more motels. In good weather, a tent, air mattress and sleeping bag would be more convenient and would create a sense of routine. I slept soundly that night for the second time in a row, didn't rouse myself from slumber until after 11:00 the next day.

Even the coolness of the night and the bright heat of the morning sun through the tent were no match for the need to sleep. I toyed with the idea of hanging around for a day, relaxing, reading, but Dog was restless, ran back and forth between the tent and the truck. An hour of his nervous energy was enough to get me moving again.

Over the next month we weren't bound by maps or schedules. I turned on the LRAD when I felt like it. Sometimes I used it to blare out *Honky Tonk Women* or *Shambala* or whichever other moldy oldie struck my fancy (by now my CD collection was to die for). Outside Tucson, at the Davis-Monthan Air Force Boneyard, I blasted *Jet Airliner* toward the sea of decommissioned planes. In Kilgore, Texas, I came across the Texas Shakespeare Festival, which, judging from the outdoor stage and the corpses in Elizabethan costumes, had been in full swing when the extinction struck. I read everyone there the Queen Mab speech from *Romeo and Juliet*, bringing dreams to those who slept. This made me feel good, made me cry a little, so I recited the speech into the LRAD recorder and let it play at a low volume for the rest of the afternoon while driving toward Louisiana.

Some days I didn't turn on the LRAD at all. Those days were no worse and no better than any others. They were just different, with different feels to them, altered rhythms.

When car crashes made roads impassable, we didn't switch vehicles. We doubled back and took smaller highways. We took our time travelling the more rustic routes, and there were good things to see there: small towns from bygone eras, old Pepsi signs, barbershop poles, the odd deer or alligator. The bad things—the clusters of death and the black clouds over burning oil pipelines—were acknowledged but weren't lingered over.

This voyage did have a destination: the United States Army Airborne School at Fort Benning, Georgia. But there were no hopes attached to the place. It was a logical spot at which to seek survivors, and whether I found them or not wasn't my call. All I could influence were the little things, the daily moments and rewards, stolen glimpses of beauty, the whole many-colored experience of travelling around one's country, even if that country was weeded over and littered with bodies. There was so much I'd never seen before, so many moments I hadn't paused long enough to take in. The end of humanity had destroyed the best part of the world, but this planet was still a blue-green orb of nature, a place with an evolving present that was forever tumbling toward an unwritten future.

At Skydive Panama City, in Blountstown, Florida, I began keeping a daily journal on a laptop that I charged off the truck battery. The entries were factual, descriptive and unforced. One day maybe I would turn the journal into a memoir, a documentation of everything that had happened since the extinction, a record for whatever intelligent being might stop here in the future. But that day hadn't arrived yet. There was no need to write stories, and anyway writing was no longer a goal, it was a hobby, something to fill empty moments, like playing solitaire or building a ship in a bottle. If writing did decide to become something larger, I would cross that bridge when I came to it. Right now I was too busy communing with the world around me to worry about it.

Between Salinas and Fort Benning, I took roughly two hundred photos and filed most of them in the glove compartment. My favorites—nature scenes, mainly, and a few shots of Dog looking regally aloof—got tacked to the sun visors, along with my old wallet photos of Ronnie and Evan. I regretted I had no snapshots of Oliver. I'd trashed all such traces of him while getting falling-down drunk shortly after he died.

I rolled up to the gates of Fort Benning on November 24th, one-hundred and twenty-eight days after leaving Great Falls. I did feel a flutter of hope as I walked onto the base, but the place showed me the usual mostly-decomposed bodies, the usual non-evidence of post-extinction habitation. Despite this, Dog and I walked all the way to the heart of the base, to the airborne school, where we saw eight different sets of remains of paratroopers who'd died while free-falling from planes. Their jumpsuited forms were disassembled messes of broken bones partially embedded in the grass. The parachutes on their backs were unopened. Other jumpers—the ones whose chutes had opened—were on the ground and in the trees. A few hung from buildings. One dangled from a rotor of a parked helicopter; his left leg had detached at the knee. The booted foot lay on the tarmac under the aircraft.

I left Fort Benning like a movie patron walking out of a bad picture at the multiplex. Why waste time on negative things? There were too many good things out there to do instead.

Like swimming with Dog in Lake Seminole. And trying inline skating in Tallahassee, and firing up the batting machine at Tropicana Field in Tampa and hitting dingers into the left-field bleachers.

And spending time in the Florida Keys, a life-long dream that I'd always put off why? Because I'd always had books to write?

In Key Largo, I took a glass-bottomed boat out to the reef and spent hours marveling at the countless varieties of marine life. At Bahia Honda Key, I snorkeled while Dog napped in the shade. I stayed in the water too long and burned my back cherry red—right through my T-shirt—and spent the next two days applying aloe vera, chugging water, and finding new and descriptive ways of calling myself intellectually compromised.

We ended up spending two full months in the Keys. While snow storms battered Montana and torrential rains drenched Seattle, Dog and I learned how to paddle board (Dog was better at it than me), fished for tarpon, ate leisurely crab dinners. In Big Pine Key, we fed the iguanas and tried to handfeed the tiny key deer that tiptoed through town in the evenings. A hurricane struck while we were there, and this prairie boy did not have enough sense to be staying in a sturdy abode with good storm windows. Dog and I spent a wet, sleepless night worrying our roof would blow off.

Loneliness intruded, of course, but I accepted it for what it was. I wanted Ronnie and Evan. I wanted mundane things like drives to the store and chats with gas-station attendants. The fact of their absence was sharp and persistent, but I always got over it thanks to time and the eternal composure of Dog, whose steadiness reinforced the value of stoicism, the very character trait that I'd spent my life in Montana trying to rise above.

I did do some work during this period. I taught myself how to filet and salt a wide variety of fish, how to start a fire with a tinder nest, how to connect a solar-panel battery to a house's main electricity line. I hit the books at the Monroe County Library and confirmed that, yes, gasoline would soon be going bad, but I also learned that diesel fuel, especially the diesel fuels used by the U.S. military, would last for up to four more years.

Four years without having to worry about power!

This knowledge was a sweet reward for having made it this far. I ditched my truck in favor of a Humvee from the Key West Naval Air Station, and I left the thing running whenever I stopped at shops for water or supplies. I also upgraded to a big-but-portable diesel generator that could power a small house for two days without a refill. Thoughts about switching to solar power got shelved. The sun would always be there when I needed it, and if it wasn't, if one day it refused to rise and Dog and I froze to death, well, that would be just one more thing we had no control over.

So I settled into this new routine, this approach to the days as a procession of moments—some good, some bad, all compulsory. I felt no need for guidance in this regard, no books on dealing with solitude, no philosophical wisdom. I allowed myself to feel rather than to think, and when the feeling didn't go well, I worked toward feeling something else, often simply by doing something else. It usually worked, usually saved me from melancholy and notions of futility.

One thing I *didn't* do was visit Ernest Hemingway House in Key West. I stayed far away from Ernie H. out of fear I might end up typing out a new literary tour de force from a standing position at his bedroom dresser while guzzling absinthe.

We left the Keys in early March, before the impossible heat of summer arrived. In Fort Myers, we stopped at Thomas Edison's treasure trove of inventions. At a museum in Savannah, we saw Forrest Gump's park bench (Forrest had no idea how right his mamma had been about never knowing what you're gonna get). In the Carolinas, the salt-water marshes were a pungent, teaming microcosm of life on Earth. Just south of Myrtle Beach, we very nearly adopted a beach house as our new-and-forever home. Instead, we turned inland and continued driving north, bypassing the Washington-Philadelphia-New York corridor because of the volume of corpses. (By this point it took no special talent to see past corpses, but every talent did have its limits.)

In late May, eleven months after the extinction, we ended up in Pleasant Point, Maine, just across the water from New Brunswick. By this time, we'd stopped dropping in on flight schools and army bases. The Humvee had a CB radio, but I didn't use it. The LRAD got left somewhere in Pennsylvania, and not once during the whole trip from Salinas had I fired off any flares. (I left the guns and cartridges on a rest-stop picnic table outside Wilmington.)

But when we got to Maine, the state had nothing of interest, no reason for being there. This wasn't Maine's fault. Travels were over. The journey had helped me solidify my truce with the world, but the procession of new places was starting to feel recycled. Moments and feelings that had once held meaning now bore a tinge of wistfulness, as if to pursue the new was to unfairly suppress the old.

Most of all, I missed my home—not just Ronnie and Evan and our little house on the tree-lined avenue, but all of it, all of Great Falls, Montana. The people were gone, much of the town had burned, a good deal of what remained had flooded—but it was home. It was my source of memories. It exerted a pull.

This didn't mean I had to ponder and philosophize and make precious decisions about The Meaning of Great Falls, Montana. It meant I had to drive there, see if the call to return was legit. If it wasn't, if Great Falls was a mirage borne of loneliness or desperation or some as-yet-unidentified emotion, I would accept that and move on.

Grant me the serenity
to accept the things I cannot change.

So I left Maine before really stopping to look at it. To get home fast, I cut a straight line through Quebec and Ontario rather than a semi-circle loop down through the eastern states. I made no stops for sightseeing or other indulgences. The travel pace was brisk but comfortable. After bisecting south-central Ontario and Lake Huron, I spilled back into the United States at Sault Ste Marie, Michigan, and rolled across Wisconsin and eastern Minnesota like a zoned-out long-haul trucker numbly at ease.

In western Minnesota, where the lakes and forests gave way to the prairie, the sense of home grew stronger—the smell of the fields, the length of the late-spring days. My driving speed increased. Without knowing why, I began paying closer attention to the wrecks on the road. It wasn't until I passed Valley City, North Dakota, that I felt an odd, hard-to-extinguish hope that some of these people might be friends or acquaintances from back in Great Falls. Prairie people, after all, were prairie people.

"What do you think, Dog? Am I losing my mind again?"

Dog ignored the question. It wasn't worth his time—and wasn't worth mine. A more important query: was my house in Great Falls still standing?

It took twelve days to cover the twenty-five-hundred miles from Maine to Montana. We approached the town from the south, on the same road I'd followed just one hour after the extinction while praying my wife and son were still alive. I recalled bandaging my cheek, driving the dead farmer's truck, struggling to absorb the new reality. The car where I thought I'd seen a post-extinction flutter of life was still there. Inside, the driver was now a languid collection of clothed but largely disconnected bones.

Closer to town, the Missouri River had claimed some flood plains, had reinvented itself. The new shallows looked like a good place to catch spring trout before the heat of summer pushed them to deeper waters.

The airport looked the same, frozen in time. On the tarmac, a pack of coyotes played tug-of-war with the bony remains of a cat-sized animal.

In town, dust covered every man-made thing: houses, vehicles, store-front benches. Weeds dominated lawns and parks. Maybe thirty percent of the houses had burned down, but in no discernible pattern. The flooding had left a silty white cake over the lawns and roads closest to the Missouri. The rooster weathervane atop Jerry Olsen's Garage had stayed wind-clean and now swayed in the breeze.

My house was still there. I parked on the street out front because it felt wrong to use the driveway. I walked inside with Dog and went straight to Ronnie's photo albums in the living room. After blowing off dust, I sat on the graying sofa to lose myself in some Kodak moments.

I didn't do this for long, didn't get maudlin or depressed. I was happy to have the albums, happy to have my family again, but I wouldn't worship them. They were just pictures on album pages. It was easy to keep this truth front and center when everything in the house was covered with half an inch of dust.

So was this place really home? Was it where I would make my last stand?

No trumpets sounded. No fireworks went off. I set about testing the water pipes for bursts caused by the freeze-and-thaw cycles of winter. If the pipes were done, I'd have to find another place to live. I'd also have to prepare for seasonal churn. Summer would peak and crest before I knew it, then the long, cold winter would return yet again. And there would be no one around to help Dog and me get through the months of short, windswept days without freezing.

36

I APPROACHED the first weeks back in Great Falls with an acolyte's composure: faithful to the process, open to wisdom. I cleaned the house, hooked up power, lugged water tanks. In the evenings, I read books, watched movies and went jogging with Dog. One morning, I visited Ronnie and Evan in the cemetery, but they weren't really buried there, only their bodies were. The same went for Oliver, in his lonely, disconnected plot. All three of them couldn't be anything other than memories.

Another morning, while driving to a bookstore downtown, I passed Ronnie's church and saw the stained-glass windows that I'd once thrown rocks through. The empty spaces where I'd knocked out Jesus' head looked meaningless at first, then started to look like vandalism. My impulse, while I sat in the truck and looked at it, was to research stained glass and to fix what I'd broken and to leave God alone. But such an over-indulged-in gesture wouldn't have changed anything. Stained-Glass Jesus couldn't be healed. Everyone who was gone couldn't be healed.

Still, the church exerted a pull. I climbed out of the truck, entered the building, and sat four rows from the altar. This wasn't symbolic rapprochement—not an attempt at anything. I was there because the church was there and Ronnie had gone there and probably would have gone there after the extinction had she survived. That fact no longer bothered me. It was just a truth that never got to play out.

But being there did stir something within me. When was the last time I'd sat in a pew? When I had *ever* sat in one without feeling a desire to oppose the faith? I looked around. There were no corpses and not a lot of dust. There were two candles on the altar, had never been lit. An open Bible sat upright on a bookstand like an invitation. The men of God must have been in the sacristy. They'd left a golden chalice on the altar. The silence all around felt appropriate and soothing even though all of my days were marked by silence.

I started to feel downright content, me in that pew—not like I was connecting to God, but like I was connecting to Ronnie, to her post-Oliver desire to attend church every day, and to her demand that we not give up on our marriage. There was nothing ironic or contradictory about the two. Capitulation to God did not have to mean blind surrender. Ronnie was too smart to accept the unacceptable. Maybe her coming here had been a form of bravery, a willingness to affirm mystery, to live with it instead of lashing out at it like her husband had done.

I sat there a while and enjoyed a feeling of release, then rose, crossed to the stained-glass windows, and picked up the rocks I'd thrown.

I walked out, then drove back to my camp on the high prairie overlooking Great Falls, the place where I'd convalesced after fleeing the town's fires and floodwaters. There was no evidence anyone had ever stood on this patch of land before. The prairie grasses were uniformly wild, and the breeze wafting down from Alberta felt warm and friendly. A coyote yipped in the distance. I walked to the edge of the field and looked down at the industrial end of town: the acres of junked cars, the storage sheds, the lined-up combines. In my mind's eye, I saw something I'd desperately wanted to see the last time I was up here: an "S.O.S." painted on the roof of the garden center. The flash of a mirror that a faraway person was tilting to get my attention. I saw myself walking down the hill toward that someone, Dog at my side, neither of us unduly elated because maybe the S.O.S. was a mirage, or if it was real, maybe it was dangerous. Maybe the person holding the mirror was demented or homicidal.

When I snapped out of this mental imagery, I was relieved to see no rooftop S.O.S. and no flashes—relieved because I was tired, didn't want to do any hiking. I wanted to go home and have some dinner and maybe watch the DVD of Oliver's first birthday party.

There were worse ways for a man to live alone.

I walked back to the truck, Dog right there with me, a spring in his step. He stared at me with pleading eyes. It was dinnertime. If I ever forgot to feed him, he would let me know about it with a glare that could turn me to stone.

I appreciated that. Dog was dependable. I would miss him if anything ever happened to him.

ABOUT THE AUTHOR

Steven Owad is an award-winning writer and editor living in Calgary, Canada. His novels have been praised in publications such as *Ellery Queen Mystery Magazine* and *Kirkus Reviews*, and his stage plays have been produced in theaters throughout North America.

In his previous life as a newspaper editor, Steven lived in Thailand and Poland, where he begged journalists not to use "impact" as a verb. Before that, there was a degree in English, with a lot of thousand-page Victorian novels. These days, shorter modern novels and plays are more his speed.

Steven loves the outdoors when there's no risk of frostbite.

YOU MIGHT ALSO ENJOY

MARGERY
Jeffrey Penn May

Introverted backpacker Jeremy wanders off trail and discovers an eccentric, otherworldly town nestled in a mountain basin.

STILL LIFE
Paul Skenazy

When his wife, Edie, dies, Will Moran abandons all he used to be, and do, to paint still life canvases of rocks and driftwood on the walls of his house.

CARNIVAL FARM
Lisa Jacob

When veterinarian Seagn Conway decides to take over a traveling carnival's petting zoo, she doesn't realize the insanity behind the scenes.

Available from Paper Angel Press in
hardcover, trade paperback, and digital editions
paperangelpress.com

Manufactured by Amazon.ca
Acheson, AB